the end

of

m i r a c l e s

the end of miracles

A Novel

MONICA STARKMAN

SHE WRITES PRESS

Published 2016
Printed in the United States of America
ISBN: 978-1-63152-054-9
Library of Congress Control Number: 2015958895

For information, address:
She Writes Press
1563 Solano Ave #546
Berkeley, CA 94707

She Writes Press is a division of SparkPoint Studio, LLC.

Book design by Stacey Aaronson

For Eduardo,
for the families we came from,
for the family we made

PART ONE

1

---

*T*he dream was always the same—a flood of babies dribbling out of her mouth, dozens, tumbling head over heels. It was like coming up from the sea sputtering a mouthful of water, salty and alive with life forms.

The dream was not frightening, not even unpleasant, but today Margo didn't want to linger with it, with the strange images, the faint sensation on her lips and tongue. Better to get up, move about, dispel all traces of it. She opened her eyes, and the babies flickered and faded as they disintegrated into the room's darkness.

Cautiously, she snaked her way to the edge of the bed. Steven savored his weekend morning sleep, and she didn't want to deprive him of it. She swung her legs to the floor, leaned her weight forward, and lifted herself out and up.

That sequence of movement—bending, extending, stretching, releasing—stirred her bodily memory. It was a pattern from the modern dance class she had taken last year at the Y: contract, release, stretch, extend, move. She could almost hear the demands of the instructor and the mono-tonous beat of the drum measuring out the rhythms, almost feel her abdomen contracting deeply into itself, and her arms stretching almost out of their sockets to touch the air beyond their reach. It was so exhilarating, that total concentration on the body—the spinning, whirling, leaping, flying. And so brutally exhausting, too: calves burning and sore thighs trembling with fatigue, for while its aim was to achieve elegance of motion and perfection of form, dance was at bottom a grubby, sweaty business. Like sex, when two people churned and ground against each other to achieve that final ecstasy. Like labor, when a woman's body groaned with effort and strained to deliver life.

No, not those thoughts either. No more this morning of babies and birthing, of unnatural dreams. Who knew what sorts of imaginings attracted bad luck?

Margo tiptoed toward the bedroom door and then descended the stairs, avoiding the loose-boarded places that set off creaks. From the front entry hall closet, she pulled out the underwear, jeans, and T-shirt she kept there to change into on weekend mornings so Steven could sleep without being disturbed by her dresser drawers squeaking open and shut. She tugged off her nightgown, grimacing disapprovingly as each level of her body was revealed in turn: thighs too flabby, hips too big, breasts too small. Never mind that Steven praised her figure and delighted in the curve of her waist. She had never approved of her body, and she disapproved of it even more now that her thirty-eight-year-old face also drooped a bit, her brown hair contained a bit of gray, and a few wrinkles had already etched fine paths around her eyes.

No, never mind, not today. Today, she must not think of
her imperfect body. Today, she would think only of flaw-
lessness, of competence, of normalcy.

In the kitchen, Margo brewed herself some coffee and
sat down with her cup at the small table in front of the
kitchen window. As she sipped, she studied how the residue
of Connecticut rain that had fallen during the night clung
to the needles of the pine trees that crowded against the
kitchen window; in the early morning light, the drops
glistened and the needles looked as if they had been dipped
in sugar. The day was clear and bright, a boon in late
winter, when the gloom of leaden skies was still to be
expected.

She fixed herself another cup of steaming coffee and
started the day's work, warmed by the sunlight streaming
through the yellow and white gingham-curtained windows
and the cheerful company of a collection of brightly colored
wooden and clay roosters that peered down at her from
their high shelves. Cleaning the cluttered refrigerator of the
bits and pieces remaining from the week's menus, Margo
saved or evicted leftovers like a judge dispensing pardons
and sentences. "At least one side of you is still beautiful,"
she said to a tomato half-blighted by mold as she wielded
her knife to rescue the healthy half; "Sorry, spaghetti," she
apologized to the soggy mass drowned in week-old grayish-
red sauce, tossing it down the disposal. By the time her
husband came down for his breakfast—early brunch by
then, really—she had completed a satisfying number of
household tasks: two loads of laundry washed and dried,

stacks of outdated magazines sifted through and pitched out, and half the bills paid.

Steven settled himself at the kitchen table, arranging his terrycloth bathrobe around his knees. "I can't believe I slept that long."

Margo came over to kiss his cheek. "My own Rip Van Winkle. So, what would you like?"

It was her habit on weekends to make breakfast for Steven. As a little girl too young yet for school, she had watched her father pour cold cereal into his bowl morning after morning while her mother stayed preoccupied with children or chores. "You know what would hit the spot on a cold morning like this?" he'd once asked her. "A hot breakfast," he continued, as he poured the packaged cornflakes into a bowl. Sitting across from her father at the kitchen table, she had imagined the bountiful breakfast she would have prepared for him, could she only reach the pantry shelves and be allowed to touch the stove. It had never occurred to Margo not to make breakfast for Steven.

She watched as he sliced through his omelet with methodical precision. It was remarkable to her how precise Steven always was; even the part in his black hair was immaculately drawn this morning, never mind that today was simply a lazy and private Saturday.

"Excellent," he said. "I like that grated nutmeg you added with the cheese."

Margo smiled at him. She always enjoyed his praise, and today she was additionally glad that she had begun the day by pleasing him.

When he was done, Steven neatly set down his knife and fork. "Well, what did you think of Amanda's young man at the party last night?"

His words were neutral, but from the down-turned set of his mouth, she could tell that his impression hadn't been a favorable one.

"He seemed all right," Margo replied as noncommittally as possible. She rose to clear off the table. "Seems like he's going to be good for her."

"Good how? Don't you think it's ridiculous? He's barely out of college. He has no real job. She said he works at that ski resort, but I guess that's a nicer way of saying he's a ski bum."

Margo cautioned herself not to leap to her friend's defense. Her task today was to keep the mood pleasant and light and overlook any minor annoyances. She turned the tap on strong until the water made a gushing sound as it sped from the faucet, and let that be her reply.

He seemed to accept her silence as a sign of acquiescence, for he turned to the newspaper and said no more.

Margo picked up the now-cool omelet pan and reached for the Teflon-safe scouring pad. A hazy memory was coalescing, coming into clearer focus as she scrubbed, a memory from far back in time, when she herself had been in a May-September match—although hers was of the usual sort: she seventeen, and he thirty.

She hadn't found any of the immature, often silly men-in-training at her school appealing. Arthur Meese was the manager at the supermarket where she clerked after school and during the summers. She admired the way he strode out of his small office, and the authority with which he communicated his instructions to the staff. She often found herself glancing at the solid square shape of his hands, and the full curve of his forearm, somehow both familiar and mysteriously attractive. In time, he noticed her interest, and began driving her home after work. The first day that he invited her into his car, her anxiety kept her mute for the entire journey, but she was thrilled by the confidences he shared with her—his plans for the store, his marriage going badly. The first time he reached over and took her hand from where it rested on her thigh, her nervousness was mingled with a sense of triumph. Weeks later, when he stopped the car in the deep woods near the pond, unbuttoned her blouse, and pressed himself against her, it seemed inevitable and good, no matter what Mrs. Byne had said in Sunday school about the fires of hell. Being with him became an obsession, and for a time her life centered on their late afternoon trysts. Yet, in the moments of stillness afterward, she held him tightly in her arms and knew, with sadness, that he was not really hers. It was never clear to her, though, why it ultimately ended; he stopped offering to drive her home, and a short time after that, she stopped clerking at the store. Months later, one Sunday afternoon, she saw him strolling on Central Street with his family, clasping his young son by the hand, while Polly, his wife, pushed a new baby in a shiny old-fashioned carriage, with a fancy hood and big chrome wheels. Margo remembered the way he had nodded his head in her direction and given her a small smile, which signaled acknowledgment but not affection. So things changed between us because his wife got pregnant, she'd thought.

And now, Steven was talking. "Remember her last one? A total bore. Why does she go out of her way to find these losers?"

Even the sports section hadn't been able to dislodge Steven's preoccupation with Amanda and her men. Again, she said nothing in reply.

There was no point in giving an answer that might potentially spark a disagreement, which might then turn into a lingering irritation with each other, so that by nightfall they would have little eagerness to lock their bodies together. This must not happen—since according to her calendar, today was the beginning of her fertile time.

No, Margo corrected herself. Fertile times were what other women had. She had only seeding times, times to be sprinkled with sperm. This entailed planning and effort and work, the way preparation of the field was work to the farmer. But for her, it seemed, there was little hope of a harvest.

Three years already since they had first achieved the title of "infertile couple." The fertility specialist had insisted they meet the criteria to the letter: "a year of adequate exposure without the use of contraceptives." At first they had found something amusing about it. Their eyes had locked in merriment.

"Adequate exposure? Does he want us to run naked in the street?" she'd said.

"He wants us to screw in public without a condom," he'd said.

It was no longer amusing after a year and a half had gone by and they were a bona fide fertility failure.

Steven then had suffered the indignities of sperm counts, masturbating himself to orgasm, collecting the semen in a see-through jar, hiding it in a small brown paper bag to hand over to the receptionist in the doctor's office. She herself had charted her body's temperature as if she were an experimental animal, and given blood and urine samples for automated laboratory machines to scrutinize her monthly hormone rhythms. The gynecologist had tested her cervical mucus for its friendliness to sperm, and examined her uterus and ovarian follicles with multiple ultrasound exams. He had explored her reproductive tract by shooting it full of contrast dye and imaging its white-washed contours; he had poked a tiny telescope through a tiny hole punched in her abdomen to look even more closely at her ovaries, peering into nooks and crannies in search of endometriosis.

There was no indication that pregnancy was totally impossible, but there were significant flaws in the delicate mechanisms required for ovulation. The biggest problem was that her ovaries weren't producing normal follicles that could effectively nourish their eggs to maturity.

So now, once again—and perhaps for the last time, if she understood her gynecologist's innuendoes correctly— she was being dosed with the ovulation-inducing medi-cations whose job it was to pry an egg out of her ungiving ovaries: to stimulate an ovarian follicle to grow and nurture its egg to maturity and then to stimulate that follicle to release its egg. An ovulation that must not be squandered, that must be perfectly timed with intercourse, so that precious egg could be bathed in sperm.

Margo quietly stacked the dishes in the dishwasher. Then, as Steven's attention was still engaged by the newspaper, she went to the small stretch of recessed countertop that served as her kitchen desk and busied herself with writing out the weekend's shopping list.

After a time, Steven walked the short distance from table to desk. He placed his hand atop her shoulder and caressed it as he spoke. "So, what are your plans for the day?"

Margo put her hand on his, rubbed it gently, and turned toward him. "A little shopping and then I have to drop by my office. Crazy computer was down again yesterday. And naturally, Rundell doesn't give a damn about that. He expects a printout of the data analysis on his desk by the crack of dawn on Monday morning."

Practically never did she abandon Steven for work on weekends. He was the one who brought home full briefcases on Friday nights and made visits to his office over the weekend. She tried to minimize her absence: "Shouldn't take me more than a couple of hours, though."

His face brightened. "That's fine with me. I also need to go to my office for a while. Since we'll both be in town, how about meeting up for an early dinner at Le Jardin?"

She nodded with enthusiasm. Tranquil, elegant, unfailingly delicious, it was his favorite restaurant and a promising way to begin the evening's rites.

◌◌

MARGO DROVE HERSELF FIRST TO THE SHOPPING MALL nearest her neighborhood. She picked up the few items she actually needed, and then drifted from store to store, completely ignoring her morning's resolution to spend some hours enjoying the sunlight. She meandered through the Sephora store aisles inspecting all the beauty products, and let herself be tempted into buying a tangerine-colored lip gloss. At Macy's, she stopped at a counter heaped with big-brimmed hats, and tried on one for which she had no use. She picked up a long velvet fairy-tale cape and settled it over her shoulders. As soon as she was certain no one was looking, Margo twirled around and around to make it fly.

When she was a child, her family had been on too tight a budget for such fine clothes. Her mother wouldn't even let her try on the delicate blouses with frilly lace-edged collars she craved. Only clothes made of sturdy, serviceable fabrics that inevitably came in dull colors or graceless prints were allowed, judged respectable and proper, as well as sufficiently durable to withstand the alterations and multiple washings necessary for them to serve as hand-me-downs for her sister.

After the time spent at the shops and among the finery, Margo's feet began to ache. It hadn't been very sensible to wear uncomfortable footwear for shopping, but she enjoyed wearing high-heeled, too-narrow leather boots, even though her toes had to pay the price.

Near the pattering fountain that was the mall's architectural highlight, she found an empty seat. There seemed to be children everywhere. She watched little girls skipping about, and boisterous boys scrambling over benches and running along the fountain's edge. The woman seated next to her grumbled about the racket they were making, but Margo did not mind their noisiness. The children's songs and shouts enriched the air, and she enjoyed their energy.

Suddenly, she felt a stinging pain on her instep. Near her boot lay the missile that had crashed against her—a small metal car, now immobile and harmless. And a little farther, a boy of five or so, bracing himself for the sharp reprimand, or worse.

Margo saw the fear in his eyes and searched for a way to relieve it. She smiled as reassuringly as she could.

"Vroom vroom," Margo chanted, and sent the little vehicle speeding back to its owner. The boy's arm shot out to catch his car. His face full of surprise and relief, he grabbed it and wheeled away.

By five o'clock Margo was at her desk in the hospital's administrative offices, and the printer began spitting out the data she had summoned up: that week's counts of the number of patients admitted each day, their diagnoses, their lengths of stay, and the billable items of care. She collected each page as it emerged and scoured the numbers on it with interest. Is this a trend? she wondered, as she spotted an interesting pattern. Chasing the clues, she entered another command, and the new analysis confirmed the presence of a trend. It seemed a kind of power, to tease out associations hidden deep in what at first glance seemed only a dense forest of numbers. It was like being able to wrest small secrets from nature. Gratified, she strode toward Rundell's office, six pages of satisfying printout in her hand.

In the chief administrator's suite, a woman from Housekeeping with a dark glass bottle and a cloth in her rubber-gloved hands was buffing his walnut desk to an opulent shine, and the smell of furniture polish was strong. Margo stopped for a moment to greet her, thinking how lonely it must be in such deserted surroundings, and then placed her packet of printouts on his administrative assistant's desk.

Not everyone in the hospital was pleased by the sumptuous surroundings of Rundell's suite, Margo knew. The doctors never ceased complaining. "Walnut and leather," they grumbled, "while we all have to economize." What the doctors didn't understand was that such furnishings were not simply luxuries, but badges of achievement in an administrative career. When shared assistants were supplanted by designated personal administrative assistants, when paint was replaced by expensive wallpaper, when industrial-grade flooring was exchanged for plush wool carpeting, it was the equivalent of adding stars and stripes to a military person's uniform. She herself shared an assistant and had only cloth-covered chairs in her office.

It was only a short wait for the elevator that would take her to her parking floor. Hospital activity was quite slow on Saturdays, with office workers off for the weekend, outpatient clinics closed, and elective new admissions not scheduled to arrive until Sunday afternoon. So, when the elevator doors slid open, she was surprised to find, instead of an empty elevator, a huge box that barred her way. A stocky male transporter stood behind it, squeezed against the back of the elevator. It was an incubator, she realized, the kind for premature babies, probably fresh from a cleaning or mechanical overhaul. Margo slid around the machine and slipped into the small space remaining at its side.

An artificial womb. She examined it closely. A heavy metal base, stolid and dull, and on top, a clear plastic dome punctured by pleated armholes that let in doctors' hands to examine, nurses' hands to cleanse and stroke. The tiny baby to be placed there would be so separate, so alone. Enclosed in so hard a shell, when once there had been the familiar comfort of a liquid hammock. In place of the sturdy, steady beat of a mother's heart, the baby would hear only hospital sounds: muffled words, mechanical beeps. Margo accompanied the machine until the elevator jolted as it halted at the fourth floor: the Obstetrics Wing and Newborn Nursery.

The transporter pushed at the incubator, grunting; it was obviously even heavier than it looked. The machine bumped over the elevator's edge and then began to roll fast, faster, its wheels on shiny vinyl now. Farther and farther it receded, into the corridor ahead. To where the babies were.

The elevator doors hesitated for a second and began to slide together, blotting the incubator from her sight. At the last fraction of a second, just before the doors shut entirely, she jammed her hands between the rubber gaskets and spread them open. Her feet moved quickly, hurrying to pick up the incubator's trail.

The transporter swiped his ID across the face of the electronic monitor guarding the door to the Obstetrics Wing. It opened for him, and Margo, directly behind, slipped through.

In their rooms, Margo knew, new mothers would be resting, recouping their energy after the arduous process of birthing, while their babies were parked for a time in the Newborn Nursery; in other rooms, mothers were hosting visitors and proudly showing off their newborns. Meanwhile, the lumbering incubator had the corridor's width all to itself. Margo followed closely behind as it rumbled along farther and farther down the hall. Until there it was, the Newborn Nursery, high plate glass almost to the ceiling. And inside, a blur of pink and white and blue.

She stepped up close to the big window and pressed her nose against the glass. Babies everywhere. A sea of little faces, mostly puckered, mostly red. All kinds of hair, some stuck up in tufts, some thick across foreheads. Bodies swaddled in flannel blankets, stretched tight and tucked firm. One little elbow suddenly stuck itself up, pushing swiftly and assertively against the taut blanket. Had it practiced that in the womb? To heave up so, like a little mountain? And here, one lay quietly awake. Clear blue eyes, mouth so pink and fine. Every so often, the round fists waved and fell on its lips, and then the face suddenly became all action, all mouth. So sweet in its desperate clumsiness. So dear.

The transporter's rubber-soled running shoes squeaked against the vinyl flooring. Margo watched as from the stacked cart parked outside the nursing station he took a clean blue paper gown, shook it loose, slipped it over his flannel shirt and blue jeans, and tied its strings. Then, with a grunt, he began to push the incubator toward the nursery door.

She stared at his feet as they plodded along, attaching, then detaching in turn from the vinyl floor. Left. Right. Left.

It would be so lovely to be immersed in that sea of little faces. The breaths and sighs must be so delicious to hear, and that new-baby fragrance to sniff.

Her feet began to inch forward, left, right, left, tracing the transporter's footsteps across the shiny polished flooring, over to the stacked cart. She pulled down a blue gown, shook it out, and slipped her arms into the full sleeves. Why not? Just for a few minutes. What harm could it do?

She tied the loose strings to the back and continued trailing the transporter as he swiped his security ID card and the doors opened for them.

Inside, she tiptoed between the babies, admiring now this one's pointy nose, now that one's delicately sculpted ears, until she reached the dear one. In repose now, the closed eyes were like slits, the eyelashes dark fringes on the pale face, the mouth a pinch of rose red, the skin so pearly, so fine. It must be soft as velvet, she thought.

"Get away from there! Who are you? You're not one of our staff!"

The nurse walked closer, her face grim as she maneuvered around the other babies toward Margo. "Carol!" the nurse called out sharply to the clerk outside at the nursing station.

"Please. I work here, in the hospital," Margo protested, fumbling at her neck for the plastic-coated identification card. "I'm in Administration."

"That doesn't give you license to walk in wherever you want."

"You're right. Of course it doesn't. I really shouldn't be here. It's just that I came in the elevator with the incubator."

"So?" The nurse hesitated, weighing the circumstances, the possibilities.

"Do you want me to call security?" the clerk asked. "Shall I start filling out an incident report?"

"Please, no. It won't happen again, I promise," Margo begged.

THAT EVENING, AT LE JARDIN, MARGO ATE HER DINNER without much enthusiasm while praising the food as she always did to please Steven, who was as proud of the chef as if he himself were the proprietor of the restaurant. At all the conversational crossroads where her input was required, she responded appropriately to keep up her end of the conversation. In between, though, she felt slightly dazed and terribly worried. The nurse had written down her name after inspecting her ID badge thoroughly. What would she do then? Would Margo soon find herself without a job?

Let it go for now, she advised herself, let it go. No use brooding over behavior she could not undo. All her energy had to be preserved for the important work yet to be done during the night.

The remainder of Saturday evening they spent quietly at home. At one minute to ten, Steven reached for the remote to turn on the evening television news. It was his ritual without fail—every night by nine forty-five he was already checking his watch.

Margo walked upstairs to prepare for her own rites. From the bed, she removed the throw pillows with their green unicorns prancing across fern forests, and folded up the quilted bedspread. She turned the shower on full strength and very warm, and with a cap to keep her hair dry, let the soothing stream of water wash over her. After toweling dry, she selected from her bedroom dresser the pale blue satin nightgown Steven loved to run his fingers down, and slipped it on. She returned to the bathroom to brush her hair, and lingered there so that she could time her walk into the bedroom just when he came up.

The tinkle of coins on wood as Steven emptied his pockets out onto the bureau top announced his arrival. Margo opened the bathroom door and walked straight into his line of vision.

He saw her and his eyes grew solemn. "Whenever I see that gown, I know it's the time of the month for mating," he said quietly, a tinge of bitterness in his voice.

"Don't you want to anyway?" She was taken aback by

his response. He'd never seemed to resent or refuse her subtle invitation for sex, either for pleasure or reproductive purposes.

"Of course I do. But right now, I'm thinking about women complaining about men just wanting them for their bodies. It seems like it's not even my body you want. It's what comes through it."

Now it was Margo who felt irritated. Yes, that was true, but wasn't he forgetting that the baby they were trying to make would be his child, too? He'd heartily welcomed the idea that it was time for them to try for a baby.

Then, deep in his eyes, she saw the pain. She suddenly understood how he must feel—like a stallion led to stud, his sexuality controlled by doctor, date, and a woman's monthly rhythm. In a way, he really was unmanned.

Steven must have seen her soften, for he reached out then and pulled her close. And soon, he ran his fingers down her satin gown, grasped her waist tightly, and pulled her to the bed.

$\mathcal{I}$t was a day of transition. The earth's hard winter crust had softened, and the wet fresh smell of early spring was in the air. As Margo left for work, she searched the planting beds near her front door for crocuses, but none were to be seen.

Each month, she noted on her calendar the date that her next period should begin, hoping each time that the day would come and go without the scarlet sign of defeat. It was now two weeks past the night she had worn the ice-blue nightgown, and the date on her calendar was one day past the red-circled one, so there was still reason for hope.

As always, her office today was in genteel disarray. Here, she enjoyed some relief from the spit-and-polish tidiness she practiced at home to alleviate Steven's discomfort when objects were not in their usual and expectable place. Here, she kept things wherever they suited her: the backs of chairs occasionally served as hangers for sweaters and scarves, and the seats served when necessary as auxiliary bookshelves. The slight mess mattered little, since no one of any importance entered her tiny quarters; she was low enough on the administrative totem pole so that it was always she who made the trek to everyone else's offices for meetings.

Her desk she did keep in order, with neat piles of computer printouts sorted according to topic: patient flow, billings, Medicaid reimbursements, expenditures, and the like, as well as the correlations and extrapolations she derived from them. A pleasant avalanche of numbers.

This morning, though, Margo had not yet attacked the piles. Instead, she was studying the memo that Sylvia, the assistant she shared with two colleagues, had wordlessly handed her in its sealed envelope labeled "Immediate Attention."

"The hospital's nurses have printed a list of grievances against the hospital administration," she read. "Today they will distribute them throughout the medical center. Tomorrow, they will give an interview to the local cable channel and the newspaper. At least they were responsible enough to notify me of that in advance."

She could almost hear Rundell's voice spitting out the words.

"We have heard rumors they are considering a strike. To counter this challenge, an all-staff administrative meeting will be held this morning at nine. Highest priority. Full attendance. No exceptions."

The only person in the conference room when Margo arrived was Mike Sherman, who'd been hired three years ago during the same month as she. Once, over an after-work drink, they'd wondered if they'd both been hired in a spasm of affirmative action: a woman and an African-American coming in to fill a quota. Margo took the seat nearest Mike's, grateful to stay close to his always supportive and reassuring presence.

"Doesn't this setup remind you of those old World War II movies?" he asked, with a broad smile. "You know, where the generals gather with their aides in the war room around tables covered with little tanks and toy soldiers to hear intelligence reports and plan attacks? It's sad, though, to think of planning attacks against our own nurses."

"You think it'll come to that? You don't think there's still a chance to cool things down?"

"Nope. Rundell won't give an inch. You know him—it would go against his grain. And right now, he can't afford to give any impression of weakness, not with the past quarter's revenues showing the hospital is heading for a big operating loss. The trustees are breathing down his neck to economize, and that doesn't include making expensive concessions."

The room began to fill with their colleagues, and they gave greetings and made light conversation until a sharp cracking sound pierced the buzz of voices. Rundell had slammed the door shut with unusual force.

He was a tall, thin man, almost gaunt, with a quick walk, though once he sat down he looked much smaller, since much of his height was in his long legs. His pale blue eyes were encircled by silver wire-rimmed glasses. His manner was as contained and taut as his body. His abilities commanded Margo's respect but not her affection; she did not particularly like him.

Without preamble, Rundell launched into an evaluation of the nurses' manifesto, summarizing their grievances.

"This is what they contend: One, the hospital administration interferes with their ability to fully practice the profession as they define it. Two, the reason the administration wants to redefine their role is in order to make the hospital more fiscally productive. Three, salaries are inadequate. Four, work shift schedules, particularly mandatory double shifts and weekend shifts, are highly disruptive and too rigidly enforced."

Margo quickly typed the gist of these points into her iPad. Salaries and work shifts, while difficult to adjust, would be the simpler problems to resolve. The other issues, the ones that touched on the nurses' sense of identity, self-image, and autonomy would be the ones Rundell would least understand, and simple remedies would not easily be found.

"What the nurses want," Rundell continued, "is to practice according to some new vision of their profession being promulgated by activist faculty in the nursing schools. What they fail to recognize is that this vision is impossible to reconcile with nursing care needs in real hospitals. In addition to being an outlet for their anger, the nurses will see a strike as something to make these instructors proud. My prediction is that the nurses will find this irresistible. In my judgment a strike is inevitable, though still a few months away."

"Told you," mumbled Mike under his breath.

"During the coming months, we must prepare well.

We'll try to avert a strike, but every position we take, every minor concession we make, will be designed to strengthen our field position."

With each point he made, he jabbed his index finger in the air.

"I myself will not take a forward position, since that could push them into action before we ourselves are sufficiently prepared. My plan is for each of you to interact with them."

Margo pictured Rundell as a giant spider, spinning a thick web and positioning himself out of sight to watch the trap in silence.

"Listen carefully," he said, as he instructed them on strategy and tactics. "Argue little. Concede nothing." Finally, he folded his hands primly on the table, a signal that he was ready to listen to their comments. Margo's colleagues around the table soon weighed in, all agreeing with Rundell.

"No question, we have to hang tough."

"Buckling in to them would destroy the hospital's capacity to survive."

"If the strike occurs, we must stand fast."

They all sounded like Roman centurions bracing against the barbarians. Margo pictured the nurses confronted by a wall of implacable armed soldiers.

Men's language, filled with metaphors of physical competition, often sounded so bellicose. When her colleagues boasted with fierce pride of having hung tough, or taken their opponents to the mat, she often imagined them as bear cubs tussling in front of a forest cave. They're large little boys, she would sometimes think.

But maybe she was wrong. Suppose this was indeed the language and behavior of success? If she spoke up now and challenged the wisdom of adopting an aggressive strategy to destroy the nurses' morale and will, would they simply exchange knowing smiles at this pitiful demonstration of female naïveté? And would they be correct?

As she ruminated on this riddle, Rundell dismissed the meeting. "That's all. Thank you."

"Ready to man your battle station?" Mike said to Margo as they walked out. She shook her head grimly. As she pictured a battlefield, the only nurse Margo saw standing upon it was her best friend, Kate, whose warm companionship made Margo feel more solid, more sound, strengthened in a way she could not exactly put into words.

BACK IN HER OFFICE, MARGO TACKLED THE MORNING'S mail. Inside one of the larger envelopes, string-closed in the back like much of the in-hospital mail, was a missive quite unlike any other piece of mail that had ever crossed her desk. "Incident Report" was written in a bold black font at the top, with the date and time prominently displayed directly below. As she began to read, Margo felt her body tighten and her fingers chill.

"Margo Kerber entered the Newborn Nursery, having followed a transporter who was bringing in an incubator.

She did have her hospital identification badge with her, but she is not authorized to be in this area. Kerber admitted that she should not have entered the space, and said it would never happen again." The report was signed by a person identifying herself as the head nurse of the Newborn Nursery.

Also enclosed was another memo: "This report will be placed in your permanent staff file."

For days, she'd been half-expecting such an incident report. But now she held the paper in her hands, a tangible thing, no longer simply a wisp of worry that could easily be brushed away.

Margo's heart raced as she considered several unnerving possibilities. Suppose a copy had also been sent to Rundell, her immediate supervisor? Suppose he soon would summon her for an interrogation? Or a firing?

Her mind sped to construct convincing arguments. "It was a momentary impulse," she could explain. "I'm not usually an impulsive person, but once in a while I do go over the line."

She was thinking of the time she'd grabbed a coloring book from the store. Whenever Margo had been sick in bed with an earache or sore throat, she could request a coloring book or a book of paper doll cutouts, and Mama would buy it for her from Kmart without a grumble about the cost or the trouble. It was the one good thing about being sick. Sometimes, though, too long a period of time went by without her falling ill. Once, she'd made her own visit to Kmart. In the children's section in the back of the store, she'd held a clutch of coloring books close to her chest. When a customer came by and kept the salesclerk busy, she slid one of them underneath her buttoned-up cardigan sweater, put the remaining books back in their place, and walked toward the door, her heart pounding harder than she'd thought possible.

"It was foolish," she'd say to Rundell, "but don't most people act on impulse at some point?" How likely was it, though, that he ever did so?

She began to search for another, better scenario—and found one. Although many incidents went unreported, a significant number were submitted, even for exceedingly minor events. So why would it not be possible that some harried office worker had made a copy to send to Margo Kerber, the staff person named, and then slipped the original into a file labeled Kerber M., a staff file among hundreds, a paper among thousands sleeping in dozens of office cabinets, a paper that would not be seen until it was time for her annual performance review, when it would be something long past, just water under the bridge.

Yes. This was the outcome she would focus on. The other, the image of the stern, judgmental, unforgiving Rundell, faded and dispersed into shredding fragments in her imagination.

With an exhale that carried away the stress, Margo pushed her chair away from the desk and headed down the corridor to the small staff kitchen to treat herself to a comforting cup of hot chocolate.

Almost there, she felt the shock of sudden wetness and

ducked into the nearby bathroom. She cleaned herself, looked at the gush of red, and flushed the toilet. It was impossible to generate any soothing alternative possibility for this, and her forehead began to throb. This month, as every other month, she had foolishly allowed hope to flourish despite the odds.

Anger joined despair. Each time her period flowed, each month her sentence as a barren woman was extended, this surge of frustration pulsed through her body, its sharpness not attenuated by familiarity. She felt angry at the body which once again had failed both herself and Steven. She felt angry at the uselessness of all the visits and tests. She felt angry at all that temperature taking, all that fornication without feeling—and for what? She ripped off the paper covering the tampon she had purchased from the dispenser on the bathroom wall and inserted it roughly.

BACK IN HER OFFICE, MARGO CALLED HER DOCTOR AND reported her status to the receptionist. Her tone was matter-of-fact and businesslike, for screams, curses, or threats of malpractice suits would not cause her empty womb to fill. She simply scheduled another appointment.

After the call, Margo's body still felt tight and her breath still came shallow and fast. She yanked a folder of work squarely in front of herself and willed her attention to the material inside. Long ago, she had discovered how to shut out unwanted feelings: stare at something hard enough and you could disappear to somewhere else, like Alice down the rabbit hole. So Margo burrowed herself into the words and numbers before her—deep, deeper, deeper still.

And soon enough the tightness in her muscles eased, and there was only the dependable solidity of crisp numbers and letters on the page.

3

The following Sunday—which preceded the Monday she was scheduled to see her gynecologist—Margo found it difficult to stay in her house. Everything was overly familiar, unable to peak her interest or grab her attention. Nothing here was novel enough to distract her from the gnawing anxiety fueled by her upcoming doctor's appointment.

The solution: another shopping expedition.

She served and cleared brunch, and then told Steven of her plan. "I don't suppose you want to come with me," she said with a knowing smile. "Right!" he replied, laughing. They did not do well shopping together. She preferred to browse, enjoying the rush of surprise and triumph when she happened upon an unanticipated and perfect find. Steven's method was quite different: he shopped only when necessary, with a very specific goal in mind, and quickly purchased the first prospect that met his minimum requirements. The female gatherer, the male hunter.

Woodchester was a midsize city with a population close to ninety thousand people, and located less than sixty miles from New Haven and Yale University. It was compact enough so that the drive to Margo's favorite shopping mall —through her suburban neighborhood to the contemporary commercial district that girdled the old central core —could be done in less than fifteen minutes. Today, she drove this route in a particularly leisurely fashion, since her aim was not efficiency but to run out the clock until the next day dawned. At the mall she trekked from end to end, avoiding only the wing containing the maternity shop. She immersed herself in the cheerful busyness and the people-watching: clusters of blue-jeaned teenagers gossiping together, running-shoed seniors pacing out the miles, and shoppers like herself trekking in and out of specialty stores. A few things she didn't actually need caught her fancy, and she purchased a bracelet constructed of glass beads that matched one of her favorite pullovers.

Late in the afternoon, satiated with shopping, Margo sought out her car, searching for the landmarks she had memorized in order to find it in the uniformity of the mall's parking lot. Her limited navigational skills served her well today, and she came across the car after only a brief reconnaissance. She did not, however, set a course toward home as she had originally intended. Instead, she steered her car toward the center of the city.

Share House was a group home for developmentally disabled teenagers where Margo volunteered for a few hours on the second and fourth Sundays of each month. This was an alternate Sunday, and Margo hadn't planned— at least not consciously—to visit Share House today, but the children's cookbook she'd just purchased at Barnes & Noble, so full of step-by-easy-step photographs and pared-down procedures, was perfect for young kitchen helpers who required simplicity. So why, she reasoned, let a schedule keep them from having the pleasure of it now? Why not provide herself with another diversion to keep anxiety at bay?

And so it was that she gifted herself with an additional opportunity to spend time with Janie, who had become the recipient of Margo's motherly affection, motherly tenderness, and motherly concern.

She rang the bell and, in the gathering dusk, patiently waited on the threshold.

"Margo! Sorry it took a while. I was in the middle of thickening the sauce." Cecilia, supervisor of the home, stood with potholder in hand. "It's lovely to see you, but weren't you here just last week?"

"I was out shopping and found this absolutely perfect cookbook." Margo held it up as proof. "And I thought, why wait to bring it?"

"And see Janie, hmm?" said Cecilia in a teasing tone of voice.

Margo, from the first, had diligently tried to obey Cecilia's orientation instruction: "Try not to make favorites. They all need somebody." And she had succeeded in finding something lovable in each one of the young residents. But there was no denying the special affection Margo had developed for Janie, and Cecilia both recognized and accepted it.

In the kitchen, a large pot of water boiled, wisps of

steam escaping from underneath the vibrating lid. Cecilia placed the new cookbook on the counter and flipped through its pages with one hand as she stirred tomato sauce with the other. Her alibi accepted, Margo slipped away to the living room.

There, several young people were stretched out on the floor completely mesmerized by the sweet, animated video streaming across the television screen. Margo threaded her way through the room between the mismatched sofas and flea-market chairs, greeting each young person as she passed. In the far corner of the room, where she sat at a sagging fiberboard card table, fourteen-year-old Janie looked up and a warm smile of welcome crossed her face. "Come see, Margo, come see," she called, beckoning with both hands.

A glow always emanated from Janie's face, which Margo had quickly experienced as a sign of Janie's ability to love, a quality that transcended her inability to learn. Being the special recipient of Janie's gentle affection Margo felt as a great privilege. She so cherished every opportunity to give Janie love, to nurture her and guide her.

"I'm coming, Janie," she said. "But I can't stay for long."

Janie's hands were dabbing paste and sticking colored pieces of construction paper on a cardboard mat. Janie pointed to her work with a paste-encrusted finger, her eyes shining with pride. "See? See?"

Margo praised, and re-praised, the colors and the shapes.

As Margo watched Janie pound with her fists yet more pieces of colored paper sticky with the white glue that seeped out from underneath their edges, she admired the near-platinum hair, the fine-boned delicate profile. How lovely Janie was.

It was Kate who'd first discovered Share House, when Arnie, a spindly sixteen-year-old boy, was recovering from severe pneumonia on her unit. Every day, a troop of young people from Arnie's group home visited him, bringing gifts of paper chains flecked with spots of glue or plates of misshapen cookies. Kate chatted with them when they came, and soon looked forward to their visits almost as much as Arnie clearly did.

After Arnie was well again and discharged home, Kate called to ask the staff director of Share House if she could volunteer there, and when the answer was an enthusiastic "yes," she enlisted Margo to volunteer as well. Kate was certain of Margo's interest, since this was one of the few commonalities they'd discovered in their childhoods, there being otherwise few given Kate's upbringing in a diverse city neighborhood and Margo's in an almost entirely Protestant Ohio small town: each of them had witnessed close up the dreary childhood of a mentally retarded cousin living in an uninspiring parental home.

Nevertheless, whenever Kate had called to set a firm date for Margo's first visit to Share House as a potential volunteer, Margo had found excuses to postpone it. Kate had finally put her finger on the reason: "Are you afraid?" And it was true. To her shame, Margo had wondered how developmentally disabled people needing to be in a semi-institutional setting might look: ugly, even a little grotesque?

"I really do want to come," Margo had explained. "I just don't know what to expect."

"Of course you don't," Kate said. "Why should anyone, since we hide them out of sight?"

Janie searched for a strip of red construction paper. She stooped and stretched, and her breasts swayed gently over the table. So richly curved, so womanly.

On the way home after her first visit to Share House, Kate had shocked her with the sterilization disgrace.

"Eugenics, they called it. So very scientific-sounding, right?" Kate's voice was thick with sarcasm. "Involuntary butchery was what it was. Keep the retarded from multiplying. Keep them from polluting the genetic grandeur of America. It was legal, too. Right here in the US of A."

As Janie contentedly smeared paste on the colored papers, Margo pictured how it would have been for her. Very early in the morning they would have come, all smiles and soft murmurs. They would have strapped her to a mobile cot and wheeled her into a big windowless room. The cloth drenched in ether would be pressed over her nose and mouth until it gagged her and choked her into unconsciousness. And when she woke, she would discover the blood-crusted gash.

The cruelty of it, the desecration, Margo thought with disgust. Mangling a perfect body because of an imperfect mind.

"Janie, look. Here's a pretty piece of yellow," she said. "Show me what you can do with the yellow."

✑

WHEN SHE LEFT SHARE HOUSE EARLY THAT EVENING, the traffic was light and she soon was turning into the driveway of her red brick colonial house. Traditional white shutters framed each window and a heavy brass knocker adorned the front door. The house had been a compromise between them: Steven had agreed to a more traditional exterior although he coveted a dramatic, glass-walled contemporary; she had agreed to crisply modern furnishings, so long as there would be no shiny chrome anywhere and the kitchen could have a country look.

Steven was still clad in his running suit after the afternoon jog that was one of his weekend luxuries. He sat in the living room surrounded by a month's worth of *Time* magazines, catching up on his reading.

"You're home so late," he said.

"After shopping, I stopped at Share House to bring over a book I bought."

"Again?" Thinking he was either a bit jealous for her weekend time, or hungry, she went over and gave him a big hug.

In the kitchen, under the gaze of the roosters, Margo considered dinner. Tonight, even though it was late, and her feet were tired, and Steven was hungry, she felt the need to create something, even if it would last no longer than the eating. She took out a box of defrosted phyllo dough and another of chopped spinach. With the help of her recipe file and the ingredients in her freezer and pantry shelves, she constructed a mushroom and spinach-encased salmon loaf wrapped in pastry. While it baked she fed Steven bits of cheese on Melba toast to dampen his hunger, and brought him a scotch and soda to make his wait more tolerable. When the oven timer finally buzzed, she called him to the table and brought over her creation with a magician's flourish.

"Definitely worth waiting for," Steven complimented her after he'd taken the first bite, even though it was well past nine.

After the dinner dishes were scraped and stacked, Margo started the dishwasher. "Clean up, Maria," she ordered. During the nights of scrubbing dinner dishes for her mother, as her hands had moved steadily in the hot and soapy sink water, Margo had daydreamed that one day she would be a princess and order her servants to do all such chores. Now, Maria the KitchenAid served that purpose well enough.

Margo joined Steven in the living room. He poured out for them the after-dinner liqueurs that were their private ritual for ushering out the weekend. Margo sipped the Cointreau he had chosen, and nibbled on a chocolate truffle brought by a guest who cared little for their weight-watching. These Sunday evenings after dinner, when they retracted their attention from the world outside and focused instead on each other, were the time of the week Margo treasured most, for it was then that they let the minor irritations of the week go and shared confidences with each other. It was on such a Sunday night that Steven revealed what Margo thought was likely the deepest humiliation of his youth.

For a long time after they'd met, Steven's life had seemed to Margo such a charmed one. Brought up as he was on New York's Upper East Side in an apartment house graced with an awning and a doorman, his youthful years had glowed in her mind as an ideal of nurturance and advantage. He was educated at the Riverdale Country Day School, and then went on to the Ivies: BA from Cornell, law degree from Yale. But then one night, early in their marriage, when they shared amusing incidents about their childhoods, his mood turned darker and he confided that during his senior year of high school, on the day when he received all three rejection letters from Harvard, Yale, and Princeton, he had careened down the paths in Central Park, yelling about the injustice of it all, until he hit a rock, flipped off his bike, and broke his wrist. "You're the first person I've ever told this to," he had said. So there are thorns even in paradise, she'd thought, as she heard the disappointment still in his voice. It had thrilled her to realize that, as she felt safe with him, he also felt safe enough with her to reveal this: something he still regarded as a failure.

Tonight, though, they spoke of things of little consequence. Margo chose to avoid spoiling the evening by reminding him of her upcoming appointment, that tomorrow she might be giving Steven his greatest disappointment yet.

Instead, she popped a Netflix disc into the DVD player and nestled into him as they watched. And after a time, they quietly went upstairs to bed.

4

———

$\mathcal{S}$ince Margo's doctor practiced in a professional building only a few blocks from the hospital, Margo could walk there and not have to contend with the slow city traffic or search for a parking space. Today, though, looking at the merchandise in the store windows along the way provided not the slightest relief from anxiety, and her heartbeat ticked faster the closer she came to his office building.

The doctor's waiting room was coolly elegant. Fine fabrics in shades of gray covered the seats of polished aluminum chairs, and glass tabletops sparkled. Margo wrote her name and arrival time on the receptionist's notepad and took her customary seat near the entrance door, where she felt less noticeable to the other women sharing the room with her and less likely to be drawn into a conversation.

In the farthest corner of the room, a youngish woman, late twenties, unfamiliar to Margo—by now she recognized many of the "regulars"—was seated on the loveseat, her well-coiffed head buried low in the sheaves of paperwork she had been given to fill out. Margo glanced at the newcomer surreptitiously, so as not to make her even more uncomfortable than she already surely was. Margo understood, of course—for hadn't she herself behaved in the very same way when she was the neophyte in this waiting room: hiding her face, fearful that someone might recognize her, fearful her impairment would become public knowledge, feeling flooded with shame? Those first few months an uneasiness came over her each time the waiting room door began to open. Suppose someone she knew came in, such as a woman from her own neighborhood?

You? the woman might think. The career woman we all thought was childless by choice? And it's really because you can't make a baby.

Suppose some physician or administrator from the hospital came to hold a conference with her gynecologist, who was a member of the medical staff? When they saw and greeted her, would their voices be heavy with pity?

Only after many visits without a single confrontation did she stop hiding behind the magazines. And after a time, Margo found that sitting in this room full of similarly afflicted women actually provided a small measure of comfort, proving that she was not the only mistake of nature.

She had, in fact, been thinking about the function and malfunction of bodies for a very long time. As a small girl, she'd had her own theories about that. One day, her mother and her aunt found her sitting on the front porch, shirtless, plucking at the skin around her tiny nipples. "Whatever are you doing?" her mother had asked. "Making them pointy," she had explained, not interrupting the rhythm of her work. The women broke out in peals of laughter and Margo felt humiliated: How could they make fun of her like that, these women whose fronts were as fluffy as cotton candy, the tips of their breasts as pointy as the bottoms of ice cream cones?

Boys had different kinds of bodies; she knew that because she had watched them in the woods. Her family's property ended where the forest came down to a narrow river, the best fishing spot in the county, and she went there often to observe the boys that gathered there. She had been forbidden to walk on the banks of the stream and she obeyed that order because she could see quite well enough from the branches of the old walnut tree growing not far from the edge of the water. She had eagerly watched the boys on the other side of the stream, not only fishing but also relieving themselves. Their pee came arching out like a rainbow, high and full. It was as forceful as the stream from a garden hose turned on strong. Afterward, she would climb down from the tree and try to go like that. She would push and try to make the stream fly and pierce the air. But instead, it just trickled to the ground, dribbling down the inside of her leg until it wet her sock and made a puddle in her shoe.

The receptionist called out a name, and the new patient rose quickly from her seat and disappeared into the doctor's consulting suite. Margo could picture the landmarks of the path the woman was now following: the two bathrooms with shelves for purses and urine specimens; the two examining rooms, one on either side of the corridor, alike as identical twins; and finally, at the end of the corridor, the doctor's study, a room that promised as much to the hopeful as the hall of the Wizard of Oz. After so many visits in the past three years, Margo was sure she could navigate the route in total darkness.

The door to the waiting room creaked slightly as it opened. In came a fortyish woman followed by a child of about three who romped after her. Margo stared at the duo. A real mother, here? Had she been fertile once and somehow fallen from grace? Or was she one of the doctor's successes, trying for another miracle?

The woman removed the boy's sweater and handed him a wooden puzzle brought forth from her tote bag. The boy fell upon the toy, and his little hands slammed the pieces into the frame. Within minutes, though, he lost interest. He sprung up and began to dart back and forth from one side of the waiting room to the other, successfully evading his mother's attempts to restrain him.

Margo watched with amusement. She still found delight in the antics of small children without being assaulted by bitterness, and for this she was grateful. Pregnant women, however, were another story: she could not see a woman heavy with child without feeling her mouth tighten with envy. Fortunately this gynecologist specialized in infertility, sparing her the sight of a waiting room full of easily pregnant women with their big bellies and dreamy smiles.

Now the receptionist called Margo's name: "Consulting room, please, with Dr. Renfield."

So. No preliminaries today. Straight to the wizard's chamber.

"Mrs. Kerber. Sit down, please," the doctor said, rising to greet her and motioning her to the chair in the conversation area by the window. A definite departure from routine: he had never before asked her to sit anywhere but in front of his desk.

He took the matching chair facing hers. "You know this was a repeat trial for this medication," he said.

She nodded.

"Let's review. The initial medication we used to induce ovulation failed. After that, the in vitro fertilization attempts failed. We've now tried a second ovulation-stimulating medication, and it too has also failed over a few cycles.

"I think we should face facts squarely. There is still the donor egg route, though given your past responses, I am not sure it would implant—and in any case, you've said you're not comfortable with that method. Although in rare cases miracles have happened when I was certain the prognosis was unfavorable, I think it would be in your best interest to accept that the chance you will conceive is quite negligible."

Margo felt cold ice spreading inside her chest.

"I know that this is a terrible disappointment," he rushed on. "You've been so diligent. Your charts have been so painstakingly kept, and you've followed instructions so carefully. You couldn't have done a better job. I think we can be comforted by the fact that we've done the very best we could."

So many times she had imagined this moment, when he finally told her it was hopeless. He was cloaking it in soft words and reassurances, but inside the gentle sentences was the hard kernel of catastrophe. So many times she had imagined crumbling, crying loud enough to be heard in the waiting room down the hall. Yet here she was, composed and listening quietly to his words.

Was it because she was hearing him, yet not hearing him? Believing him, but not believing him—at least not yet?

"There's one more thing I want to recommend," he was saying. "A psychiatrist who specializes in women's issues, including infertility. I would like you to see her."

So did he think her mind was as crippled as her body? If I believed that, she thought, I'd feel twice as inadequate as I already do. I won't believe that. I can't.

"It will give you the opportunity to talk about your situation," he continued, "to explore your thoughts about being a mother, about being a woman."

Let another doctor poke and probe in yet another one of her private places? No, Margo thought, no.

"I recommend that you and your husband see her soon."

Steven, too? He had to be kidding. Steven had little interest in psychology. This was to her advantage, though. Steven would veto the recommendation, she was certain, and that would be that.

"Once you verbalize your thoughts and feelings, you can start to work them out."

You don't even know the proper terminology, Margo

thought. Work them through: that was what the magazine article she'd read by a psychologist had called this process.

"I hope you find it helpful," Dr. Renfield said as he rose from his chair. He walked to the door and opened it wide, indicating the appointment was over. He shook her hand firmly as she walked out.

Margo made her way slowly down the corridor, past the examining rooms, past the bathrooms. She entered the waiting room and wondered what the women sitting there could read in her face.

5

———

The poached fish and the asparagus soufflé had been prepared and dined upon; the dishes were being showered by Maria the dishwasher; and Steven, well-sated and fortified for several more hours of work, had sequestered himself in his study surrounded by briefs and books. Her evening work done, Margo moved to the living room, where she turned on the TV to bring sound into the uncomfortable silence, and then let herself sink into the sofa.

She hadn't yet cried. At work, where she must not show tears under any circumstances, Margo had plodded on automatic pilot through the afternoon's activities. Once home, where she could cry, no tears came, only thoughts weighted with sorrow. Never to initiate life? Never to feel life moving inside her? Never to bring forth life and nourish it with sustenance from her own body? How could she accept this?

The idea of baby-making was a kind of magic that had enchanted her ever since the summer of her fifth year. During those long hot summer days out on the big white porch, with flies buzzing aimlessly around her and the scent of the cornfield sweetening the air, she was thinking about babies.

The porch had wound around the entire house, sectioned off by invisible but strictly enforced divisions. The space near the front door was for grown-ups. On the other side of the house, the side facing the vegetable garden, the roofed porch was reserved for quiet play. Board games were stacked on an old card table and a blanket was spread on the porch's slats. Sprinkled with old pillows, it was a good place for a child to nestle and read or daydream.

She lay there thinking about babies because when Mama peeled off her housedress, she could see clearly that Mama's stomach was big, the skin stretched like a thick balloon. Her body was swollen again, and she looked like the hippopotamus in the animal picture book. And when Mama would be regular again, there would be another screaming baby outside, sucking on her chest. And Daddy would come to look at it a lot, his face proud.

She lay there wondering how Mama actually got the babies. They grew in her stomach, she knew that, and then they came out when they were big enough. Her mother had told her it had something to do with eggs, that eggs grew into babies, and that daddies had something to do with it, that they gave a seed for the egg. But it was her daddy who had the eggs, so Mama must have told it wrong. Every day, her daddy ate two hard-boiled eggs for lunch. During the week Mama had packed them into his lunchbox; on the weekends Margo would watch Daddy crack them on the edge of his plate, roll them hard between his hands, then pick off the bits of shell. Every day he ate them, so he had to have a lot of eggs by now. And so, when he pushed one of them into Mama, she got a baby. He gave Mama an egg, he gave her a baby. This was the way it worked, so if Margo herself could get one of his eggs inside her, could she also get a baby?

Margo stiffened and firmed her muscles to help disperse these memories into filmy fragments in her mind.

She couldn't have a baby, and there was nothing any gynecologist or psychiatrist could do about it. And despite that bitter reality, they wanted to subject her to yet another investigative procedure. For what? What use would it be to see the psychiatrist and dredge up from her childhood memories of things like magic eggs? Why shine a floodlight on all her unfulfilled hopes, when what she needed was to forget all of that?

The cheers and applause from the television chef's studio audience interrupted her thoughts and reminded Margo of the lateness of the hour. And she had not yet said anything to Steven of the doctor's final pronouncement.

How, though? How to tell him that because of her inadequate body, he would never glory in his wife's big belly, proof of his virility and life-giving semen? How to tell him that because of her defective body, he would never see a child whose chin was shaped square and firm like his own. How to tell him that baby-making was a magic neither of them would ever know?

She finally mustered up sufficient courage to get up from the couch and walk to Steven's study. "I'm sorry to interrupt, but we really need to talk."

A puzzled look spread across his face—likely because she never announced a conversation, just launched right into it—but he said nothing and simply followed as she led him into the living room.

There, she turned off the TV, sat herself down on the sofa, and patted the cushion to her left. Steven sat down and silently waited.

"I went to the doctor today." Margo nervously brushed back the hair from her brow. "He told me there wasn't any point in continuing on this drug. Or trying another one." She cleared her throat. "Miracles do happen sometimes, he said, but we shouldn't count on it."

Steven remained silent, as if waiting for her to continue. She saw neither sadness nor anger in his eyes, but his face looked drained of color. So was it even worse? Was he sorry to have married her at all? Back in the bliss of early love she had wondered: Why had this remarkable man chosen her? In between the kisses and caresses of courtship, without being asked, he had murmured some of the reasons. He loved the way she felt things so intensely, he said. He loved her passionate responses to the small details and incidents of life. Life with her would never be boring, he said. But now life with her was sterile, in the most elemental way it could be. Was his face drained of blood because he was realizing that because of her, he would not see a child made of his body, a child who would have been his immortality, his triumph over death?

"It's all my fault," Margo said, her mouth quivering as she said the words. "I'm sorry."

"Look, it's not such a great surprise, is it?" Steven said evenly, as if attempting to supply rationality for them both. "The doctor's implied as much before. It's not a matter of fault, it's a matter of facts." His arm moved around her. "We have each other, and that's the most important fact of all."

The tightness in her chest eased, and she pillowed her head in the hollow of his shoulder.

"Steven," she said, after a few quiet moments went by. "The doctor said one more thing. About a psychiatrist in town who specializes in women's issues and infertile couples. He's referring his new patients to her, and he wants me to go. You, too."

Steven rubbed his index finger back and forth across his lips like a saw, as he usually did when he was concentrating hard on something.

"If that's the doctor's recommendation," he said.

Margo was startled by his easy acquiescence. "But all we would do there is sit and talk about our feelings. And it won't really change anything."

"The doctor recommended it, so there must be a valid purpose to it," Steven said. "It could help us sort things out. Put things in perspective."

"Can a therapist make me not want to get pregnant? Can a therapist undo the trouble with my eggs, my hormones, and whatever else isn't working? I can't help it, but it feels like an insult for the doctor to send me there. Like telling people with cancer they can think themselves healthy if they try hard enough to visualize their immune cells as little sharks gobbling up the tumor. It's just blaming the victim."

"No one's blaming you, Margo." Steven cleared his throat. "Let's just do it, okay? How bad can it be? So why don't you call my office tomorrow and we'll check out some days and times we both could make?"

Hearing nothing further from her, he rose from the sofa and walked back to the work piled on his desk.

AT FIVE TO TEN, STEVEN CAME OUT OF HIS STUDY AND switched on the television to his favorite news channel. Margo did not want to watch. The world would still be in its usual chaos, and the news would bring only additional reports of murders, famines, riots, genocides. What was the point of steeping oneself in all that global grief? Did it help anyone or change anything?

And wasn't the local news bad enough? That on Pine View Drive, here in this very house, the drought persisted and the crops had failed?

She went upstairs and proceeded through her nightly cleansing and creaming ritual. From underneath her pillow, she pulled out the nightgown stored there, pulled it on, and slipped under the covers. To distract herself, Margo reached for the novel on her nightstand and opened it to where the bookmark lay. Charles the Second was on a royal hunt. Banners of royal purple whipped in the wind. Dogs barked, horns blared, sweat-soaked horses breathed heavily as they galloped fast through shifting mists, through forests thick with trees.

But it was no use. She could picture none of it, couldn't join the hunting party. She felt the twenty-first-century sheet smooth and cool beneath her, and saw her bedroom bathed in bright light from the lamp. Tonight, no book would have sufficient power to transport her away. She set the book back on the table and shut her eyes.

Soon, Steven came up, washed, changed, and turned off the light. Once in bed, he fit the length of himself tightly against her back, nuzzling his nose into the nape of her neck, pressing his pelvis firmly against her buttocks. She made herself motionless, dampening the slightest flickering of her muscles. Not tonight. She felt sorry to disappoint him further, but right now she wanted nothing to do with bodies.

Steven hesitated for a moment, then cleared away from her body so fast she heard the bed squeak.

6

It was predictable that the psychiatrist's office would be located in the tallest apartment building in Woodchester. Half the mental health professionals in the city rented office space there, and a number of Margo's acquaintances and friends seemed to come for psychotherapy there.

It was amazing to her how many people talked about their clinical treatment. Some would detail endlessly the minute-to-minute proceedings of their last therapy session; some gloried in boasting of the amazing insights of their analysts, while others delighted in demeaning them. She herself would have undertaken almost any subterfuge to make certain her need for such a treatment remained secret. She admired the friends who easily disclosed their need for psychotherapy. For herself, though, being seen here would feel like being found out, like an exposure of the fact that she was damaged in yet one more way.

As Margo waited with Steven for one of the elevators to open its doors, she glanced anxiously at the people milling through the lobby. Suppose she encountered someone she knew? Considering the demography of the building, they would surely suspect that she was there to see one of the resident shrinks. And if they recognized Steven as her husband, they might even assume that their marriage was in trouble.

At last, an elevator arrived. Margo rushed inside almost before the doors had opened completely, eager to escape the visibility of the lobby. It mattered not at all that anyone who might suspect she was here to visit a shrink was equally likely to be in this building for the same purpose.

"I don't like this already," she mumbled to Steven, stepping back against the far wall.

Finally, their floor. She sped along the carpeted corridor well ahead of Steven. Locating the office, she threw the door open to get herself safely inside before some acquaintance might possibly emerge from another psychiatrist's office that might possibly be situated in the same corridor.

Dr. Taynor's waiting room was small and sparely furnished. There was scarcely space for the two narrow chairs separated by a small Parsons table on which non-political magazines—*National Geographic, Smithsonian,* and *Architectural Digest*—were neatly arranged. On the one wall large enough to accommodate it, hung a vivid abstract painting.

Margo sat down and gazed intently at the painting, hoping to distract herself by entering its swirling masses of color.

In a moment, Steven came in and sat down beside her. They were ten minutes early.

7

*E*xactly on the hour, the door to the inner office opened, revealing a lean, middle-aged woman with calm blue eyes and salt-and-pepper hair cut short into a smooth cap. She was dressed in a well-cut black pantsuit, enlivened with a soft gray blouse in a delicate herringbone pattern, and had low-heeled black pumps on her feet.

"Mrs. Kerber, Mr. Kerber. I'm Dr. Taynor." The woman smiled pleasantly and shook hands with each of them. "Please come in."

The doctor's consulting room was of good size, furnished with three upholstered chairs pulled into a conversational grouping. Nearby stood an antique kneehole desk topped with a vase of spring daffodils, a folder, a pad of lined yellow legal paper, and a pen and pencil. By the window were two plant stands overflowing with lush green ivy and philodendron plants, and on a small corner table was a bromeliad plant with a single bud looking ripe and ready to open in some color it still kept secret.

Lots of healthy, living things, Margo thought.

Dr. Taynor motioned for them to sit. She picked up the pad of paper and a pencil, and seated herself in the remaining chair. "You've been referred to me because of your long-standing problem with infertility. Is that right?"

"Correct," answered Steven.

"Then let me explain the purpose of this consultation. I've seen many couples who are struggling with infertility. For many of them, our work together has been helpful, I think. The reproductive function is such a complicated one, and we still have only a partial understanding of its complex physiology and psychology. What we do know is that there is an important relationship between the biological and emotional aspects of reproduction. Emotions may affect the physiology of reproductive hormones. Just as importantly, the condition of infertility can have a vast impact on a person's self-image and emotional health."

I already know that, Margo thought.

"What I'd like to do today," the doctor said, "is an initial evaluation. If it appears that further work could be useful to you, I'll recommend that we continue, and we can set up additional sessions. I know something about the medical situation from Dr. Renfield. So let's start with your orienting me to the basics: your ages, how long you've been married, what you do."

Margo's eyes and the tilt of her head communicated a message to Steven: you do the talking. He launched into an extensive response that both met the doctor's request and was as organized, precise, and detailed as his usual mode of thinking. He gave her the significant vital statistics, as well as describing their professional activities and recreational pursuits.

To all of this Dr. Taynor listened attentively, occasionally making notes on her pad of yellow lined paper.

When Steven said nothing more, Dr. Taynor turned to Margo. "Please tell me about your experience with the treatments."

Seeing no alternative to taking her turn, Margo went directly to the heart of the matter. "It's been three years since we started being seen for infertility," she said. "I'm the problem. Steven is completely fine. I've had hormone treatments and the in vitro hasn't worked. Once, the doctor thought there was an implantation for a few days, but then I lost it. Just before he referred us to you, he said there was no point in repeating any of it."

"And what about other options?"

"We've considered them all," Margo said. "Donor egg —the doctor's not very confident it would implant, but he said he'd be willing to try if we wanted to. But, to me, and I know this may sound silly, Steven's sperm with another woman's egg would feel like he was cheating." Or feel like a kind of alien impregnation—but this was a thought so completely ridiculous that Margo didn't want to reveal she'd even had it.

"What are your thoughts about a surrogate?"

"Not so great, either. The thing is, for me, it's really important to *be* pregnant. Sure it's about getting a baby, but for me it's also about *growing* a baby."

Margo paused then, overcome with feelings of longing and need.

Dr. Taynor watched the workings of Margo's face; to a

psychiatrist, this was always a reliable signpost of something that needed further exploration. She noticed something telling, but left it for now and moved on to another subject.

"And what about adoption?"

Steven jumped in now. "We've talked about adoption, of course. Margo's already said how badly she wants to be pregnant, so to her adoption means a personal defeat, but she's somewhat okay with it, because then we'd have a child. I'm the one that has the concerns with it. There have been too many instances of problems, big problems, such as a child harmed prenatally by the birth mother's alcoholism. Or the child growing up and developing an illness like schizophrenia because the mother likely had the disease and that was the reason the child was available to be adopted in the first place. And then there are the children from foreign countries who are developmentally disabled because of poor care in their orphanages.

"I know many adoptions turn out fine," Steven said almost apologetically, "but it's the uncertainty. For me, there's too great of a risk for very serious problems. So, you see, Dr. Taynor, each option is objectionable to at least one of us."

Dr. Taynor made a few more notes on her pad. "All right," she said. "I have a sense of your current situation, so let's go back to earlier times in your lives. I'd like each of you to think back to your childhood and your families of origin, since feelings about parenthood have such important roots there.

"Why don't you tell me about your mother and father

—what they were like as people, as parents?" She looked at Margo.

"Steven, why don't you start?" Margo said quickly.

Steven shrugged, and took the conversational lead. "I can describe my mother most concisely by saying that she is an old-fashioned Germanic woman. The kind of person who is very concerned about keeping a clean house." He paused for a moment. "Not much sense of humor. She was very strict, but to her credit, my sister and I never doubted that she cared very much for us.

"Since I was the firstborn and the only son, she doted on me, and I must admit that I liked that. Except when she dressed me up like a boy from an old-fashioned family, despite my protests. When the other boys pointed at me and howled with laughter, as I knew they would, I didn't like her very much.

"My father was relatively uninvolved. He's a quiet man, a good man. He saw his responsibility to family fulfilled once he brought home the paycheck. He let my mother do all the rest. She didn't mind. In fact, she liked having all that control. My mother was the one most involved with all family matters, and I suppose that's normal enough, or at least it was at that time and not different from other families we knew. So I suppose it's logical that she is now the parent most disappointed that we have no children. Or it also could be that she's just the one who talks to me about it."

Steven looked over at Margo, concern registering on his face. Never before had he spoken so directly in her hearing of his mother's dissatisfaction. He needn't worry, Margo thought, this was no startling surprise. She had long since deciphered the resentment coded in her mother-in-law's pronouncements about "modern working women."

"And how did your parents take responsibility for your sex education?" the doctor was asking Steven.

Her questions are so intrusive, Margo thought, even if it's part of her job. She remembered Mama's stern instructions: "Don't tell family things to strangers." Margo had always obeyed this caution.

"Oh, Mother did that," answered Steven easily, apparently not at all uncomfortable with the question. "It probably would have been more appropriate for my father to do it, but it would have been too uncomfortable for him to talk about such things. Not that she was comfortable, but she was so worried about my coming down with a sexually transmitted disease that she made sure I got the proper warnings."

Proper warnings—the words resonated in Margo's mind.

The trouble was that Mama didn't ask or talk enough about the important things, or give the proper warnings. Why hadn't Mama ever told her about menstrual periods? One day when she was twelve, Margo had gone to the toilet and been horrified to see the toilet paper streaked with blood. How had she hurt herself? Even more scary to contemplate, what part of herself had she hurt? She kept silent until the blood soaked through her pants and the fear of bleeding to death finally pushed aside embarrassment and shame. And when she came to Mama and blurted out her fears, Mama had laughed. Margo had stared at her in disbelief; how could a mother be beside herself with laughter when her own daughter might be bleeding to death, and from there?

Steven had stopped speaking and Dr. Taynor did not prod him further. They were both looking at Margo now.

"Can you tell me about your early life and your family?" Dr. Taynor asked pleasantly.

Margo heard the unspoken demand behind the soft words. She searched for something to say that was not too revealing or too painful.

"Well, my parents got married young. They were only eighteen and seventeen. I was born first—after a respectable ten months had gone by, so it wasn't a shotgun affair. Lucille, my sister, came along a year later, and then my brothers, three of them in seven years. It seemed like my mother was pregnant all the time."

Margo hoped Dr. Taynor was not going to make a big deal of this, suggesting that she was having difficulty dealing with infertility because her own mother had been such a prolific producer.

"We lived in a big white house at the end of a private road in the Ohio countryside. The school was in town, and so we spent a lot of time on the school bus. We kids played with each other a lot, because our house was kind of isolated."

"How do you think your mother felt about herself as a woman, and as a mother?"

"I know she was proud of being a mother. And proud

of her family. Even though she complained a lot, and kept telling us how difficult we made her life, we knew she thought she was doing something important."

"And what did she communicate, verbally or nonverbally, about being a woman?"

Margo pictured Mama standing at the stove, her face covered with cream. People were supposed to use creams mostly at night, she knew, because that's what all the ads said to do. But not Mama. She protected her face with thick layers of it during the day, and kept her face washed clean and glowing in the evening. At night she also sat and brushed her beautiful hair. Mama's hair was thick, dark, and wavy, and unless she was cooking, she wore it loose and full. Daddy often ran his hands over it whenever he was near enough. Mama kept Margo's hair in braids, which were correct for a schoolgirl: neat and trim, she said. And ugly, Margo thought. Why did Mama want a neat and ugly daughter?

"How she felt about being a woman? She was always checking her face when she passed by a mirror, so I guess her looks were important to her," Margo said.

And what did her mother communicate about being a woman? A bitter memory, too private to share, came to Margo's mind. One day Mama had taken Lucille shopping and they had returned with two teen-sized bras, one already fastened around her sister's pea-sized breasts, the other set down on Lucille's bureau. Granted, Margo's own breasts were still dormant, even though she was almost a year older than Lucille. But was there that much size difference between a pea and a seed? Couldn't Mama have foreseen that her oldest daughter would feel humiliated? Couldn't she have bought a third bra for Margo, even though it would have covered nothing?

"And your father?" Dr. Taynor pressed on.

How could she say what he was like? He was as changeable as a chameleon: now bright and bold, then faded and fearful. But of his love she was certain. Probably he had not loved her as fiercely as she had loved him, but it was enough so that she had felt secure in it.

"He loved me, and I loved him," Margo said. That was the simple truth, never mind all the rest.

"What aspirations did your father have for the girls in his family?"

This was much less difficult to talk about. "He always encouraged us in our studies. He was proud of my good grades. He never finished high school, not because he wasn't smart but because he had to earn money. He thought it was very important that his children get good educations. I heard him say that many times. For all of us, girls and boys alike. It was a real passion with him.

"He died very young, only thirty-two. But by then my mother had already been convinced by his insistence on schooling, so she saw to it that all of us were well educated, even though she had to work multiple jobs to make that happen."

Now these memories were making her uncomfortable again. Please let this be enough to satisfy her, Margo hoped. Please let her change the subject again, or say it's time to go.

"We haven't gotten as far as I would have liked, but we've made a good start," Dr. Taynor said. "We can plan to meet again next week."

Margo protested silently. Why? For what purpose? But Steven was nodding his head in agreement. Margo kept her face as expressionless as she could make it.

"Why don't you talk it over and let me know," Dr. Taynor said.

They discussed it on the way down in the empty elevator, and in the car driving home. They argued about it over breakfast the next morning.

Steven wanted to give it a try, while Margo was vigorously opposed. "There's nothing to be gained," she said. "Just more questions, more anxiety, more stress."

Steven's mild interest in the process was not enough to motivate him to try to sway Margo's opinion. He said nothing more.

"Maybe if it turns out we really need to, we can go back," Margo said, trying to soften things.

But they did not return to the room with the ivy and the philodendron and the bromeliad again.

At least, not then.

8

Several weeks had passed since Margo received her copy of the incident report, and there had been no repercussions whatsoever. She reassured herself it was increasingly likely that the Human Resources department reviewing the report had concluded that no further action need be taken. She was beginning to feel a sense of safety.

This was her thinking—until she received a call from Rundell's assistant, summoning her to come to his office that very afternoon, for no work-related reason she could fathom. Margo's anxiety suddenly rose and she felt her chest heaving out and in. She tried to reassure herself: don't be paranoid, probably he just has a new project to assign. Still, though, as she walked to his office, she began preparing herself for the worst.

"Sit down, Margo," he said as soon as the assistant motioned her in, "and shut the door behind you."

She did as he directed.

"I've been quite preoccupied with major problems in the hospital, as you well know."

Margo nodded solemnly.

"I've developed a backlog of less pressing items and I'm taking care of one of them now. I was made aware of one rather odd incident involving you, and I was asked by HR to follow up. I'm sure you know what I'm referring to. The Newborn Nursery."

"Yes, I'm so embarrassed," she whispered.

"What was *that* all about?"

She mustered her courage and spoke plainly and without defensiveness. "That Saturday, I came in to work on getting data ready for our next meeting. I didn't plan on going to the nursery. It just happened. The elevator I got on had an incubator in it. The transporter stopped and got out on the nursery floor, and without thinking I just followed him. I love looking at little babies. I always have. So I followed him into the nursery and looked at them. That's all I did."

"Well, that was enough for you to get written up in an incident report."

"They were right. I had no reason to be there. I told them it was just an impulse after I got on that particular elevator, not something I planned. But I really didn't have any excuse then, and I don't have one now. I hope you can understand."

"I can't say I understand, but I accept the explanation. Just make sure it never happens again. Because if it does, there will have to be consequences."

"It will definitely never happen again."

"All right, Margo. Now let's both get back to work."

Her stress dissipated into one big exhalation of breath.

How fortunate that he hadn't asked for any explanation of her behavior, for how could she explain it to him when she still couldn't explain it to herself? He could have asked, she knew, because he was entitled to do so, unlike illegal questions about her plans for childbearing. Luckily, Rundell believed that guarding everyone's privacy as much as possible was best for the workplace; he did not pry uninvited into the thoughts or private lives of those he supervised or reveal much about himself, either, although she knew he had two children and a wife who didn't work outside the home.

"Thank you," she said, trying to keep her voice professional and not crack from the intense relief and gratitude she felt.

She almost skipped back to her office, so buoyant were her steps.

9

*T*hough nothing could truly substitute for the self-esteem lost by being declared irreversibly infertile, success at work now became something more for Margo than simply experiencing the satisfaction of a job well done, or scoring a leg up in the ever-present workplace competition with colleagues. Work became something that could mute the blow, or at least provide a distraction from it.

Throwing oneself into one's work is a classic self-treatment for sorrow and disappointment, but genuine affection for one's work is required, as well as the ability to quarantine grief and anger. Margo's qualifications in this regard were impeccable. Compartmentalizing bits and pieces of her emotional life was second nature to her. Long ago, she had discovered that relegating hurts to storage in some deep and inaccessible place in her mind could stifle emotions that otherwise flooded her without warning. And as for enjoying her work, numbers had always been her forte and her fascination. She was gifted mathematically. Solving equations gave her the sort of pleasure that solving crossword puzzles gave those who love words.

Not that she didn't find pleasure in words. Even as a child, reading books transported her into the lives of others. She met in books words she never heard at home, long words that were beautiful to look at and say out loud, words she would look up in the big dictionary the next time she returned to the library. She loved words too, but from numbers emanated a kind of stability, order, and consistency that seemed to temper and counterbalance some disorganized thing in herself that she could not name.

And Margo loved to work at the hospital. Even after three years, she still felt fortunate to have landed such a plum of a job. It was exciting to work where it really mattered, where birth and healing were the daily events of the enterprise, where illness and death were the adversaries. The constant flow of activity and purpose energized her. So when she slipped into longer workdays, it scarcely seemed the self-prescribed narcotic that it really was.

At the beginning of each month, Margo still continued to circle the day she calculated that her period should arrive. It was solely a matter of personal hygiene now, so that she would not be caught unprepared in light-colored clothes or without a supply of tampons. It was nothing more than that; the date remained ordinary, no longer imbued with any special magic or promise.

It was therefore with a sense of shock that she opened her calendar one Wednesday evening in early September to record the date of a newly received dinner invitation, and noted that although the date marked by the red circle was several days past, there had still been no sign of her period.

Quickly, she dismissed the thought that she might be pregnant. Better to sequester the dream of pregnancy securely away in a storeroom deep in her mind. She had thrown away her pregnancy test kits because it was safer to remain beyond hope.

The following evening, when the day's work was completed, she called Steven to advise him that the stuffed green peppers in the refrigerator needed only four minutes in the microwave, and there was still one more cup of raspberry mousse in the freezer for dessert. From the bottom drawer of her filing cabinet, she pulled out her hospital volunteer's pink-and-white-striped bib apron, and replenished its front kangaroo pouch with little peppermint candy canes.

Two Thursday nights a month, Margo volunteered in a children's unit at the hospital: 3-West Pediatrics. She had sought this out as a way to participate in the "real" work of the hospital, the clinical work. And she kept at it, with a kind of religious dedication, even though it was sometimes even more wrenching than she had imagined; pain was always cruel, but it was cruelest when it came to children. Sometimes she would see a child she recognized from a prior hospitalization going through the admissions procedure, crying not in the indignant, frightened way the first-timers cried, but weeping silently as if grieving the inevitable separation and pain to come. Sometimes, when she saw against a bleached-white pillowcase the wizened face of a child yellowed by the bilirubin backed out of his cancer-riddled liver, the unfairness of it slammed into her and tightened her gut. These were things no child should ever have to experience.

Six thirty now, and the unit was quiet. Missing was the daytime bustle of medical staff making their rounds and orderlies carting patients to and from diagnostic and therapeutic appointments. There were only three nurses, a clerk at the nursing station desk, and two already-exhausted resident physicians restarting infiltrated intravenous lines.

The head nurse sat working at her computer. "You're here already!" she greeted Margo. "God, the time's really flying—two late admissions and a kid just back from the recovery room. Haven't had a minute to think about your assignments. Just start with anyone you've seen before, and then find a new kid or two who needs company."

From a small storage closet nearby, Margo pulled out an empty cart and stocked it with puzzles, board games, and puppets from the closet's shelves. She wheeled it down the hall, avoiding the disinfectant-wet side of the corridor so as not to spoil the janitor's handiwork with footprints.

At Jonathan's room, she stopped at the threshold, and he waved to welcome her in. Only ten, Jonathan had already been in his hospital room for three weeks with an infection in one of the long bones of his left leg that required continuous intravenous antibiotic therapy and other attentions. His parents lived a two-hour car ride from the hospital and so could come to visit only on the weekends. During the week, the evening volunteers were the closest thing to family he had.

"What would you like to play tonight?" Margo asked. "I've got Battleship, Clue, and Mastermind, but I don't know how to play that one."

"You got Mastermind? I'm real good at it. I can teach you."

"You're the boss. You want Mastermind, you've got Mastermind." She knew there were precious few things kids could be boss over during a hospital stay.

He won each round fair and square, with not a bit of game-throwing on Margo's part. He was, indeed, very good at it.

After half an hour, Margo rose from the chair she had drawn over to his bedside. "That's it for now, I'm afraid. My watch says it's time for me to go." He helped her pack up the game, with a wistful look in his eyes.

"If you're still here next Thursday, you can beat me at Mastermind again," she said, trying to ease the parting.

In the next room, an unfamiliar pink-cheeked elf of a boy sat up in bed. He looked no older than eight. Margo hoped the color in his face was from improving health and not from fever.

"Hi. Want some company?" she called from the doorway. "I've got good games."

He said nothing, but he had not turned his head away, so she persisted gently with her overtures. "I've got puppets, too. Doctors. Nurses. You can be anyone you like."

Now he looked with interest at the cart, so she wheeled it in and showed him the assortment of characters. Her hand fingered the candy canes in her apron, but she dared not risk giving candy to a diabetic or special-diet child, and she would not ask the overwhelmed nurse about him on such a hectic night.

"So what's your name?"

"Freddie."

"Mine's Margo."

He selected the nurse puppet and slipped it over his right hand. He made it strut up and down on his bed, his wrist bouncing across the bed sheet. With his other hand, he yanked Margo's arm closer. "It'll be easy and quick if you don't pull away. I'll count backward from three. Ready? Three, two, one." He jammed his white-outfitted index finger into her arm. His face was grim as he applied himself to the task, just for once turning the tables and being the aggressor rather than the victim. She let him poke her as much as he wished, until at last he had satisfied himself.

When it was nearly nine, Margo said goodnight to Freddie, smiling and waving at him from the door to let him know that despite all that poking, everything was all right between them.

She rolled the cart back into the closet and unloaded its wares onto the shelves, then backtracked to Jonathan's room to say goodnight, but he was already asleep. She placed a candy cane on his bedside stand so that he would see it in the morning when he woke.

Before she went out to her car for the trip home, Margo

made a stop at the bathroom. Still not the slightest sign of her period.

Really, it isn't possible, she reminded herself. Hadn't the doctor said that the chances had diminished to almost zero?

1 0

———

$\mathcal{S}$ummer. Season of unfettered feet; of family picnics on cloths spread like stamps across an envelope of grass; of burgers sizzling on blackened grates; of thick-sliced tomatoes, slaw, and ease.

On a Saturday mid-September, still officially summer and with the weather warm enough to prove it, Margo and Steven arrived at his sister Liza's house for a luncheon of porterhouse steaks served with *pommes de terre* covered with French Dijon mustard dressing.

As she passed through the gate of the ironwork fence, Margo fingered its intricate curves, swirl after swirl. The design had been carefully chosen by Liza after much poring over photographs of stately British homes, where such gates usually signaled that horses would be found beyond, even hounds. A grand illusion here, of course, since all that lay beyond was simply half an acre of Scarsdale, New York, suburbia.

Liza ran at them, her long honey-colored skirt barely clearing the bluestone path. "Hi, guys!" She smiled broadly in welcome.

Carter, Liza's four-year-old son, loved both his aunt and uncle, but it was Margo's legs that he wrapped his arms around. Like most children, who quickly peg the adults that genuinely delight in their company, Carter had long recognized that Aunt Margo was such a one for him. When she bent down and kissed his cheek, Carter took this opportunity to peek into her shopping bag. With a smile, Margo pulled out a Lego set that she hadn't wrapped just so he'd have less of a wait to see what it was. From the way his eyes sparkled, Margo knew she had made the right choice; picking a Lego set for Carter was an assured slam dunk of a gift.

At Liza's reminder, Carter said his "Thank you" and ran off with his new treasure.

"I have something for you, too," Margo said to Liza, reaching down again into the shopping bag. She'd purchased another miniature nutmeg grater identical to the one Kate had enjoyed so greatly, this time along with a container of whole nutmegs with a label that boasted, "Imported from Granada."

Liza remarked on the loveliness of the silver-foil paper and carefully unwrapped the gift. "This will be just perfect for the eggnog at our Christmas party. Freshly grated nutmeg from Granada, the Spice Island, you know it's called. My guests will love it. Thanks so much, Margo." She escorted them to the tree-shaded patio. "Mother and Dad are here already, and you're just in time for a fresh batch of drinks. Paul sends his apologies—he had to stay longer than he expected on his business trip."

Steven bent to greet his mother, and the senior Mrs. Kerber basked in his kiss. "Steven! All that hard work must agree with you—you look just wonderful."

How marvelous it must be, Margo thought, as she grazed her mother-in-law's powdery cheek with her lips, to be so satisfied with the adult child you bore and raised.

"Hello, Margo dear. Such a nice summery dress," her mother-in-law said.

"Thank you so much," replied Margo.

"Where's Dad?" Steven's eyes were already searching along the edges of Liza's property.

"Never mind, I see him. Dad!" Steven waved toward a shady bed of multicolored impatiens and began to walk toward him.

Liza soon brought out platters of smoked oysters, shrimp curled atop a crystal bowl filled with lemon slices and shaved ice, and a molded pâté. "You've simply got to try this," she said, proffering pâté-covered Melba rounds. "It's the Dean and DeLuca feature this month. The Madeira in it gives the pâté such an unusual flavor, don't you think?"

Liza set the tray down and settled into a lawn chair, folding her billowing skirt around her legs. "How do you like Carter's outfit, Mother? It's Armani for Children."

"It's lovely. I must say, I fail to understand why most people nowadays dress their little boys in denim, like cowhands, for any and all occasions. I saw to it that Steven was dressed properly, and even more so for special occasions, no matter what his age. Steven, remember that little blue suit?

The one you wore with that white shirt with the big round collar and bow?"

"I know exactly the one you mean, Mother."

"You looked like a little prince in it."

"You did think so."

"You didn't?"

"I looked like a little clown in it."

Steven's mother turned to Margo. "What do men know about style? He looked like a little prince in it. Navy wool with white piping. I've still got it packed away. Come over and see it, Margo. You'll inherit it when you have your own son."

So here it is again, Margo thought. Steven's mother knew nothing of their problem. All through the years of trying, Margo had begged Steven to withhold from his mother all information about their failed attempts. Margo preferred bearing her mother-in-law's unsubtle hints, like this one, to explaining and then feeling humiliated before her. She didn't doubt that her mother-in-law had confronted Steven more than once with the direct question: "When?" But he'd never mentioned it to her, and she'd avoided asking him.

Soon, the steaks were well seared and properly medium rare. Liza heaped their plates with black-peppered meat, yellow-dressed potato salad, and deeply orange steamed baby carrots, the colors vibrant against ebony-black dishes.

"Look how beautiful this is, Steven," Margo said, as she passed him his plate.

Steven's father, a quiet man who usually spoke little and preferred to have his wife press conversation forward, did not let this opportunity to praise his daughter's abilities pass. "It *is* beautiful, and I'm sure it tastes as good as it looks."

The group became silent as they devoted themselves to the fine food. Carter had been served first, with a small hamburger, and soon cleaned his plate.

"Now can I have a pupcake, Mom?"

His grandmother's mouth twitched. "A what, Carter?" she asked.

"A pupcake."

"Next time I go in the house I'll bring you one," Liza promised.

"Carter," his grandmother said beguilingly, "can you sing us that new song you learned in nursery school? You know, the one you sang for Grandpa and me before Uncle Steven and Aunt Margo came?"

The child began to belt out the lyrics, his face shining with pride: *"Davee . . . Davee Crockett . . . King of the Wild Front Teeth."*

Carter's grandmother burst out in paroxysms of laughter; Liza struggled to keep her face straight, pursing her lips, but failed. Like two teenage girls, mother and daughter fell into rounds and rounds of helpless giggling.

The child stood stock still, immobilized by confusion as his sweet pride crumbled. His eyes filled with tears, he turned around, and his round sturdy legs pumped frantically and propelled him toward the house.

"Carter! Carter!" Liza called out, going after him. "It's all right, sweetie, it's all right."

Margo, no stranger to feelings of humiliation, smoldered at those words. No, it wasn't all right. It was bad enough when the challenges of life brought feelings of shame, quite another thing when your own family set a trap to humiliate you.

After a few minutes, Liza returned with a tray of gold-rimmed demitasse cups full of sweet-smelling cappuccino. She pointed to Carter sitting hunched over on the deck. "He refuses to come back out."

Margo leaned forward in her chair. "I'll go stay with him for a while."

"No. Don't anyone coddle him," commanded her mother-in-law. "He has to learn not to be so sensitive. You'll see, he'll come back by himself."

Reluctantly, Margo leaned back in her chair.

Steven's mother next turned her attention to her adored son. "So, Steven, tell me about all the wonderful things you're up to."

"The practice is doing fine, Mother." Steven raised his chin as he spoke, as she had taught him to do so long ago. "There's a steady stream of referrals coming in. Good cases and plenty of variety."

"Wonderful, son," said his father.

Margo excused herself, knowing her absence at this point would scarcely be noticed or matter to her mother-in-law, now happily hearing about her son's triumphs.

She headed for the bathroom. It was not that nature was calling her to use it; it was the urgent need to know the status—present or absent—of her delayed menstrual period.

And, amazingly, there was still not the slightest sign of it.

LATER IN THE AFTERNOON, MARGO HUGGED LIZA goodbye, congratulating and thanking her for the wonderful feast. She gave her mother-in-law a kiss on the cheek, and knelt down to receive and return Carter's embrace. Steven gently clapped his father on the back and kissed his mother on both cheeks the way she liked it. He solemnly shook Carter's hand goodbye.

During the trip home, Margo longed to tell Steven about the missed period. She longed to, but at the same time she feared setting him up for yet another disappointment by raising false possibilities and false hopes.

And, in any event, why invite bad luck by rejoicing about a possible miracle?

So, instead, Margo listened to the continuation of Steven's tales about his work successes, and took her pleasure by sharing in his satisfaction.

*T*hrough the rest of the weekend, Margo kept herself as busy as she could. Whenever the suspicion she might be pregnant managed to surface despite vigorous efforts at distraction, she gave herself a stern lecture: "This is just a prank played by a uterus too lazy to do its monthly chore."

Sunday morning, she and Steven sat together at the kitchen table over cups of coffee and traded the many sections of the Sunday newspaper between them, pointing out to each other articles that should not be overlooked. She caught up on unpaid bills, and even started the much-disliked task of purging piles of papers of unessential mail, outdated magazines, and no-longer-necessary notes to herself. Out in the garden, Margo removed faded annuals to give space and nutrients to the budding chrysanthemums, and listened to the excited cries of neighborhood children doing wheelies on their bikes. The afternoon was filled with the sounds of household machinery whirring as Margo washed and dried clothing, and in the evening she cooked soup and a stew for weeknight meals to come.

But on Monday she rose from bed with a curiously different feeling in her body—a sweet and heavy fatigue, a slight uneasiness in her stomach. At that moment, standing beside the sleep-crumpled sheets, she stopped waging a battle against hope. With a deep certainty, she knew she was pregnant. Margo sat back on the edge of the bed and remained there for a few minutes, awed.

Then, with the background sound of Steven showering, she reached for the phone perched on the night table, looked up the name, and made the call.

It was early enough that her gynecologist was not yet at his office. His answering service put her straight through to him after she told them it was important.

"Hello. It's Margo Kerber. Thanks for taking my call. I'd like to come in today. Because I'm pregnant." The joy bubbled up so fierce and strong she could scarcely pronounce the words.

"Well. I don't know." He sounded dubious. "You took a pregnancy test?"

"Not yet. After our last meeting, I thought throwing them away was a good idea."

"All right. Do a pregnancy test tonight, and come tomorrow morning. I'll phone the receptionist to squeeze you in before my first appointment."

Margo readied herself for work, pulling clothing from drawers and closets. How odd it was, she thought, to be so absolutely sure. It must be instinct to know like this, she thought, like robins know when it's time to collect twigs and bits of grass for nests.

Still, after work she went to the drugstore to buy a fresh pregnancy test. The results were positive—a lovely confirmation, she thought, but in no way a surprise.

THE DISPOSABLE WHITE PAPER SHEET ATOP THE doctor's examining table crunched and crackled with each slight movement she made in response to his pokings and proddings. Finally, the doctor's instruments clanked into the metal basin. He arose from his place on the stool between her legs, and came to stand beside her.

"Well," he said. His face wore a chastened look, and there was a note of surprise in his voice. "The cervix is soft, and with the positive home test you report, it's likely you're pregnant. We'll get a definitive blood test, and I'll have the results for you tomorrow."

"All right, doctor," she replied, sweetly. She could afford to be magnanimous with him today. Tomorrow, she would be accepting his congratulations.

THE MORNING CITY TRAFFIC WAS STILL THICK AS SHE drove from the doctor's office to work.

Stuck in a slow-moving lane, Margo pictured how it would be when she told Steven about the baby. So many times during the years, she had imagined coming home and blurting out the joyful tidings. An immediate phone call would not do, because she wanted to be there and watch the glow come over his dear face.

Tonight, though, she would say nothing. It was better to wait until the test results were back. Like her gynecologist, Steven too would require the scientific corroboration.

She arrived at her office late, but with plenty of time left to have a productive morning. From the folders on her desk, she selected the one that contained the first item on her to-do list: commodity budget for the surgical subspecialties. On the printout she checked number against number, actual expenditures against estimated ones.

Or tried to. For very soon her mind unfastened itself from the columns of dollars and cents and floated far away from the figures.

All the while I'm sitting here in my office, she thought, I'm changing—every instant—becoming more and more pregnant. She imagined herself rising like a bowlful of yeasty dough. How incredible, that although she seemed to be simply sitting quietly at her desk, she was steadily transforming into a new state of being, through a physical process as absolute and definitive as the transformation of water into ice. From now on, she thought, *everything* I do, every simple little thing, like combing my hair or talking on the phone, will happen while my uterus is expanding. A baby is growing there. Little nails are forming, little ears.

Margo was startled to suddenly find her assistant in the room, standing and watching her. "Sylvia. What's going on?"

"That's what I was about to ask you. You've been sitting

for almost half an hour, staring at nothing, with your pen in the air."

"Everything's fine. Really." Sylvia did not answer, but her eyebrows rose.

"Well, all right, there's something," Margo said. "I can't tell you what yet. But it's something good!"

After Sylvia left, Margo moved her pen back and forth over the data sheet, making imaginary jottings, so as to look gainfully occupied while she continued on with her reveries.

She visualized her body succulent and lush, a fount of nourishment. She pictured her uterus ripe and full of fruit, and her bloodstream a nutrient express train shuttling to the baby calcium and vitamins and sugar and everything else it needed.

Magic. A secret magic, since at this moment the pregnancy was a secret knowledge shared only between the two of them, herself and the baby, that tiny precious parasite burrowing relentlessly deeper into the furrows of her womb, connected to her in the most intimate embrace two humans could ever share.

But now something stirred in her mind, spreading like a film of viscous black oil, some unfocused uneasiness, even dread. It formed itself into one dark thought: be wary, be stealthy, do not display happiness, just in case.

Stop! Margo quickly steered her mind away from the morbid warning. Sylvia was right; she had accomplished next to nothing all morning.

Margo willed herself to focus on the columns of

numbers on the page in front of her, and did not stop until she completed the final reconciliation.

Like so many weekly meetings that were the bane of mid-level administrators, today's Tuesday afternoon fiscal overview was dreary and tedious. As usual, attendance was obligatory but active participation from the ranks was neither required nor expected. Today, Margo delighted in this dispensability. While the voices at the head of the table droned on, she let her thoughts slip loose and, for a full hour, luxuriated in dreaming about the miracle baby unfolding inside her.

At home that evening, Margo was high-spirited and entertained Steven with amusing anecdotes from magazine articles she'd read; that night in bed, her desire came alive. Steven, the happy beneficiary, nestled closer to his wife's body as he drifted together with her into sleep, and likely assumed, Margo thought with some pleasure, that it was so much better now that they had finally put the idea of having a baby to rest.

TWO NIGHTS LATER, AFTER DINNER, MARGO ASKED Steven to join her on the sofa in the living room. When they were sitting there side by side, she took his hand in hers and looked into his face. "An absolutely wonderful thing has happened. I'm just going to blurt it right out. I'm pregnant! We're going to have a baby!"

For a moment, Steven sat as if frozen, and then his eyes

opened wide, his eyebrows arched, and his neck craned forward. "What? Would you repeat that, please?"

She realized that while she'd had weeks to adjust to even the possibility of a pregnancy, he'd just had a few seconds to absorb a starting new reality.

"I'm pregnant! I know the doctor said it was impossible, but obviously it wasn't, because here I am with a baby—our baby—growing inside me." Margo felt as if her whole body was aglow.

"And it's not just his opinion based on an examination of you? He did all the pregnancy tests, and they came back positive?"

"Yes! Absolutely, definitely positive."

Margo watched the expression on his face transfigure from wary astonishment to jubilation. Tears came to both of their eyes. Then came a volley of questions: "Since when have you been pregnant? Did the doctor say everything was proceeding normally? Do you feel like throwing up? When's the due date?"

Margo laughed at the rapid-fire barrage, and answered each question in turn.

He rose, gently reached under her arms to lift her up into the air, and carefully spun her around. She laughed and laughed.

They sat down on the couch, as near to each other as they possibly could, and burst into conversation.

"Do we want to know if it's a boy or a girl?"

"Soon we'll have a playpen in this room!"

After a time, their excited conversation came to a halt

and they simply held hands, peaceful and close, each lost in their own reveries.

Eventually Margo said, "Let's not tell anyone yet. Okay?"

Steven looked surprised. "I thought you'd be on the phone all night."

Many of her friends had indeed made the announcement the very day their pregnancies were confirmed; one had confessed she'd even shared the glad tidings with a stranger on the street. But Margo had been thinking a thought that refused to be ignored.

Suppose she told everyone and then had a miscarriage? It would be yet another agonizing humiliation.

"Not all pregnancies stick, you know," she said to Steven. "It's still so early on. I just couldn't stand telling people we were going to have a baby, and then lose it."

"Of course, we'll do whatever you want," he said, and kissed her gently on the forehead. "You're the boss."

And then they simply sat together, smiling at each other, and then smiling some more.

$\mathcal{F}$our weeks later, for the first time, Margo set about telling someone other than Steven of her semi-miraculous conception. It would be Kate, of course. Kate was the only person to whom she'd confided the details of her infertility: the failed treatments, the dashed hopes. Kate, two years younger, with a biological clock that had not ticked away as much time as Margo's had and who still relied on contraception to delay the motherhood she looked forward to in the future, had understood and empathized with Margo's pain. After she confided in Kate, Margo always felt calmer, more secure, even protected.

Now, in the small diner not far from the hospital, she was sitting at a table for two. Propelled by nervousness to leave her desk early, she arrived well before the noontime rush and snagged a premium table near the front window. Arriving early, though, prolonged the time she needed to wait alone, and waiting had its psychological perils today. Ordinarily, there was never much risk in telling Kate anything, since Kate never envied or demeaned or tried to aggrandize herself at someone else's expense. But this would be no ordinary telling. Revealing her pregnancy would partake of mystery and magic.

To distract herself, she examined details of the décor to which she had never previously given even a passing glance. Why did the tiny wildflower garlands on the wallpaper start out straight and then suddenly collide at the top? How many inches of additional fabric would it have taken to get those skewed cafe curtains to meet properly at the middle of the window?

The waitress appeared, order pad in hand, pencil poised. "A cup of coffee, please," Margo said. "There's one more person still coming." The busy waitress glowered and left. Kate was late, not unusual or unexpected, since a nurse could not simply walk away from essential patient care just because the clock said it was twelve noon.

Around Margo, conversation began to buzz and plates clattered as they were placed atop Formica tables. This familiar cacophony of sounds only jangled her already-unsettled nerves. She quickly directed her attention away from herself and to the prospective diners crowded into the restaurant's tiny waiting area, and determined they fell into two groups: fresh-faced youths in jeans, and young executives clad in their work uniforms: tan pants and navy jackets. After that, she scrutinized the line of people gathering outside, and decided that it reminded her of the chain of dividing amoebae she had observed under a microscope in her college biology class.

Observing people and constructing fantasies about them had always been one of Margo's most reliable ways to escape unpleasantness or boredom. Even as a small child, on the obligatory Sunday visits to her grandmother's house, she had parked herself on a chair by the parlor window and gazed out at the town park beyond. She transformed old women strewing breadcrumbs for the birds into queens graciously bestowing gifts on their subjects; alcoholics stumbling along in tattered clothes became clowns feigning clumsiness for the delight of their audience. She could turn the world into a magical place and transform the people in it into helpful heroes.

But now, the people-watching did not serve its intended purpose. Now, no reassuring heroes appeared. Instead, some darker part of her mind manufactured a warning: Be careful! Don't stir up trouble!

Ridiculous! she chastised herself. From what pool of dread were such morbid ideas surfacing?

Fortunately, Kate arrived then, and the sight of her dispelled the dark thoughts into nothingness. "So sorry I'm late," she said, as she flung herself into the seat. "And I'm afraid I absolutely have to start back in half an hour."

The waitress spotted Kate's arrival and came over to their table. They ordered quickly, and the waitress sped away.

"I'm glad you suggested a fun lunch here," said Kate. "With a strike coming, we're going to need to stick together. It's going to get pretty nasty."

Margo couldn't even think about such things. Her mind was on a different track, and Kate's presence freed up the joy.

"The reason I asked you to lunch was because I've got

something personal—something terrific—to tell you. You're the first person I'm telling."

She took a big breath, like a diver about to go under. "I'm pregnant. I'm really going to have a baby."

Kate's response was instantaneous and exuberant. "Holy shit!" she shrieked. "That's fantastic." At tables nearby, heads turned. "What did Steven say when you told him?" she asked in a more subdued tone.

"He stared at me as if I was announcing something completely irrational, like a virgin birth or something."

In response to this, Kate roared.

"And then, when it sank in that we were really going to have a baby, he picked me up and danced around with me. Can you imagine Steven doing that?"

The waitress brought their food. Margo had optimistically ordered a cup of chicken noodle soup and a plain baked potato, but after a few tablespoons of the soup, the queasy fullness in her stomach intensified, so she switched to nibbling on the accompanying cracker, which was still the only food item she could reliably tolerate.

Then she felt a chill sweep across her skin, as if the windowpane had cracked and a draft slipped in.

"Kate, I'm really excited but I'm worried too. The first twelve weeks are the dangerous ones, right? If I lost the baby now, I couldn't stand it. Especially since it's a miracle I ever got pregnant in the first place."

"There's a chance of that, but most pregnancies stick. So focus on the good odds and think about all the babies that make it. Let's toast. To you. To Steven. To the baby!"

Kate raised her water glass high. "And to not worrying," she added.

Margo took a deep breath and nodded her head. "Okay."

They clinked their glasses together, and the celebratory sound unleashed a flood of happy conversation about birth plans, christenings, and godparents.

Too soon came the time for Kate to leave. So they paid the bill and walked out of the restaurant, leaving a very generous tip for the waitress.

13

The weeks that followed were something of a dreamlike blur, with heavy fatigue softening and slowing everything Margo undertook. Much of the time she felt drugged; and in a way she was, the cells of her body saturated by the powerful placental hormones circulating in her blood. Chorionic gonadotropins, her pregnancy encyclopedia called them. Even the name was tranquilizing.

This fatigue was unlike any she had ever experienced. With the insistence and power of an ocean undertow, the call to sleep tugged at her, and she was helpless to resist. Arriving home from work, she would head directly for the bed, and, as if obeying some deeply implanted hypnotic command, slide immediately into sleep.

One Thursday evening, emerging from such an obligatory nap, Margo woke to a vinegary smell permeating the house. She followed her nose to the source and found that Steven had heated up two sauerbraten dinners she had made and frozen several months ago. Overheated them, actually, for they looked quite desiccated and forlorn in their aluminum foil coffins.

"Good, you're up. I was just about to come and get you. I'm becoming quite the chef, aren't I?" He led her proudly to the table.

Margo was not in the least bit hungry. Her appetite had paled, and her stomach always felt full and heavy, as if it were crammed with metal weights. Still, she forced herself to eat some strings of the dried-out meat, so as not to spoil Steven's pleasure or deprive the growing baby of needed nourishment.

After dinner, Steven postponed his usual trip to his study and sat together with Margo on the sofa as she dipped into the handiwork bag on the side table and retrieved from it a partially crocheted square for the white and yellow crib blanket she was making. He watched as her fingers worked the hook in and out, looping and pulling the yarn.

Margo noticed his gaze turning to her body, scanning her torso up and down, back and forth. Was he disappointed, she wondered, since there was nothing yet to see? He brushed his right index finger lightly across her abdomen, like a blind reader fingering braille. It thrilled her, how he was already trying to make contact with their child. Bending over, he kissed her abdomen. "Hello, little one. Make yourself right at home in there."

Margo ruffled Steven's hair, delighting in his playfulness. This sweet strand of his nature was too often hidden by the more serious bent of his personality, and when it shone through like this, it took her breath away.

Like in Hawaii, she thought, and the memory came

alive. On their fifth anniversary, he had taken her to that magical place, where they watched sunsets wash the sky with softly shifting oranges and mauves, and marveled at transparent fish that floated around their feet waiting to be fed bits of bread. She had brought two nightgowns for the occasion: one a black lace-edged affair that cinched tightly around the curves of her body, one a pale peachy froth that barely cleared her hips. Each night they left the balcony door open so they could hear the surf lapping against the sand. And once, when the wind was high and the waves pounded against the beach, he had smoothed her hair and whispered (after having proved it so): "Sex is like a storm. It gathers, it roars, and then it settles into stillness." He could be a poet like that.

Margo continued with her crocheting as the evening wore on. From a tiny nubbin, each square grew steadily in size. Something out of nothing, she thought, the perfect parallel for pregnancy. At ten, Steven returned from his study to watch the nightly news. Margo put away the yarn and hook and went upstairs, leaving him engrossed in the daily dose of local murders and overseas chaos.

She turned on the shower as hot as she dared and let the water flow over her and soothe her body. Drying herself with a rough towel, she rubbed hard until she reached her lower abdomen, where she pressed the towel gently so as not to disturb the baby in its nest. In the bedroom, she reached far back into her lingerie drawer where she kept seldom-used slips and bras of special hues and sizes, and pulled out the peachy, frothy gown.

Steven came upstairs, saw her, and grinned broadly, as if he, too, was remembering Hawaii. And soon, the gown lay softly crumpled on the floor.

Steven's lovemaking seemed to her this time less like a storm and more like a sun shower, gentle and softly tender. And though this night he spoke little, she could feel the poetry in his touch.

14

———

"Good morning." Sylvia greeted her from her seat at the desk in the tiny cubicle that served as an anteroom to several staff offices. "I've piled some things for you to take care of on your desk."

Two hours later, despite her good intentions, Margo had accomplished next to nothing. Fatigue infiltrated her body. Her eyelids drooped and fluttered, so that the numbers on her computer and on hard copy printouts blurred and ran together.

Margo did not like being unproductive, no matter what the reason, no matter that this morning she could blame her torpor on the sedating gonadotropins circulating through her veins. Since it was now obvious that she could not work with her brain this morning, she decided to make use of her legs. From the "out" basket on her desk, she retrieved a few items that would ordinarily have been sent out through the hospital mail system. Today, they would go special delivery: she would be the messenger service and the packets would be given over by her own hand.

Margo very much enjoyed being out in the hospital.

Sometimes, though, she felt a bit guilty about her pleasure. There seemed something vaguely strange about feeling happy here. It was, after all, a place of so much suffering. But like most other administrative staff, she usually took little notice of the darker side of the hospital. The doors to the blood bank and the unmarked-but-known autopsy area had for her become simply landmarks along her navigational course. When she took shortcuts through basement corridors in which patients on carts or in wheelchairs were being transported to various tests or procedures, her mind was usually preoccupied with data and time pressures, and she perceived the patients vaguely as mobile obstacles not to be bumped into. But sometimes a child in a wheelchair, with the chalk-white anemic skin and thinned-out hair that were the sure sign of drug or radiation therapy for cancer, arrested her eye. Or, in the elevator, she would notice a knot of visitors, their faces pinched with grief. Then, the particularity of her workplace came upon her with full force, and she felt chastened by the silent sorrow of others.

Today, her destination was the Respiratory Intensive Care Unit on the sixth floor. Her journey there through corridors and elevators confronted her with the usual bustle of people seriously going about the business of being patients or hospital staff members, but nothing was obviously disturbing enough to arrest her attention.

In the RICU, Margo handed her packets over to the unit clerk. She looked for staff members she knew so that she could exchange a few words and feel more closely attached to the clinical world of the hospital, but she spied none. The unfamiliar nurse sitting at the central nursing station in fact took no note of her presence, instead scanning the semicircle of glass-fronted patient rooms, much like a lifeguard searching the sea.

In these rooms, Margo could see doctors and nurses going about their daily work. Here in the unit, they struggled to rescue patients drowning in the frothy body fluids that filled both lungs when a heart weakened; to help the breathless after bacteria had destroyed delicate lacy lung tissue and changed it into solid airless chunks; to make a path for oxygen delivery in someone whose infection-swollen voice box choked and stifled all flow of air. It was overwhelming to her to think of the very many different ways a person could smother to death—and the many ways the skilled doctors and nurses of her hospital could avert that horror.

The rooms were also crammed with stainless steel machines and intravenous poles studded with bags of fluids. And on the beds lay the hapless patients, fragile and slight compared to these wonders of modern technology. There they lay, disoriented to time in a world illuminated by twenty-four-hour fluorescent suns, fed around the clock by liquid food running through thin plastic tubes, and drained of liquid waste by catheters stuck into the most private of places. What a struggle it must be just to hold on to a scrap of personal dignity in this place, Margo thought.

It was now close to noon, according to the big clock on the nursing station wall, and therefore time for lunch. She had no appetite but knew she must try to eat, for having had only salted crackers to quell her nausea, her body and baby surely needed nutrients by now.

Once Margo reached the entrance of the cafeteria, though, a barrage of sweet-smelling food wafted into her nose and set her stomach churning. She quickly turned away and retraced her steps into the corridor, quickly breathing lungfuls of fresher air until her nausea abated.

She headed for her office, this time saving the stash of crackers in her paper bag and taking some instead from the big box in her file cabinet drawer. Her stomach soothed. And then she let her thoughts fly to their hub, like metal chips streaming toward a magnet.

The baby. That lovely miracle in her womb, that tiny person suspended in its watery bed, its cells multiplying zealously, its tiny organs structuring themselves into complicated factories of functions.

Then, suddenly, the shapeless dread came again, seeping and spreading across her consciousness. Within its inky dark, an image began to take shape: the Evil Eye, its jealous, clouded pupil staring balefully at her.

The Evil Eye? That superstitious Mediterranean notion fervently believed in by her next-door neighbor's live-in Turkish mother-in-law? Having coffee with the women next door meant being subjected to well-intended warnings and earnest advice about the importance of wearing the appropriate amulets around one's neck and carefully watching one's words. Such an archaic notion, Margo had always thought. Yet here it was, commanding the center of her own mind.

Why? Was it from her stroll through the RICU, being reminded of how much can go wrong in the human body? From thinking that seemingly random illness and tragedy were always lying in wait? Or was it because she had crowed about the baby with Kate and recklessly broadcast her joy?

Margo marshaled all her energy and attention to attack the image and wipe it from her consciousness. She concentrated hard on the tasks before her, enumerating them, prioritizing them. She systematically tackled the folders on her desk and in her computer. Soon, she lost herself in the assortments and arrangements of numbers. Quietly and effectively, these symbols displaced the unpleasant image in her mind.

On the way home, after Steven picked her up, Margo silently resolved to tell yet more people of her great joy, her mother first of all. But somehow, in the days that followed, she found no time to call. Dangerous to tell her own mother? She scoffed at this ridiculous idea. Yet Margo couldn't bring herself to call until a week later, when Steven prevailed upon her to share the news.

15

$\mathscr{A}$t Share House, strange ideas were commonplace. As were emotion-laden outbursts and episodes of eccentric and even bizarre behavior. The six teens and young adults who inhabited the group home were missing key neurologic connections or optimal levels of neuro-chemicals, and were thus frequently buffeted by tumultuous emotions they could not control.

And so, on a typical Monday afternoon, when Janie dragged a chair into the corner of the dayroom and sat with her nose pushed flat into the damp crack where the drywall seams were separating—right through Easy Bingo and juice time, and Blues Clues on TV—it had not raised much concern. The staff were by now accustomed to all sorts of idiosyncrasies: tufts of hair tugged out of the scalp from anxiety, thumbs thrust for comfort into nineteen-year-old mouths, soup pots stuck over heads for privacy. As long as they did no damage to themselves or to others, the young people were often allowed the solace of their rituals.

After half an hour, Cecilia approached Janie. "Is anything wrong?"

Janie's lips trembled, but she did not reply.

"Anything I can do to help?"

Janie shook her head.

When the dinner hour neared, Cecilia busied herself helping her staff assistant chop squares of onions and green peppers to add to the large hunk of ground beef defrosted for dinner. She showed Tony, the resident helper of the day, how to mix the meat and vegetable chunks together, and then together they stuffed the loaf pans full.

When the evening's meal was set in the oven for baking, Cecilia came to check once more on the young hermit, taking care to position herself as unobtrusively as possible on the outskirts of Janie's space. Respecting her charges' dignity was for Cecilia an article of faith, forged during two unnerving years as a social worker at Connecticut's largest placement for the developmentally disabled. She recoiled from the institutional regimentation, even while recognizing its inevitability in the face of overcrowding and under-staffing.

Seeing that Janie was engaged in nothing more dangerous or destructive than simply sitting silent and still, Cecilia returned to the kitchen to help cook the rice and cut salad greens.

"Dinnertime! Dinner," she came into the dayroom to announce when all was done. "Dinnertime!" the glad cry was taken up. The stampede to the dinner table was the highlight of the young people's day, even though the menu cycled with unerring regularity through pizza, meat loaf, baked chicken, and spaghetti. Cecilia returned to the kitchen to carefully spoon out the rice, for her charges were quite competent when it came to comparing equality of portion size.

"Tony, please tell Janie to come for dinner," she directed.

And then the shrieks began, piercing through the buzz of expectant laughter.

Cecilia rushed into the dayroom to see Tony—thick-necked, sausage-fingered, fifteen—stolidly parked at Janie's side and tugging at her sleeve. "She screams, she screams," he protested indignantly.

"Let go, Tony," she ordered, calm authority in her voice.

He obeyed, but still the shrieks swelled and ebbed like sirens.

"She screams. But why? I try help," Tony said, his face reflecting both confusion and indignation.

"It's not you, Tony. You did well. It's just that Janie isn't ready yet." Cecilia turned and smiled at Janie and let her be.

After dinner, after the quiet group games and the good-night songs, when the denizens of the home trooped upstairs to bed, Janie left her corner and followed the last of the line up the stairs. The staff members nodded at each other as they observed once again the efficacy of establishing habits and routine. Upstairs, the group went through their evening cleansing rituals and then were escorted to their rooms. The night shift staff arrived, and Cecilia retired to her room. Her night table was stacked high with old magazines and books. Cecilia read one of the magazines until her eyes grew heavy and the letters blurred. She pressed down the page's corner, put out the light, and dropped into sleep.

The house was night-still, except for an occasional creak from a wood joint somewhere. Once in a while, the heating ducts rumbled and pinged as they labored to dispel the late November chill.

Then shrieks, sharp with terror, penetrated the walls. The two on-duty staff members rushed up the stairs, and Cecilia's feet hit the floor. Down the bare-wooded hall she ran and was the first to reach Janie's room. She threw open the door. Her fingers rapidly found the switch. Between the blinking of her light-assaulted eyes, she saw a figure sitting stiff and straight on her bed, and a wide, wailing mouth.

"Janie, honey, Janie," she murmured as she came close and smoothed Janie's hair with her hand. At the touch, Janie's upper body jolted; her shoulders curved together, her arms crossed on her chest.

"Sh, sh, Janie," Cecilia crooned. At the same time, she looked at the gross tremors of the girl's fingers, the hugely pupiled eyes. It was necessary to refocus Janie, away from her terrors. "Janie!" she said loudly. "It was just a dream."

"No! Not dream!" roared Janie. "Not dream."

"All right, honey. All right." She put her hands on Janie's shoulders. "Let me help you lie down and get comfy, okay?"

"No! No!" Janie screeched.

Cecilia reared back. "All right, then just lie down, and I'll pull the covers up to make you warm and cozy."

Janie, unmoving, stared at Cecilia intently, her forehead creased in furrows, her eyelids hooded and low.

Janie evidently had reached a decision. Slowly, she

curled herself down until she lay supine on the bed, still keeping her arms folded protectively across her chest. Without protest, she allowed the blanket to fall against her, staring up at the ceiling even as Cecilia murmured "Good night."

As Cecilia worked to calm Janie, the night shift personnel comforted the frightened young people huddling in their own rooms. Once Janie quieted, the others settled down, and the team conferred quietly in the hallway.

"Something's definitely wrong with Janie, and it's been wrong all day. Hopefully a good sleep will be the end of it. For now, though, one of you should definitely sit up here the rest of the night. I'm going to go back to bed. Maybe I can even get to sleep," Cecilia said.

Before breakfast, Cecilia rose from her bed, dashed water on her face, and took two Advils to fend off a brewing migraine headache. She went downstairs to help the night staff set out plastic bowls and tumblers, the last duties of their shift.

Soon the group came bouncing down the stairs. Unmindful of the night's disturbance, they happily ran toward the individual boxes of cereal to make one of the most important choices of their day.

Only Janie shunned the dining room and went to sit once more in her corner. When all the bowls were filled, and milk and orange juice poured, Cecilia fetched the thermometer. "Open your mouth, honey. Let's see if maybe you're sick." She crouched in front of Janie, the thermometer delicately poised between her fingertips and moving toward Janie's face.

Fast as a trap suddenly sprung, Janie clamped shut her mouth.

"C'mon, Janie, you've had your temperature taken before. Remember, it's kind of like having a peppermint stick in your mouth? No? All right, then, let me feel your forehead."

Cecilia steered her fingers slowly toward Janie's face.

"Don't touch!" Janie's shriek was riddled with panic. Her hands flew up, palms out again like shields.

This was not the whining irritability born of sore throats. This was terror talking.

"All right, Janie. All right."

AFTER THE BREAKFAST RESIDUE WAS CLEARED, CECILIA settled the others at the big table and handed out their journals. Into brightly covered notebooks, those who could write laboriously recorded in their own ways that there was no more Special K and that Janie made big crying in the night, and those who couldn't write made pictures filled with heavy reds and blacks.

Cecilia waited until she was certain the young people were deeply engaged in their morning's work. Then she picked up the phone and made a call to Margo.

"Sorry to bother you at work, and with your pregnancy I don't want to stress you out with this, but something's wrong with Janie. Is there any way you can come see her when you're done there?"

"What's wrong?"

"Something's terrifying her, but I don't know what it is. She screamed during the night and now she's panicking."

"Oh, no."

"I can't get a handle on what's scaring her. That's why I need you."

"But what can I do that you can't?"

"She trusts you, maybe she'll talk to you. It's worth a try. Otherwise, I'm completely in the dark."

"Okay, I'll be there right after work. Please tell her I'm coming as soon as I can."

"I don't know if she'll hear me. It's that bad."

After Cecilia hung up, Margo held on to the phone. "Please, not that bad," she whispered.

16

———

By Thursday Margo was ready to implement her plan for unlocking the secrets underlying Janie's worrisome behavior. On her previous visits earlier in the week, Janie had clung to her and sobbed, but would say nothing to help explain the mystery of her agitation and sorrow. At 5:00 p.m., after work, Margo put on her volunteer's apron and went to the Pediatrics Unit to take the dolls—to borrow them, she told herself. She approached the nursing station and conspicuously shifted the large tote bag on her arm. At the clerk's desk, she opened it to reveal to her the blue cardigan stuffed inside, and asked, "Do you feel warm, too? The hospital seems so overheated I've been stripping off clothing all day."

The clerk shrugged her shoulders. Margo gave her a friendly smile and walked on toward her destination.

One shelf in the toy closet on the unit was reserved for the child psychiatrist summoned by the pediatricians whenever a consultation for a patient was needed. This shelf held an assortment of games and toys not unlike those one might find in any Toys "R" Us store; to the uninitiated, they gave no hint of the powerful investigative tools they could be.

Margo had learned of their potency during an educa-
tional in-service teaching seminar given by the psychiatrist
for the pediatric staff. Regular volunteers were also
welcome to attend, and Margo had attended and listened
with great interest.

"We use specially designed animal and people dolls, but
almost any toy or game can be used. Here's an example
using Checkers. An eight-year-old patient who came weekly
to my office almost immediately would set out the checker-
board. Every time he would cheat in order to take more of
my checkers; and every time, when he was right on the
verge of winning, he'd sacrifice his checkers and make
himself lose.

"Why would he do this?" she asked, and then answered
her own question. "Anxiety. He wanted so badly to beat me
that he would cheat, but he was so anxious about defeating
me that he couldn't allow himself to do it. Of course the
clinical question was: Where did that anxiety come from?
Here's where the puppets and dolls come in.

"Puppet and doll play is a way for children to express
their feelings, impulses, and anxieties in a safe way. This
boy assigned a larger animal puppet to be Papa Bear and a
smaller one to be Baby Bear. The Baby Bear stole not only
Papa Bear's chair but his food bowl, and his bed, and his
tools. Again, the stealing.

"So now I had two sets of observations I could engage
his curiosity about, and I invited him to work with me in
trying to understand what was going on."

As Margo had pondered Cecilia's plea for her to uncover the source of Janie's fear, the memory of the psychiatrist's puppet play technique popped into her mind. With mounting excitement, Margo realized that this would be a perfect tool. Today she had no need of animal puppets. She sifted through the dolls till she found a blonde-tressed girl, a young boy, a middle-aged woman, and a stocky man. She stuffed the dolls deep into her tote bag and covered them with the sweater. Then she walked out into the unit and closed the closet door firmly.

The nursing staff were busy with their patients and paid her no attention. After some time had passed, so the front desk clerk would assume she'd actually been working with the children, Margo sauntered by as nonchalantly as she could. I'm taking them just for tonight, she reassured herself as she walked quickly down the hall. Janie needs these just as much as any other child.

"AGAIN?" STEVEN ASKED, WHEN SHE TOLD HIM AT dinner that she'd be going over to Share House. "You've gone there twice already this week."

Could he be jealous of her being away from home so much? "I told you how she is," Margo explained patiently. "Last night she trembled so hard you could actually see the shaking. Like some kind of seizure."

"Just because you work at the hospital doesn't make you a diagnostician. She should see a neurologist."

"That's not the problem, Steven. I just used the word seizure to describe how it looked. Cecilia doesn't suspect anything like that, and she's had a lot of experience. She thinks something must have happened to Janie. Or Janie saw something happen."

"Then why not give her a chance to get over it? Isn't it possible your overconcern is making things worse? With all these visits, aren't you communicating you agree something is terribly wrong? Their memories are probably short, so why not let that be an advantage for her now and let her be?"

"No, she needs help and I *do* help. Last night we had a little conversation, nothing important, just about which skirt and blouse she would wear in the morning. But Cecilia said it was the first time she's really talked to anybody. And when I was leaving, Janie begged me to come again today."

"Don't you see? Your daily visits are becoming a reward for her behavior, so why should she give it up?"

So who's being the diagnostician now? Margo thought, but kept this to herself.

"I don't think that's it. She trusts me, so she's letting down her guard. I think she's getting ready to let me in on what's troubling her. That's why I'm bringing the dolls."

"The dolls?"

"Psychotherapists use them to help children communicate problems."

"You're getting out of your league. What right do you have to experiment on Janie? You've got the best of intentions, Margo, but it's not wise to overstep. It could even be a legal risk."

"The pediatric nurses use them with kids before surgery, and they're not trained psychologists, either."

"Look, you're already working as hard as ever at your job. In your condition, you should take better care of yourself. I never thought I'd have to tell *you* that."

Your mother has already told me that, Margo thought. "Maybe you should take a break from work," she'd said. "Stress hormones can harm babies in the uterus, I read."

Steven continued, "And has it ever occurred to you that your preoccupation with Janie altogether is a bit unusual? Like she was your surrogate child or something?"

Margo chose not to let herself become angry at his remarks. He was clearly jealous about something; it was best to just ignore it.

"I'll be fine, dear. It's an easy car ride there. And it really would be worse for me just to sit at home and worry."

17

I'm so glad you could make it," Cecilia said. She guided Margo between the TV watchers sprawled on the floor to the small room at the end of the living room. "I'm putting you in here because there's a door that can be closed."

Cecilia pulled out one of the chairs around the card table and let Margo settle herself. "I'll go get her."

Margo set the tote bag atop the table gingerly. How many secrets had these dolls already pried out from carefully guarded hiding places? How many secrets smoldered inside each one?

Janie walked into the room, pale and beautiful. Her hair, newly washed, no longer hung in clumps, and her crisp light blue blouse was neatly tucked into her jeans. Her gaze was fixed on the floor.

Margo was immediately filled with both affection and concern. Yes, Janie was a kind of foster daughter to her. And tonight she would do all in her power to help, as any mother would.

"Hello, Janie. Come, come sit at the table with me."

Janie sat down and Margo asked what she'd done that day.

"I take shower. I do cutouts. Cecilia make me come down for lunch. Peanut butter. But she let me go back after."

"That's good."

"Not good, Margo. Not good." Janie's eyes, fixed on Margo's own, held such anguish in them that it was all Margo could do not to look away.

"What's not good, Janie?"

But Janie said nothing more.

Margo pushed over the tote bag. "Look what I brought today. Would you like to open it and see?"

"You," Janie whispered, pushing the bag back to Margo. Margo opened the tote bag wide, and Janie peered inside.

"Dolls," Janie said, a little smile softening her face. In her bedroom, dolls lined the dresser top and bookshelves, including an aging Raggedy Ann and Curious George taken from home when her parents had brought her to this place where she might better prosper.

"Let's take them all out," Margo said. One by one, they extricated the four dolls and laid them out across the table.

"Let's tell stories with them, Janie, okay?"

"You," Janie said shyly.

"All right, I'll be first, then you."

Margo picked up the teen doll, sweet-faced, clad in jeans. "Oh my goodness, I'm so worried," she said in a breathy voice. "I wish I had someone to tell."

She walked the doll along the table and stopped her in front of the slender lady doll, chosen because its hair was brown like Margo's own, its face fixed forever in a pleasant smile. "Can I talk to you, lady? Can I tell you something I'm worried about?" Margo said in a pleading falsetto voice.

"Yes, you can," Margo answered, the voice now her own. "Let's go over there, where it's private and quiet."

She bounce-walked the two figures together over to a corner of the table. "Let's sit down." Margo sat the lady doll on the edge of the table, bending its legs so they curled firmly around the table's edge. "Tell me all about it."

Margo handed Janie the teenager. "You take this one, Janie, and say the rest of the story."

Janie grabbed the doll with unexpected urgency and perched the doll next to Margo's.

"I'm so worried," she said, mimicking not only Margo's words but also the breathy falsetto voice.

"Mrs. Corsen dog bark." And now the voice was Janie's own. "That dog, I like him, he like me. He always lick my hand. I know I'm not suppose to go out without telling. But Cecilia and everyone in other room. So I go outside. Dog down street, not far. I play with dog, dog play with me.

"Then man come. He smile. He say he know me. Know my house." Janie's voice picked up speed and pitch. "He say he show me something. He take me to a secret place between buildings, a place he call a alley."

No! Margo screamed inside her head, wishing her mind could put on earplugs.

Janie grabbed the man doll, dressed in sporty shirt and slacks. "Man put hand here," she said, her voice quavering, pushing the man doll's stiff tiny hands against the teen doll's red sweater. "Then he take my hand"—she pushed the teen doll's hand onto the man doll's crotch—"and put it here. Inside the pants," she wailed. "And it feel ugly. Like chicken skin before it cook."

Ashen, Janie dropped both dolls to the floor. "Bad! Bad!"

"Who's bad?" Margo forced herself to speak, although she wondered how speech could come when her throat was so constricted.

"Man bad. Janie bad."

Margo's mind whirled. Her thoughts were spinning in circles. She sat frozen as Janie wailed beside her. Cecilia ran in. She pulled Janie up from her chair and hugged her close, rocking together with her slowly, gently.

Janie kept on screaming but didn't resist Cecilia's touch.

Margo watched them sway back and forth. Her eyes tracked their rocking bodies: back and forth, back and forth. She was paralyzed, she was mute. What kind of a caregiver am I? she thought.

All Margo could do was try to calm herself, lose herself in their rocking. Back and forth, back and forth.

18

---

*M*argo's night was sleepless. Images of Janie flashed
continuously across her mind: Janie in the alley,
Janie screaming amidst the dolls. Images of herself too:
shocked, paralyzed, and utterly useless.

During the following day, Margo tiredly yet doggedly
seized on work meant to distract her from these discon-
certing images, such as unnecessarily reviewing action plans
for every project in which she was engaged. Once home,
she concentrated on dinner and then weeded through stacks
of unsorted clippings while watching TV. She told Steven
nothing about the prior night's revelations and reactions—
in part to avoid re-experiencing them, in part to avoid a
lecture about protecting herself from stress. Sheer exhaustion allowed her to finally drop into a deep sleep.

Saturday morning, Cecilia called. "Thank God you
found out what's wrong. We brought in a psychologist yesterday. She's going to come every day, as long as necessary."
Cecilia did not request that Margo make a visit, and Margo
did not volunteer one. Images of Janie's despair reappeared
in Margo's mind. She raked herself with self-reproach:

What kind of caregiver was I when I was most needed? And what kind of mother does that mean I'm going to be?

Margo went for a walk to distract herself. The last golden leaves on the neighborhood's sugar maple trees had already been harvested by brisk winds and lay in unattractive heaps on lawns and streets, transformed by the night rain into soggy masses underfoot. The few remaining leaves hung shriveled on the trees, edges curled in on themselves. A host of blackbirds congregated on the treetops, pausing a while before resuming their exodus to warmer climes; they clamored raucously as if complaining of the enormous undertaking just ahead of them.

It was chillier outside than Margo expected, and she soon turned back home. Once inside, she made a quick trip to the bathroom, while enumerating the weekend housecleaning chores ahead of her: straighten the linen closet, throw out long-outdated catalogs, file the thinned-out stacks of clippings. Blood had stained her underwear, leaving dried patches that were purply-brown, like the sediment of old wine. She swayed, felt certain she was falling, although her feet remained firmly planted on the tile floor. With great effort she pushed air in and out of her lungs. Terror disheveled her mind and sent her thoughts into a scramble.

She fled the bathroom that now felt claustrophobically small and sank onto the edge of her bed. She pressed the back of her right hand against her teeth, the only way she knew to stem the chaos in her mind: start a sharpness, feel it, be it. Steady now, steady, she willed herself.

As soon as she felt able to talk, she called her obstetrician. An anonymous mellifluous female voice from his answering service responded.

"You've got to get a hold of the doctor immediately. It's an emergency!"

"I'll contact him right away," the voice replied calmly.

As she waited, Margo clung to this promise of speed. Within minutes, the phone rang.

She stammered out the news: "I found bloodstains." Then answered his questions: "No, it's brownish, not bright red." "No, no cramps at all."

"From the sound of it, it may be fine," he said. "But we should take a look, of course. I've got no staff in my office today. Go to the emergency room now, and I'll meet you there."

"Is it all right for me to drive? My husband's not home and I don't know how soon he can get back to the house." Please let it be all right, she thought; she couldn't stay there one more minute.

"You can drive yourself, unless the bleeding becomes heavy."

"The emergency room," she repeated, to be sure she heard correctly.

"Right. Don't drive too fast. From the sound of it, it isn't that kind of emergency."

She changed into less ratty clothes and got into her car. Despite the doctor's advice, she pulled out of the driveway too abruptly and drove much too fast. She navigated the road automatically while her thoughts skipped back and forth, as if controlled by a drunken railroad master wildly switching trains from one track to another.

It could be fine, he said. And he had plenty of clinical experience to go by to make that judgment. How many identical calls must he have handled in his professional career?

But if it wasn't an emergency, why did he want her at the emergency room *now*?

Though he said it was safe to drive, and certainly a person in a dangerous bleeding condition would be told to wait for an ambulance, wouldn't they?

But he didn't say it was *not* an emergency. He said it wasn't *that kind* of an emergency. So what kind of emergency was it?

An answer came to her: it was an Evil Eye kind of emergency.

19

At the emergency room entrance, she pulled her car into one of the spaces reserved for patients. Despite her haste, she walked toward the entry door carefully.

Once inside, she continued her small, cautious steps. Perhaps it was dangerous to make large and jarring movements. Probably she should never have changed her clothes. All that twisting and bending to get in and out of pant legs and armholes. Could that have done harm?

"Sit here, please," directed the ER triage nurse as she motioned Margo to the seat alongside her desk.

The role of an emergency room triage nurse, Margo knew, was to make a rapid screening decision in order to sort out the critical cases from the less important ones. Such an uneven variety of disorders poured in: nose bleeds, pneumonias, ingrown toenails, heart attacks, scalps split in domestic arguments, car accidents, sore throats—all of which had to be sorted out according to the speed at which treatment needed to be rendered.

The nurse made her rapid assessment of Margo: no signs of shock, pulse a bit fast but not thready, blood pressure normal—no need to be rushed in for immediate care.

"Go into the third treatment room on the right and put on a gown," the nurse said casually. Margo felt soothed by the lack of concern, but then as she began the walk down the corridor, the nurse called after her, "Your doctor's already arrived. I'll let him know you're here."

Margo's thoughts switched tracks again. Already arrived? Why such haste? Was her situation more serious than he had told her?

The treatment room was completely colorless. Against the stark white walls stood gray metal cabinets, sterile gauze pads visible through the glass doors. A white-sheeted examining table stood dead center, surrounded by white enamel tables covered with chrome instruments. Better not to look at those too closely.

An aide brought in a paper gown and left. Margo changed cautiously, careful not to stretch too far or too fast. She messaged Steven on her cell phone. "I've got a problem but my doctor doesn't think it's going to be serious. I saw some bloodstains, so I called him. He wanted to check me over, so I'm at the emergency room. Please come." She stepped up onto the treatment table and waited.

A tap on the door. Her doctor came in, a staff nurse trailing behind him. He listened carefully as she repeated what had happened.

"Any cramps or pain of any sort since we spoke on the phone?"

"I'm so nervous my stomach hurts here," she said,

pointing to the place underneath her rib cage where her stomach was in a knot. "But that's all."

"All right, let's have a look, then," he said briskly, motioning to the nurse to help Margo into the stirrups, then putting on his gloves and arranging his instruments.

Margo lay back, trying to keep her mind clear of disturbing thoughts. She concentrated on the whiteness of the ceiling above her: white, whiter, whitest.

The cold hard metal of the speculum was in her. What was he seeing? Chains of fearful images flashed through her imagination: A purplish blob for a uterus? Maroon blood clots, like chunks of grape jelly?

"Looks good," the doctor was saying as he slid the cold steel out of her.

Her body loosened all at once, like a marionette whose strings were suddenly let slack.

"The cervix is well closed, as it should be," he continued, stripping the gloves from his hands. "I don't see any fresh bleeding at all. It was probably just a tiny peripheral bleed from the placenta."

Looks good, she repeated to herself. Looks good.

"Go home and stay in bed the rest of the weekend. Monday too. Give me a call Monday afternoon and we'll decide about the rest of the week. No intercourse."

She would have agreed to anything he asked of her.

"You might see a few more spots of dark blood. That's not unexpected, so don't be alarmed. But if the color should turn bright red or the flow increases, give me a call right away."

Again, she nodded, and the doctor departed. The nurse helped her slide off the table, and left Margo to dress, which she did as fast as she dared. She walked into the corridor, retraced her steps to the triage desk, and then to the waiting room beyond.

Steven was sitting straight in a chair against the wall. As soon as he spotted her, he jumped up and strode toward her.

"Everything's good," Margo said immediately, so he wouldn't have to worry an instant more than necessary. As they walked hand in hand to the parking lot, she told him the doctor's explanations and his orders.

Steven settled Margo into the driver's seat of her car and then took his place behind the wheel of his. He waited for her to begin driving, then started up his ignition.

*O*nce home, Steven escorted Margo up the stairs, his hand firmly supporting her elbow. Under his watchful eyes she washed her face and brushed her teeth as if it were bedtime, slipped into a loose warm nightgown, and slid under the warm blanket. Steven pulled the drapes shut. "I'll make you something warm," he said. He left the door open, so he could hear her if she called.

The room was dim and peaceful, the bed enveloping and soft. Steven soon brought in a cup of hot herbal tea and a plate of crackers. He sat on the edge of the bed and watched her sip and munch. "Everything all right?"

"I think so, but I should go and check." Cautiously, she rose from the bed. In the bathroom she marshaled her courage and looked at her underwear.

"Yes, everything's okay," she called out loudly.

He helped her settle back into the pillows and tucked the blanket around her. "Then I'll go get some takeout, and we'll have a picnic right here on the bed."

Steven hated it when she brought so much as a piece of fruit or a cookie into bed to nibble on when she read at night. This offer of a meal on the sheets she recognized as a truly selfless act.

"Thank you, my love," she said. "You've already made me feel a lot better."

"Want me to bring you anything else?"

"No thanks, I'm fine."

After Steven left, Margo pulled the blanket up to her chin and snuggled her face into his pillow so she could sniff the scent of him that lingered there.

Soon, in the familiar warmth and scent of her bed, the tension began to drain from her body, and her mind began to drift.

꩜

THE *PICNIC-SUR-LE-BED* WAS DELIGHTFUL DESPITE THE circumstance that had elicited it. Steven spread a tablecloth over the quilt and they munched on souvlaki sandwiches and baklava desserts. Also, Steven presented her with an unexpected gift: an assortment of women's magazines. Not paper dolls, Margo thought, but close enough.

When they were done eating, Steven cleared up the remains of the picnic, taking pains to search out every last crumb of food. He took the tray downstairs and returned to lie beside her and stroke her hair.

"You're a wonderful man, you know that?" she murmured, planting a kiss on his neck. Wonderful, she meant, not just because of his caregiving, but also because he hadn't once hinted she'd let herself get overly stressed, never implied that she'd done anything wrong. Warmed by the blanket and her husband's body pressed close, Margo fell into a deep sleep that erased memory and misgiving.

THE NEXT MORNING WAS AS BRIGHT AND CLEAR AS ANY jogger could hope for. The sky was deeply blue without a speck of cloud, and the pavement sparkled and glinted in the unfiltered sun. Steven was chafing at the bit to be out the door and running, but he checked with Margo first: "Everything still look good?" She nodded reassuringly. Nevertheless, ten minutes later, he was still in the house and checked with her again. "Go already," she said, and with a wave of her hand motioned him out into the crisp cold to pit himself against the miles.

Less than forty-five minutes later he returned, tugging at his clothes to indicate he dared not come any closer until he had showered. She laughed and waved him away again, this time with mock disgust.

Afterward, when his skin bore the sweeter scents of soap and aftershave lotion, he bent over the bed and stroked her hair. "Everything still okay?"

She smiled broadly. "Fine."

He went out once more, this time to buy their Sunday brunch and bring in the newspaper.

"Start working on this," he said when he returned, heaving the weighty Sunday *New York Times* onto the middle of their bed, "and I'll be back with food in a minute."

On a wedding-gift silver tray, he brought up sliced bagels cut and stacked into two neat piles, a small glass dish filled with whipped cream cheese, and a plate with slices of smoked salmon. She praised the abundance of the spread and was once again touched by his sweet willingness to tolerate the abundance of crumbs that would soon litter their bed.

Brunch eaten, they tackled the fat newspaper, dividing the many sections between them. Steven devoured the sports and financial sections but soon turned restive again.

"I'd better work on my briefs before Kate and Walt come over. Anything I can do for you before I go downstairs?"

"Nothing, love, I'm fine."

After Steven left, Margo scuttled the rest of the paper onto the floor and burrowed deep down into the bed again, pulling the blanket over her face against the window's light. Today's news section would undoubtedly be full of the usual dismal reports of problems far and wide. Better to rejoice that she was fine, that twenty-four hours had passed and, but for one small faint purply-brown spot, there was no sign of trouble. Her good luck was holding.

The dark thoughts came again, seeping and sliding across her mind. Careful! Careful! Beware the Evil Eye, put on a sad face.

"Stop it now!" Margo exclaimed aloud as she struggled to snuff out the pernicious ideas. She would tell Kate about them right away, as soon as Kate arrived. Kate would laugh at the superstitious neighbor woman who glanced furtively about at anyone's brazen boast of good fortune and mumbled incantations under her breath. Kate had her feet firmly planted in science, not sorcery; Kate believed in molecules, not magic.

She fixed her mind on an image of Kate sitting at her bedside, laughing hard, her eyes filled with mirth. Kate would come soon and heap scorn on the primitive superstition. And then the Evil Eye would be forced to close its gaping lid and flee from Margo's mind into oblivion.

2 1

The following Thursday, Margo followed her obstetrician's recommendation and went back to work.

It frightened her to be there. Five days of sequestering herself in bed seemed not nearly long enough to guarantee the safety of her pregnancy. At home she had created a cocoon of tranquility. But at work she would be bombarded by demands.

She worried that even a sudden stretch to reach across her desk for a pencil might be just enough to dislodge a necessary tiny clot. But in the end she had complied with her doctor's recommendation to return to work because it was more threatening to think he was not the omniscient, infallible obstetrician she needed him to be.

Thursday and Friday she kept to her office and did her best to avoid time pressure and aggravation. On Saturday she gratefully retreated to her home once more and spent a slow and languorous weekend, sipping herbal teas and doing little more strenuous than choosing movies to watch while curled up on her living room sofa.

By Sunday afternoon she felt tranquil enough to call Cecilia and ask her how Janie was.

"The psychologist says it's a textbook case of post-traumatic stress. The withdrawal, the nightmares, the screaming when something jogs her memory of the incident, it's all typical. She's getting treatment sessions twice a week. And she's getting better, sleeping well and eating more."

"That's so great to hear," Margo said with relief.

"The psychologist says Janie understands she needs to talk about it, even though it's horrible and scary. We're lucky, she told me, because that degree of cooperation with treatment is unusual when cognitive skills are as limited as Janie's are. And *you* deserve a lot of credit, Margo, for unlocking that awful secret."

Margo could not be soothed by the compliment.

Credit for what? For becoming useless when Janie disclosed the horror? For letting Cecilia comfort her while she herself fled?

"Please tell Janie I love her. And tell her I'm so glad she's feeling better."

But Margo did not volunteer to visit—and Cecilia did not ask her to come.

ON MONDAY MORNING, MARGO ROSE FROM HER BED feeling confident. More than a week had now gone by, and in the last few days, there had not been a stain or a spot.

She dressed with care for the weekly staff meeting with the pleasant anticipation of rejoining her colleagues and a worry-free day at work. She put on her best pantsuit, the dove-gray one with the trouser buttons resewn quite a few inches over to better accommodate her thickened waist, and a shimmer of silver jewelry to brighten the lapel. Then she prepared for Steven and herself a breakfast of omelets and fruit, and set off to the hospital.

The morning meeting turned out to be tense and troubling. "The nurses informed me they've set up a formal grievance committee," Rundell announced immediately. "From the tone of it, I suspect they are getting professional advice. My best guess is it's from the American Nursing Association or, maybe worse, a union hoping to organize them."

Margo was as surprised by this as were her colleagues. While she hadn't seen Kate in the past week, she knew her friend would rightly have kept silent until the nurses decided to make this development public.

"Let's all start thinking of scenarios we might face if they decide to strike," Rundell said. "And come up with some action recommendations. We'll have a special meeting at the end of the week with this as the only item on the agenda."

It's beginning, Margo thought soberly. It'll be a mess for the hospital, and what is going to happen to Kate? When the meeting ended, she returned to her office and immediately called Kate to ask her to lunch the next day. She was already scheduled then, but agreed to Wednesday at their usual restaurant.

⟡

"IS EVERYTHING ALL RIGHT WITH YOU?" KATE ASKED AS soon as Margo arrived and sat down across from her.

"Definitely. Not a single sign of bleeding."

Kate looked visibly relieved. "I was worried you had something bad to tell me."

"In a way I do, but it's not about me. At our staff meeting Monday, Rundell announced he'd gotten a letter from the nurses' grievance committee, and that there's a chance of a nursing strike."

"A chance? If that's what he told you, then Rundell doesn't have a clue about how serious things really are this time. I can pretty much guarantee that soon you and I are going to be on opposite sides of a helluva fight."

That was just what Margo was afraid of. A chill passed across her skin, her body reacting at the thought of some disruption in the friendship with Kate she found so nourishing.

"You want to know why I couldn't make lunch yesterday?" Kate said. "Because we had a meeting with all the nurses that could free themselves up at noon. I'll try to repeat as verbatim as I can what was said, so you'll know how high the anger level is."

Kate put up her hands to tick each point off on her fingers.

"How many times do we have to tell them our staffing levels are inadequate?

"All they do is set up one meeting after another. What's been accomplished? Zero.

"They just tell us to come up with more 'creative'"—
and here Kate made quotation marks in the air with her
fingers—"ways of staffing and using who we've already got.

"They keep crying about the hospital budget. Now
they're hinting about freezing our salaries. Or giving us a
little raise but at the same time decreasing their contri-
butions to our pension plan. Do they think we're stupid?

"I'm sick of them screwing us. It's time to be more in
their faces. If we don't strike—or at least threaten to—
nothing is going to happen."

Kate ran out of fingers on the one hand and switched
to her other one.

"And here's one more that makes me really angry."
Kate's voice picked up in tempo and volume. "We're being
prevented from practicing our profession as we define it."

"What does that mean exactly?" Margo asked.

"It means people in power at the hospital make their
own definition of nursing and then force us to limit what
we do to what *they* think we should do."

"Like what?"

"For instance, the chief of Medicine doesn't want *his*
nurses to waste precious nursing time counseling patients
about stress. But stress is a risk factor for disease, and
anxiety increases length of hospital stay. We're trained to
work with patients to lessen stress, but the chief of
Medicine wants us to stick to passing out pills.

"And how about this? You go to your supply closet for
the four-by-ten-inch gauze pads you always need to
reinforce a certain dressing, and they're not there. Why?

Because some junior administrator fresh out of business school, who has never seen a surgical wound in his life, decided it's cheaper to order larger quantities of four-by-sixes. Without even asking us!"

"Everyone in the hospital is trying to do the job they were trained and hired to do," said Margo gently.

"Right! That's just what I'm saying! That's exactly what we want, too. But it looks like we have to strike in order to get it."

Kate took a few sips of water.

"Not that we aren't worried about the strike, about keeping our jobs. Some nurses are afraid that when the administrators bring in replacements, they might decide to hire them permanently and get rid of us. But my take is that experienced nurses aren't easy to find. We're the ones who know the small details about how this hospital runs. All that knowledge and the resulting efficiency disappear if we disappear. And even if they were foolish enough to fire us, Yale-New Haven would fall all over itself trying to recruit a bunch of skilled, experienced nurses like us.

"My biggest problem with a strike is that patients will suffer. There's just no way around it: going on strike means abandoning patients. People already here will get shipped to other hospitals. No new patients will get admitted except for emergencies. And it'll be because of us, because our decision has slammed the door in their faces!"

Margo nodded sympathetically. "That *is* a bad feeling to have."

"But here's how I justify it. We're just half an hour

from two fine hospitals. Sure, our patients prefer our hospital, but their care elsewhere will be good. In fact, from what we know about our understaffing problem, it might even be better.

"And that brings me to a really big issue we have. We've told them over and over again that insufficient nursing staff puts patients at real risk. We're collecting specific instances of that, and even *we* are amazed at how much unnecessary risk there is to patients in our hospital."

"I agree, Kate," said Margo. "Despite all our best efforts, too many patients are at unnecessary risk. Too many hospital-acquired infections. Too many drug-dose errors. The administration wants to do its part in fixing them."

"Then why doesn't it fix the nursing understaffing problem?"

"I'm not sure what percent of that risk is due to insufficient numbers of nurses," Margo said as gently as she could.

"More than you think. We don't get enough in-service training time to become expert enough on new procedures and equipment before we have to use them on a patient. Another thing is that I've been getting assigned too many patients, so for the first time in my career, there are too many days when I don't feel on top of things, when I don't know enough about my patients. That's also not a good feeling. The bottom line is that it's not safe: not for us and not for our patients."

I know that feeling too well, Margo thought. I don't want Kate to feel that way, to feel incapable, powerless.

The two busied themselves with their Greek salads, their forks chiming inside ceramic bowls and ice clinking against their water glasses.

Margo chose her next words carefully. "Something's a little confusing, though. Rundell told us he sent out a team months ago to investigate just those concerns. He said they didn't find significant safety issues related to understaffing of nurses."

Kate put down her fork. "*We're* the ones on the front lines, and *we* see what happens every day. It's not the same as a few administrators doing a spot check here and there. Not to speak of them knowing in advance what their conclusions are going to be."

"It wasn't just administrators. There were doctors in the group, too," Margo said softly.

"Believe me, it's not safe!" There was no mistaking the irritation in Kate's voice.

"Even when we work during our so-called rest breaks, it's still not enough. If we're tied up with one patient, the others get insufficient attention. No one can convince me that's safe.

"And here's something else you can tell your precious Rundell. He should realize that what's unsafe for the patients is also not safe for him. He may think he's saving money by not increasing staffing, but when he faces big payouts for negligence, his insurance premiums are going to shoot sky-high.

"Anyway, is there any doubt that Rundell will keep stonewalling everything we're asking for?"

They were now at the crux of Margo's concern. "Suppose he doesn't respond to the grievance committee the way the nurses would like?"

"Then we'll have no choice but to strike. I hope you understand that it'll happen because we have no other choice."

"Kate, if only the hospital had the dollars to keep all units fully staffed with nurses all the time," Margo said. "But times have changed for the worse. Rundell's trying to deal with constant pressure from Medicare and private pay to cut costs and billings to them. And then, they don't make full reimbursements on what we bill. And the hospital just can't operate in the red for long, or there won't *be* a hospital."

"Clinically, times have changed too," said Kate, her voice rising. "Patients are older so they get sicker, because they have chronic conditions underneath whatever acute illness they get. So taking care of them is much more difficult and time-consuming. The nurse-patient ratio everyone's used for years just doesn't work anymore."

Margo felt the gap between them widening. She searched for something to say to narrow it.

"You're right, understaffing is to no one's advantage. What makes it hard, though, is that nurses' salaries are already one of the biggest items in the hospital budget. The problem is how to staff for the unpredictable peak times without overstaffing the rest of the time."

Kate abruptly reached for her handbag. She counted out the dollars and dropped them on the table. "Got to go.

This should cover my meal plus the tip. Take good care of yourself, Margo."

Kate stood up and headed for the door, leaving Margo staring openmouthed at her rapidly receding form.

Margo sat at the table alone after Kate left, ordering cup after cup of decaf tea. She was shocked by Kate's vehemence. She'd hoped they would be able to strengthen the bond between them by empathizing with the other's point of view. She'd hoped to prevent a rift from forming between them and instead had initiated one.

How had she gone wrong?

22

The following Monday, Margo had an important mission: she had set herself the task of shifting Rundell's perspective.

This morning a staff meeting was scheduled, and Margo was determined to attempt the seemingly impossible: to open Rundell's mind. She had to, because the risk of a strike was too great, bringing with it the risk of a real rupture with Kate, with her stalwart, dependable, loving Kate. It was not only about how much she enjoyed Kate's companionship, Margo realized, but that Kate's friendship buoyed her own positive sense of herself. And now, especially, she needed Kate's levelheadedness and support to help keep her own anxieties at bay. What she was about to do was itself a risk, but it was one Margo had to take.

As soon as Margo arrived at her office and seated herself at her desk, she reviewed and revised one last time the notes she had worked on over the weekend, trying to find the very best way to phrase her words so they sounded more like observations and less like dissent.

Then, it was time.

She arrived at the conference room slightly before the appointed hour. Already seated were Rundell at the head of the table, and at its foot Jim McLaren, the second-in-command. Margo took a place toward the center of the table. While she waited, she soothed herself by thinking about her baby and resting her right hand gently on her lower belly atop the firm swelling, close to the tiny hands, the delicately curved body, the dear little feet.

The staff room soon filled, and Rundell started right on the hour. "I'll begin with a brief update, and then I want to hear from you. The nurses are stepping up the pressure. They are threatening that they're closer to a decision to strike. Their demands remain unreasonable: insisting they want higher staffing levels but not at the price of a pay freeze to make that possible. The Board of Directors allocates us a finite amount of money to run the hospital. I'm an administrator not an alchemist. I can't make gold out of lead."

Rundell fell silent, and then Jim McLaren spoke up. "Contrast their demands with what the doctors do. They keep the same staffing numbers even when every single bed is filled and the acuity level is very high. They work as hard as necessary to take care of their patients. They just do it. That's professionalism. The nurses say we owe them respect as professionals, so how can they consider a strike that will instantly cause severe understaffing? It's illogical. And it's unethical."

"Exactly," said Larry White, a mid-level administrator who stood not much higher than Margo on the authority

ladder. "They say it's not the money, but we know it's about
the money. And if we add up the value of all the benefits
they're getting, the total is pretty damn good: extra pay for
holidays, bonuses, great health insurance, excellent pen-
sions."

Margo listened intently, looking for the optimal moment
to make her own remarks. Meanwhile, Rundell posed a
question to the group: "What are your thoughts about our
strategy, given the potential of a strike?"

"There are only two alternatives here," said Richard
Sloan. "If the nurses are so concerned about patient safety,
let them stay on the job. If they choose to strike instead,
fire them. There are plenty of other nurses out there who'd
be glad to get a permanent job with the kind of com-
pensation our nurses already have."

"The quicker we force them to make a move, the better.
They'll be caught off balance," said Larry White.

"Though not acting quickly might have some benefits
for us," said Sam Shapiro. "They might think we're ambi-
valent. And if we let them think there's a chance we might
just give in to their demands, we could lull them into a false
sense of security and then confront them with our refusal
exactly when the timing is best for us."

Rundell nodded in Sam's direction.

When no one else volunteered an opinion, he fixed his
gaze on Margo. "Your duties take you out on the nursing
units. Have you obtained any inside information that might
help us plan?"

She felt a huge swell of relief. This question was a gift,

shifting the potentially subversive remarks she was about to make into a cooperative response to his request.

"I did hear some things that help clarify their dissatisfaction. For example, they object to our managers making changes in their purchase requests without consulting them first. Like which sizes of gauze pads to order."

A burst of laughter broke out around the table.

"I know it seems petty, but it directly affects their clinical work. And to them it means they're not being respected as professionals."

Rundell seemed unperturbed. His pale blue eyes remained contemplative and calm. Perhaps he really was open to the nurses' concerns, to resolving this conflict in a thoughtful way.

Margo continued, more confident now. "Professional autonomy is a big concern of theirs. They resent doctors telling nurses how they should and shouldn't spend their professional time. Many say that their leaders should not have to report to a hospital administrator but rather to a chief nurse, the way the doctors report to their physician chief of staff."

And now Rundell exploded. "If they reported to the director of Nursing, she'd immediately hire double the number of nurses. And they want our managers to waste time on what size gauzes to order. It's laughable, it's ridiculous."

The room was hushed.

Margo, unable to stop herself, rushed into the rest of the remarks she'd prepared. Didn't a team player sometimes have to bring uncomfortable truths and unpopular points of view?

"The nurses mean well, not just for themselves but for the hospital and our patients. Also, since a big part of their issue is wanting to be respected, if we show them we at least respect their point of view, I think we should see a lot more conciliation from them."

"Unlikely," said Rundell. "They want a confrontation. They *need* to strike."

He turned his face from her.

"Sam, Larry, you seem closest to the mark. I want you to work with Jim and me as I interact with their grievance committee and design specific strategies to deal with all the possible scenarios that may play out. We cannot allow the nurses to control the process of negotiation. If they can't be dissuaded from striking, we must maneuver them to do so when it is to *our* best advantage.

"And we all have to be on the same page about this," he said with firmness in his voice as he glanced around the room. "All of us."

Rundell rose from his seat, his customary way of signaling there was no more he wanted to speak about—or listen to. "Thank you all," he said.

Unable to stop the gathering tears, Margo picked up her notepad and pen and fled to her office. There she chastised herself: What have I accomplished? Nothing, except making the nurses look like a band of idiots and making myself look naïve and out of my depth in the big leagues.

She pummeled herself with invectives: ineffective, incompetent, totally inadequate.

No. Her hand crept to her belly; her fingertips pressed through the fabric and found the reassuring protuberance of her womb. Ineffective, yes, but totally inadequate? No. For here, under her fingers, lay the proof.

She turned to her computer and opened the book-marked website that illustrated the week-by-week miraculous process by which a fertilized egg developed into a fully formed and functioning human being. These were the transformations that were happening in her own womb while she looked at spreadsheets, cooked, and slept. Every day when she arrived at work and turned on her computer, she summoned it up for yet another peek at the trans-formation happening in her womb. Now she consulted it for distraction and solace.

She searched out the appropriate week. At fifteen weeks of pregnancy, the baby's bones were starting to develop, and it would very soon be making sucking movements with its little mouth.

"Hello, hello," she crooned to the baby now, entering a communion in which there was no unpleasantness or defeat.

23

That evening, Margo heated up a frozen leftover beef stew as a substitute for concocting an original dinner, given that her mind was totally preoccupied with more pressing matters.

As soon as she heard the smack of the door announcing Steven's arrival home, she ran to greet him and invited him to sit right down at the dining room table, as dinner was ready. Returning to the kitchen, she spooned out the steaming stew onto a mound of brown rice and brought it to him, together with the tossed green salad she took from the refrigerator. After making her own plateful, she went to join him.

Steven was usually the one with the more interesting stories to tell of the day at work, but he characteristically waited with them until he'd eaten much of his main course. Margo was able to eat well again, her nausea having entirely disappeared so she could nourish herself and the baby with pleasure. But tonight, she was more hungry to unburden herself to Steven than to enjoy a meal.

"Steven, I'm worried. It's the strike business. Rundell

and Kate. I tried to defend each one to the other one, and now I've screwed it up with both of them."

"Give me some concrete examples here," Steven said.

"Today at the staff meeting I made a fool of myself the way I tried to defend the nurses. I told Rundell the nurses were upset that management decided arbitrarily what size gauze pads to order, because I know this is a point of resentment for them, that they weren't even consulted about a decision that affects clinical care. I told him they wanted respect, that they should be reporting to a chief nurse, not one of our administrators. He really blew up at that one. So instead of helping to divert a strike, I probably made Rundell even more inflexible than he already was."

"Margo, you never could have done that. He was already mad as hell."

"Did I ruin it? I couldn't bear it if I did."

"Look, the situation's not good, but it's not ruined. You'll have to work to repair things and act in ways that make it very plain to him you're his ally, that what you say and do are meant to help him."

After dinner was over, after she had scraped the dishes and loaded the dishwasher, Margo went to consult once more with Steven, who had retreated to his study to lean into his evening's work.

"Steven, I'm worried about Kate."

A quiet sigh from Steven. He swiveled his desk chair around to face her and listened.

"She's already distanced herself from me before a strike has even started."

"How do you know that?"

"The other day she and I just happened to be in the gift shop at the same time, and she smiled at me, but it wasn't really genuine. And another time, in a corridor, she was talking to someone, and when I walked by she just gave me a quick wave and went right back to her conversation. She didn't motion for me to come over like she usually does."

"Maybe that conversation was confidential."

"Maybe, but she didn't even pretend to smile that time. How can I fix it with her?"

"I don't know. I'm sure you'll find a way."

Steven rotated his chair back to face the desk. "Sorry, I have to get to this or I'll be up all night."

Find a way? She saw no way, no way at all.

Margo's eyes fixed on the blackness of Steven's wool sweater as he bent over his keyboard, and she summoned up the memory of the first time she'd seen Kate.

That day two years ago had begun as an ordinary sunny summer morning. Suddenly a savage wind came up, and within minutes, the sky darkened to a murky blackish green. Margo had barely finished parking when the thunder erupted, peal after peal splitting the air with cracking sounds. She raced to the parapet over the nearest entrance to the hospital, and then through the doors to safety inside, her skin and clothes dampened by the first waves of rain.

A crowd was pressed against the window walls to watch, and she had joined them. The rain fell hard, massing in layers like sheets of glass. The pace of the wind increased and the trees arched sharply, their terminal branches flying straight out like unruly hair. Outdoor lamps with automatic light sensors came on then—it had become almost as dark as night—but the denseness of the rain quenched their light. And outside, under the parapet, in the midst of all that wildness, a solitary woman stood, sturdy and bright in her nurse's clothing, stretching out her arms as if to catch a bit of the wind.

Five minutes of violence, and suddenly the storm passed, leaving a dilute sky above and streets littered with leaves and branches like a forest floor. The nurse came in then, laughing, as she wiped her face with her hands. Margo looked at her and felt admiration for this professional woman who was so spirited and alive to the world, so free of fear and full of joy.

How lucky she'd felt when she'd been introduced to Kate soon thereafter, and they'd quickly become close friends. But now?

Margo pictured herself standing on a raft of logs, icy water seeping through the cracks. The wind gusted harshly, stirring up currents that pushed the raft farther and farther from the darkening bank where Kate was standing, farther and farther, until Kate disappeared entirely from sight.

24

The following Tuesday, at the front entrance of the hospital, in the weak light of an early December sunrise, a band of nurses marched in a tight circle. Their arms swung briskly and their feet hit the pavement smartly. "We're Fighting For Your Health," placards on their backs announced in crisply printed block letters. "Nurses Need Respect," read others.

The previous morning, while Rundell and his staff in their Monday morning meeting continued discussion of a possible strike, the nurses' executive council had voted to go ahead with it. By noon, they had notified Rundell of their decision, their timetable, and their conditions: they would continue staffing the Intensive Care Units, the ER, and one operating room for emergency surgery. For all other nursing areas, coverage would cease in twenty-four hours, which would provide time for the noncritical patients to be discharged or transferred to other hospitals.

Calls and e-mails marked "urgent" had gone out to every member of Rundell's staff. "Come to the conference room immediately." All afternoon they had discussed options, priorities, and arm-twisting. The major decision-makers remained to continue their work into the evening. All others, including Margo, were to go home and prepare for the chaotic day to come.

Arriving early Tuesday morning, Margo found a parking spot easily and walked toward the hospital entrance. She heard the nurses' chants and read their defiant placards. Instead of hurrying past them, she stood still, immobilized.

Never cross a picket line.

It was a command she'd always honored, ever since the long-ago day when her father had walked with her to a big dreary building at the edge of town, a building with dirty windows and chipped wooden doors like those in the factory where her father worked. Burly men in work clothes paced back and forth, yelling and spitting in the dirt as they hoisted cardboard signs with crayoned wobbly letters. The words were difficult for a six-year-old who had just started reading to decipher, but her father read them to her as the men swung their signs in the air like swords.

Her father instructed her then about bosses and laborers, about exploitation and loyalty to your coworkers. There was fervor in his voice, like in the preacher's voice at church. He had pulled her by the hand and walked with her in a purposely wide detour around the men. She was awed by his fierceness and grateful he had shared such a passionate commitment with her. *Never cross a picket line.* Never had she disobeyed this admonition.

Now she was struggling with it, and with herself.

This was a picket line, a worker's picket line. But Rundell needed her, was expecting her, and this picket line was barring her way. But these were workers, and she knew personally that they had legitimate complaints and reasons for striking. A conundrum of contradictions. She was unmindful of the cold as her mind bounced back and forth between two competing conclusions—until, at last, she arrived at the solution.

Show solidarity with your colleagues. He hadn't phrased it exactly this way, but it was the underlying message of her father's teaching. Colleagues were what the factory workers were to him. And colleagues were what Rundell and the others were to her. So, in the end, she must choose to support her own colleagues.

Margo began to walk. She circled around the strikers. Still, she was not able to look them in the face. She could only pray that Kate was not amongst them.

Once inside the hospital, she half-ran to her office, quickly pulled off her coat, and hurried to the conference room. The chairs around the huge walnut table were already filled, so Margo slipped into an empty chair against the wall.

"The news is not good," Rundell reported, his face disapproving and stern. "The ER technicians have been contacted to help replace the nurses, but almost all seem to have fallen ill at the same time and said they had to stay home. Much of Housekeeping is out, as are many unit clerks.

"People, get out there now and pick up the slack," Rundell ordered. "Do whatever needs to be done."

Some administrators became part of Housekeeping and were dispatched to wipe up spills that for safety's sake had to be cleaned and dried immediately. Others became transporters and pushed patients to Radiology and elsewhere. Since lunch had to be provided for patients on solid diets, and many in Food Services had also called in sick, by ten thirty Margo was in the underground hospital kitchen setting out rows of whole wheat bread ready for a filling of cheese slices or tuna fish salad.

After the sandwich making was done, Margo returned to her office. From her window she could see ambulances pulling up like so many rescue boats come to fetch the shipwrecked. Slumped in wheelchairs, patients clutched blankets to warm themselves against the biting cold as they waited their turn to be loaded up and ferried home or to other hospitals.

Margo watched and mourned. The intricate fabric of her hospital was shredding faster than she could have imagined.

*M*argo was living in two separate but parallel worlds. Her primary world was that of her pregnancy. In this world, she lived in a deep mystical bond with her child. In this world, she lived to nourish and care for herself well enough to nourish her child. Her secondary world was everything else.

Today was the second day of the strike, but it was also the date for her scheduled quadruple marker blood test and sonogram. She informed Sylvia and Rundell's assistant that she had a medical appointment and would be coming in somewhat later in the morning. Margo was waiting to tell people she was pregnant until these test results were back, although she assumed those who saw her regularly had already guessed.

In her obstetrician's suite, Steven sat near the lab while Margo's blood was being drawn, and then the two of them were ushered to the sonography area. They shook hands with the technician, who looked impossibly young, thought Margo, for someone about to perform such a crucial task.

"Before we start, would you like me to tell you the gender of the baby?"

"We'd rather not," answered Margo.

She'd thought about it as the ultrasound date grew closer, and concluded that keeping the gender secret would better preserve the mysteriousness of pregnancy—and the discovery at birth would increase the excitement they'd be feeling as they first met their baby. "It's your call," Steven had said in agreement.

The procedure went just as they had read it would: glasses of water to expand her bladder, gel drizzled all over her abdomen to smooth the path of the sonogram wand.

And then, "There's your baby. See the arm?"

"It's moving its arms," Margo said. Despite all the YouTube videos she'd watched, the miraculous movements of her own baby in her own uterus filled her with awe.

"There's the spine, and the head, and the skull. See the face? I'll get a picture for you."

"I see it! I see it!" exclaimed Steven.

"Wow, it's incredible." Margo couldn't contain her elation.

"Besides waving its arms it could be urinating. They do that a lot."

"Already?" said Steven.

"See the left leg? And here's the heart beating."

Both Margo and Steven were silent through the rest of the viewing, speechless with amazement. When the technician was through, they were sent back to the doctor's office to hear his opinion of the results.

"The sonogram is perfectly normal. Baby looks good, and so does the placenta. Everything's going well. I'll have the results of the quad marker in a few days to confirm that for you."

Margo breathed a deep sigh of relief. So much for the Evil Eye. "Any sign of what caused the bleeding?"

"No, and I wouldn't expect there to be any," the doctor said. "With small amounts of bleeding and a quick resolution, it was probably just a minor tear in the placenta. Most of the time we haven't the slightest idea why it starts, or how it stops."

He tilted back in his chair. "In any event, rejoice. All looks well." His hands parted in the air like a clergyman invoking a blessing, and Margo rejoiced.

In the car Steven kissed Margo, and she nuzzled his neck and breathed in his smell. As he drove, they basked silently together in their joy.

Steven dropped her off at the hospital, and Margo walked toward the entrance, clutching tight her handbag, which now contained a copy of the precious ultrasound images. In early December, Connecticut weather is already quite chilly, and Margo shivered against the morning air even though she had wrapped herself up well in a heavy fisherman's cardigan and knitted cap. She had a distinct aversion to cold weather and felt the cold on her face as a stinging pain.

At the front of the hospital, the nurses, too, were dealing with the chill. They hugged themselves as best they could, in hopes of keeping a bit more warmth in their bodies as the bitter wind pushed against them. Margo quickened her step and headed toward the entry door. Crossing the picket line was easier the second time around.

She was hungry for work, but little had come in from the clinical areas since most units had shut down and bed occupancy was dwindling. The Coronary Care Unit, though, was still open and well staffed, and had sent her some data. Margo eagerly uploaded those numbers into a spreadsheet. She ran the usual analyses and additional unnecessary ones as well, comparing the results with the daily profile from last month and last year. But even so, she was done in twenty minutes.

Elsewhere in the hospital, there was no longer any kitchen work to do, since the patients still remaining required primarily intravenous feeding, and staff were expected to brown-bag their lunch or call for pizza delivery. With nothing else to do, and with no reason to feel guilty about neglecting anything, she pulled the magical sonogram pictures from her handbag and immersed herself in the pleasure of contemplating every little part of her baby, her treasure, her own.

But the hours passed slowly. By mid-afternoon, Margo's body felt restless and in need of some physical activity, as well as the need to see for herself what was transpiring in the hospital.

She walked through the near-deserted lobby and the corridor that led to the inpatient wing of the hospital. She pressed the button for Level 5, one of the Internal

Medicine units she followed and knew well. It was directly above the Obstetrics Wing.

Once she entered, it was immediately clear that this unit was not one of the ones kept open for those patients who couldn't safely be moved out of the hospital. The place was totally empty and silent. A dim pall hung over it, as all the lights were out but one. The beds showed evidence of occupants hastily dismissed and not expected back: sheets rumpled, blankets flung aside. Cardiac monitor screens had gone blank, stripped of the lively electrocardiographic patterns that normally jiggled across their screens. Intravenous poles, shorn of the fluid-filled plastic sacks that usually adorned them, stood bare as dead trees.

The unit was simply a ghost town.

Margo's thoughts flew to the floor directly below, the one that had recently become the most important part of the hospital for her: Obstetrics. It must look just as forlorn and useless. She pictured the bassinets empty and pushed willy-nilly against the walls, the baby blankets piled on shelves instead of swaddled around little bodies.

And what of the pregnant women who depended on it should they need admission for rapidly progressing labor, for preeclamptic toxemia, for premature contractions, for bleeding, for all the things that might go wrong in a pregnancy?

Margo walked back to her office and phoned her obstetrician. His receptionist must have noticed the anxiety in her voice, because Margo had to wait only a few moments before he picked up the phone and listened to her concerns.

"There are other good hospitals close by," he replied. "I don't have admitting privileges for them, but I know excellent obstetricians who do. If it would make you feel any better, I could give you some names."

She did not find this answer the least bit reassuring. She trusted *this* obstetrician. He had proven his clinical skill by accurately predicting the outcome of her bleeding episode. She had confidence in his judgment and his ready availability.

She didn't want any other obstetrician. In case of need, she wanted to come to *her* hospital and be taken care of by *her* doctor. But she thanked him and politely told him she'd take the list of names just in case.

26

The following morning at six thirty, Margo was in her bathroom pulling off her nightgown and worrying about the hospital but also delighting at the sight of the growing bulge of her belly. At the same time, Dr. Julius Crane was moving through the entrance to the hospital's surgical suite on the third floor.

He strode swiftly to the main bulletin board and scanned the master sheet of operating room assignments for the morning. Black ink crossed out the names of eighteen patients originally scheduled for elective surgery today, including three of his who had been on the schedule for weeks.

At the scrub sink, Dr. Crane pushed the water flow release valve with his knee, and began the ten-minute soaping ritual of hands and forearms, raking the scrub brush across his skin. Today, only this urgent case—a bleeding ulcer—remained on the operating room schedule.

All the surgeons, including Dr. Crane, were infuriated. Even if the strike ended the next day, it would take weeks to get all the canceled patients new spots on the always-tight schedule, if they had not already sought out other surgeons who operated in other hospitals.

Arms aloft and still dripping water, Dr. Crane pressed with his elbow the metal plate that signaled the operating room door to open. A short and burly man who radiated an air of self-assurance, he gave no greeting to the scrub nurse, just grabbed the sterile towel she held out to him, and plunged his hands into the surgical gloves she held open. He performed another of the bold yet meticulous operations for which he was justly renowned. The surgery resident doctor assisting Dr. Crane watched the skillful way his hands moved as he tied off the small bleeding vessels, dissected out the diseased portion of the stomach, and sutured with delicate stitches the remaining stomach to the small intestine.

Only when the last suture to close the skin incision had been taken did the hurricane hit in Operating Room Number Three. Dr. Crane threw his gloves on the floor. "Damn the nurses, who in hell do they think they are?" He followed with a litany of vituperation for the hospital administrators, the hospital attorneys, the trustees, the unions, the system, and the Democrats. Only the resident and the still-unconscious patient escaped his wrath.

AT 9:30 A.M. MARGO AND HER COLLEAGUES WERE DEEP in damage control mode. The conference room had rapidly taken on the tenor of a headquarters under siege. Half a dozen easels had been set up around the room, covered

with Magic Markered problem lists. Discarded sheets of paper littered the carpet.

Rundell was assessing the severity of the previous day's wounds. "Too much negative coverage by the media," he snapped. "We need better damage control." This new item was inked onto the problem lists.

A knock at the door and Rundell's administrative assistant rushed in, shutting the door behind her. "Dr. Crane's outside," she said, her voice strained. "I said you were still in conference, and couldn't be disturbed. But he says he can't wait. And won't."

The conference room door flew open, and Crane strode in.

Dr. Crane was a hospital legend. Even the lowliest of administrators knew of him—the clinical wizard, the magnetic service chief, the canny hospital politician who wielded words as skillfully as he did scalpels. Margo had always found his powerful energy exciting.

"Do you realize how many patients have been canceled at the last moment, except for emergencies? And an operation for cancer doesn't count as that kind of emergency. Are patients supposed to sit calmly and not worry that tumor cells are growing by the day until the nurses decide it's time for their exciting rebellion to end?"

"No!" bellowed the doctor. "If they have any sense at all, they'll go find a surgeon affiliated with a hospital that functions like a hospital and not like a damn kindergarten!"

Rundell sat unmoving. His eyes seemed to look through, rather than at, his inquisitor.

"Have you people"—and here Dr. Crane jabbed his long index finger into the air and circled it slowly around the table—"taken a good look at those nurses out there? They look like camp kids in a color war with their slogans and fight songs. That's professionalism? What the hell are they talking about? Professional nurses are supposed to be taking care of patients!"

He aimed his finger now straight at Rundell. "And professional administrators should have the guts and the balls to do something about it when they don't. I want you to do something about it! And I want you to do it now!"

Dr. Crane wheeled on his heels and marched out of the room. Margo could almost see the air parting to make way for him.

"Asshole," Rundell hissed.

Intakes of breath were audible around the table. Never had Margo, or, she assumed, her colleagues, heard Rundell swear. His eyes were transfigured, fierce and wildly blue.

"Does that bastard seriously think I am not aware of the situation?" Rundell shot out of his chair and slammed the door shut against their shocked faces.

Then, an explosion of voices: "Bring in the riot squad." "Hitler versus Mussolini." "Godzilla meets King Kong." "We should have videotaped it."

Margo found no humor in the situation, only distress. Amidst the cacophony she sat quietly, twisting a strand of hair at the side of her face. Crane and Rundell, two of her hospital's pillars of strength, were crumbling in front of her eyes. Who knew how it all would end?

*M*argo felt powerless to repair the breach with Kate, and much else was skittering beyond her control, but there was one thing she could put to right. The following day, she placed a call to Cecilia.

"How's Janie doing?"

"She's so much better. Making steady progress, the psychologist says, though there's still a lot of sadness there."

"My doctor says I'm fine, so I could come over if you think it would help."

"It would be great. But I don't want to put any pressure on you."

"You're not. I feel bad about staying away."

"Don't. You were right not to come. You need to take care of yourself. When Janie asked for you, we told her you were a little sick and would come when you were better. She accepted that."

Accepted it, thought Margo, because in Janie, generosity of spirit filled the places where intelligence was lacking.

"So what's a good night for me to come?" Margo asked.

Cecilia orchestrated the evening to provide Margo and Janie with the privacy they would need. She took her charges for an outing to the local bowling alley, courtesy of the generous members of the Lions Club, who paid the fees and sent representatives to press fingers into bowling balls and clap enthusiastically whether pins went down or not. Her assistant Nina, who worked the afternoon shift at Share House, would stay with Janie until Margo arrived at seven and would then disappear upstairs.

The route to Share House wove deeply into the city's old central core. Margo drove along streets that progressively narrowed and became increasingly littered with newsprint, candy wrappers, emptied six-pack beer containers. Shards of glass glittered under her headlights, slivers that threatened her tires and thus, in these potentially violent streets, her life.

Nearing Share House, she released her foot's pressure on the accelerator so as to slow her speed. Now she was getting closer to the alley, closer to the stalker's lair. For the past two nights, a disturbing dream had startled Margo from sleep: The Man in his hairy nakedness pinned against Cecilia's kitchen table, struggling against the restraining ropes that bit into his flesh, while Margo gave Janie a bat to beat him with and boiling water for scalding him. Each night Margo had tossed back and forth in the darkness, waiting for morning to come and erase the images with sunlight and work.

Margo slipped into a spot directly under a street lamp

whose weak light promised some security for her vehicle and for herself. Even though no one was to be seen, she ran the few steps to the door, pumped the doorbell, and was thankful that Nina was there in an instant. Margo stuffed her coat into the overfilled front closet, and despite knowing it was ridiculous, glanced into the darkened kitchen to reassure herself the table was topped by nothing more sinister than a pair of salt and pepper shakers.

In the darkened living room, Janie sat in front of the television console watching a DVD, her face bathed in the light emanating from the screen. She heard Margo enter, and strained in the dim light to see her.

Margo, in turn, searched Janie's face, fearing to see signs that Janie had learned not only that life could be frightening and people cruel, but also that trusted friends could be unreliable and even disappear.

"Hi, Margo. Margo, you like Janie?" she whispered.

It was Janie, of course, who had the greater fear and the greater need. Margo raised her arms and opened them wide, and Janie sprang from the floor, and nestled herself against Margo's chest.

Margo walked them to the sofa, sat Janie down, and sat herself close. "I like Janie. Very, very much."

"Not mad at Janie?"

"No, of course not."

Janie swallowed hard and tightened her fists. "Even because the man?" Janie's mouth trembled and her eyes welled with tears.

Margo seethed. Beatings were too good for him. His

skin should be sliced off inch by inch. He should be beheaded with a dull and rusty knife.

"I'm mad at the man, Janie—not you. That man touched you and scared you, and that was bad."

"Man bad, Margo?"

"Very bad."

"Very bad," echoed Janie. "Very bad." All was silent as Janie took some time to process this.

"Now let's go to the kitchen and make ourselves a treat," said Margo. "How about the special hot chocolate?" At Share House, cocoa, which was usually served to celebrate birthdays and holidays, had the cachet of caviar. Margo helped Janie spoon out heaping tablespoons of the thick powder into two mugs, and heated milk in a saucepan until tiny bubbles formed. They sat themselves at the table to sip the dark elixir.

With natural grace, Janie wiped away with her pinkie the thin trails of drink that trickled down her chin. "Why we get hot chocolate now?" she asked.

"Because we deserve it. We deserve a happy time."

"A happy time," Janie echoed, smiling.

After they were done, Margo carried the empty cups to the sink and rinsed them out. "Would you like to paste now, Janie? Would you like to make something beautiful?"

"Mm hmm, mm hmm." The ends of Janie's long blond hair rose and fell as she nodded enthusiastically.

In the living room, Margo flipped on the switch of the standing floor lamp, a Hydra-like relic from the 1950s with multiple goosenecks and parchment shades. White light soon dotted the room. From the shelves where Cecilia stored arts and crafts materials—outdated wallpaper samples, fabric remnants and the like—Margo took sheets of colored construction paper, a pair of blunted scissors, and a jar of paste.

"Come on, follow me," she said gaily, "let's sit here at the table."

When Cecilia returned with her band of bowlers, she found the house aglow with light. And tacked on the display corkboard, a new collage, bright with patches of pink and spring-fresh green, and, in its center, a big orange circle sun.

28

On the seventh day of the strike, Margo sat in her office with almost nothing to occupy her: no new e-mails, no pregnancy websites she hadn't already looked at earlier. She'd packed some unread magazines from home in her bag, but drew the line at bringing her crocheting.

Early in the afternoon, her office phone rang. "Kate's here," announced Sylvia.

Margo pulled in a deep breath. Kate, who'd been avoiding her? To whom she'd hardly spoken for weeks? Kate's unit had been closed down the first day, and she was not on the list of nurses authorized by the strike council to work.

So why was she in the hospital? And why in this particular spot? Please, Margo thought, please let this not get ugly.

Kate flew through the doorway, dressed in her standard working attire. "You're shocked I'm here, right?"

Margo nodded.

"You're not the only one." Kate sat down on the edge of the spare chair. "I absolutely never expected to break ranks."

Calm washed over Margo as she realized this was going to be far from a confrontation.

"Where are you working? What are you doing?" she asked.

"Burn Unit. There aren't enough step-down convalescent burn units like ours nearby, so the strike council authorized ours to stay open, with a skeleton crew. But burn care is tough, and those nurses are already exhausted. One of them's a friend—Julia—maybe you know her? She called and said she was wiped, that they desperately needed more staff.

"So when I heard that, I knew I had to come in. Not just to make sure the patients were well cared for, but that Julia was, too.

"But when I crossed that picket line where friends are marching, I could see they resented me. I could see their anger."

"But why, since it's an authorized unit?"

"The authorized nurses are regular Burn staff, and they're okayed by the council to work. The other Burn nurses won't buck the quota the council established. I'm not a Burn Unit nurse, but I can still help them out. What the council sees as my biggest sin is that I didn't ask for permission, though I did e-mail them as soon as I got to the unit. I just wanted to come in as soon as I could.

"So they e-mailed me back to tell me not to attend their group meetings anymore. Like I'm some kind of Trojan horse or something." Kate's eyes brimmed with tears.

Margo understood that Kate had come in order to

confide and be comforted. She reached over to take her friend's hand.

"People can be so dense," Margo said. "It's nothing like what's happening to you, but when I tried in our staff meeting to explain the gauze size thing and about how nurses feel devalued, everyone laughed. And since then, Rundell doesn't ask for my opinion anymore."

"That's it!" Kate said. "People want to make it black and white. You're either for or against. And it's just not that simple."

So began a ritual. Once each day, Kate came to Margo's office for comforting.

"Take your shoes off, put your feet up," Margo would say, pulling over a stack of books for Kate to use as a hassock.

Margo felt joy on many levels when Kate visited her: joy that she was giving solace to her dearest friend, and joy that the reconciliation she had longed for was here at last.

The evening after the first day Kate came to her, Margo shared her relief and happiness with Steven as soon as he came home.

Later in the evening, though, her concerns came back to the fore. She waited to tell him until the ten o'clock news was over. "The tragedy of this strike is not just that both sides are right, but that it's dragging on too long. And that's not fair to the patients counting on the hospital's being there for them today, tomorrow, and the day after that."

Margo's voice picked up speed and intensity. "You can't just tell people to go to some strange doctor who practices in some strange hospital. Trust in your doctor counts for a lot. It's not like picking a plumber off the Internet at random."

"You're worried about yourself, right? In case you need the hospital? But you're doing fine. That's what the doctor said. By the time you need the hospital for your delivery, the strike will long be over."

She nodded her head a few times, trying to believe his reassurances.

"Let's go upstairs," Steven said. "It's getting late."

In the bathroom, Margo took a warm shower. She pulled the flannel nightgown over her head, moisturized her face, and walked into the bedroom.

Steven was already in bed. He patted the empty space on her side. "Come to bed, and I'll help you forget about 'fair.'"

$\mathcal{S}$ince its conception, the baby was growing day by day, week by week, in so many ways. The diagrams in the books and the YouTube videos showed Margo that her baby, now at almost seventeen weeks of pregnancy, was growing tiny toenails, starting to store fat to provide itself with energy and warmth, and on the verge of beginning to hear. Every day she bent close to her belly and whispered words of encouragement: you're so smart, so hardworking.

Margo's days at the hospital followed a routine much less satisfying. Park her car. Note the unlit windows of rooms currently unavailable to patients. Cross the picket line. Do the half hour's worth of work that was all she had to do now. Clean out a file cabinet drawer of outdated and unnecessary folders. Call Cecilia to see how Janie was doing. The strike was still pernicious, but it elicited less of a sense of peril for Margo. Kate came every day and was as warm and close as ever, and the pregnancy was progressing well and not in need of any medical miracles.

In Rundell's conference room, however, the pressure

had only increased with each passing day. Daily negotiating sessions were now taking place among the critical decision-makers from each side. Margo and most of her colleagues were far from that level of seniority, so they knew next to nothing about what was transpiring behind the closed doors. A clamp of secrecy had been imposed on the negotiations, and so they pounced on any bit of evidence, however minor, that might be a clue to the goings-on inside.

On Monday afternoon, the beginning of the third week of the strike, several people noticed that the do-not-disturb slide tab was displayed on the conference room. At the end of the day, the door was still shut, the do-not-disturb tab still in place. Next morning, when they arrived at eight o'clock the tab was displayed—and Margo and her colleagues could only guess whether the negotiators had pulled a college-style all-nighter or had arrived before dawn broke.

Tuesday noon, a rumor began to circulate that the nurses were preparing to vote on a negotiated agreement.

At four thirty that afternoon, an e-mail marked "urgent" and addressed to all hospital employees appeared on Margo's computer. Cowritten by Rundell and the chairperson of the nurses' strike council, it read: "We are pleased to announce that complete nursing coverage will resume tomorrow morning. We anticipate full resumption of all hospital activities on Thursday."

Her colleagues emerged from offices and gathered in the adjoining hallway, slapping each other's backs and giving high fives. Margo hurried through the hospital corridors until she reached the Burn Unit. There, in full view of other staff and patients, she bear-hugged Kate until Kate laughingly pled for mercy: "Oh my God, enough, I can't breathe."

Thursday morning, Rundell assembled his staff for an extended briefing. "You've already learned some of the story from the press and local television. Here is the full agreement: a two-percent pay increase and no cuts in funding of their retirement pension this year—but no guarantee of increases in the following years. The head nurse of each nursing unit will report directly to the director of Nursing regarding acute problems, including sudden understaffing because of increased patient volume. Her assessment will become key in making the decision to close beds there temporarily—and I emphasize temporarily —when staffing is deemed insufficient.

"Of course we could not—and did not—commit to permanent overstaffing. And we will not endorse any document that sets out their views on professional autonomy or defines what the practice of nursing includes, such as dedicated time for patient and family counseling. We don't think it appropriate to endorse or not endorse any professional group's self-definition. In fact, requesting our endorsement contradicts the very autonomy they seek."

The following afternoon, in the hospital's largest auditorium, Rundell spoke to all hospital staff who'd accepted his invitation to come and hear his remarks.

"All of us who are part of this hospital have suffered during this strike," he said. "Now, we must all focus on restoring and further strengthening our professional and personal ties. We owe that to ourselves. More importantly, we owe that to our patients."

Later that day, Rundell met only with his own administrative staff. "Make sure not to leave enemies," he cautioned, "especially not with people you have to work with. We need all our skilled nurses. Make sure the nurses who chose to strike feel welcome here."

Margo celebrated that night with Steven at Le Jardin.

"I'm so pleasantly surprised," she said, as they sipped wine and ginger ale and awaited their dinners. "I thought Rundell would be a lot more vindictive."

he middle three months of pregnancy are characteristically joyful and comfortable ones, and Margo
enjoyed their pleasures. Metabolic changes sent oxygen and
energy coursing through her body. She began to feel
vigorous and physically spry. She donned maternity clothes
and shyly announced her status. People seemed genuinely
delighted, gave congratulations, and said she had a special
glow about her.

In the days following the strike's end, Margo sought a
reason to justify a trip into the clinical areas of the hospital.
Walking about, she could see for herself that this center of
healing, this dynamic community from which she drew
energy and meaning, was clearly mending. She was filled
with matchless relief, like a child reprieved from the threat
of parental divorce.

At home, Steven frequently murmured that she had
never been more beautiful. Her body was blossoming, and
Steven could scarcely keep his hands off her, his fingers
seeking out not only the areas that brought erotic delight,
but the protuberant swell of her belly as well. She told

Steven she was increasingly certain she felt their baby moving. "It's like champagne bubbles on your lips. And like the fluttering of a butterfly." Excitedly she mirrored his wide grin.

Margo's mother called her often. They were becoming closer in a way that Margo had not anticipated. And Margo's mother-in-law had roared into action soon after Steven had given her the news that she was soon to have another grandchild. Weekly, she'd dispatch an e-mail with tidbits of information gleaned from the Internet, such as the dangers to pregnant women in certain cleaning products. Monthly, a carton of vitamin-packed fresh fruit from Florida or Georgia arrived.

Steven joined Margo on her shopping expeditions to examine baby furniture and infant attire. They cheerfully argued over the merits of this style of crib and that design on draperies.

On New Year's Day, Margo and Steven were resting in their family room before a fire in the hearth. They had spent the day wallpapering the new nursery, formerly a corner guest bedroom, which had two large windows that would let in plenty of light and fresh air. Steven sipped a snifter of brandy, Margo a glass of freshly squeezed orange juice.

"Putting up wallpaper, they say, is an iron test of marriage," she teased, recalling the fervor of their argument about the best way to seam the cherub-strewn paper so that the babes would not end up looking like Siamese twins.

"A perceptive piece of folk wisdom."

She nuzzled his neck. "We passed that marriage test with flying colors. And I think we're going to be pretty good in the parenting department, too. At least you will. You're going to be an amazing father. I bet you won't even pressure the kid about his or her profession. No problem— either corporate or criminal law will be fine with you, right?"

He laughed and colored a little.

Steven sipped his brandy silently, and Margo happily guessed that he was savoring the possibility of talking shop with his son or daughter.

She shifted her position slightly to give her back a bit more support. "Really, you'll be terrific."

A shower of cinders exploded in the fireplace. As she gazed at their erratic tracks, she let her thoughts flow and drift. Steven would provide steadiness and stability; he'd be an anchor for his child.

And in that he would be totally unlike her own father.

DADDY WAS PHYSICALLY SOLID, WITH A BARREL-SHAPED chest connecting broad shoulders to a thick waist. His hair was reddish-brown, and wavy curls fell over onto his forehead while tight wiry ones matted together on his chest. When he called out her name in his deep, resonant voice, she ran so fast that she arrived breathless. He would laugh and say she was a champion sprinter. They went for long walks at the edge of the woods, singing their special songs.

Before bedtime, he would pretend he was a bucking bronco and let her ride on his back. She would giggle and shriek with excitement. There was also a special bedtime story he had made up just for her and recited every night when he was the one to put her to bed, a story about a girl and a boy encountering one scary obstacle after another: yawning pits, fire-breathing dragons, all requiring feats of courage and amazing athleticism. He would tell it slowly, stopping and waiting at all the places where it was her contribution to utter the whoops and groans that were the sound effects.

She adored him.

Once her sister was born and shared her room, much of that specialness ended. The same story was told, but now her sister heard it as well, and Daddy meant for her to hear. Margo still listened in the dark and responded in the right places, but she felt a sense of loss and more than a touch of resentment.

When she was older, about nine, her father stopped telling stories and inviting her for walks, and no longer asked her what books she was reading. Returning home from work, he slowly climbed the stairs to his room and, except for a quick dinner where he kept silent, would not be seen again until he left for work the following morning. If Margo called him from outside the closed bedroom door, no answer came, nothing at all. If she cracked the door open and peeked into the room, she saw him lying on the bed fully clothed, shoes and all. If she shoved the door open and ran to his side, he would glance at her out of the corner of his eye but then look up at the ceiling again, giving no sign that he acknowledged, much less welcomed, her presence.

Then, she would run outside to her special tree, the big walnut with crinkly dark bark, fling her arms around it, rest her cheek against its rough, familiar trunk, and let the grief flow out from some place deep in her chest.

One day when she was twelve, she came home from school to find three unfamiliar cars outside the house. Inside, it was strangely silent. Her mother was not in the kitchen preparing the children's after-school milk and cookies. The parlor, with its dark-colored furniture perched on wooden feet that looked like tiger paws, was empty. Where were the visitors that had come in the cars?

Upstairs, the door to her parents' bedroom was ajar. She heard the murmur of hushed voices and slipped inside. In the seconds before she was noticed and roughly pushed out of the room, she caught sight of a crumpled person-shape on the floor, a collar of leather around the neck. Although the hair was reddish-brown and curly, it couldn't really be her father, could it?

For days after his suicide, she refused to think about him. He had abandoned her without a word, without a sign of affection or regret. Now she would abandon him just as ruthlessly, refusing to talk about or even bring him to mind.

Yet at the funeral—so people told her, for she remembered nothing of this—she had tried to climb into the coffin.

MARGO LET HER EYES REST ON STEVEN. HE WOULD NEVER abandon a wife and child like that, or in any way. Of this she was certain; it would be an act of irresponsibility completely foreign to his nature. It was one of the things that had drawn her to Steven: that she could count on him.

"What are you looking at?" he asked.

"The father of my fortunate child," she said, her smile radiant and sure.

THAT NIGHT THERE WAS A WINTER RAINSTORM. A PEAL of thunder roused Margo out of a deep sleep. Finding herself unable to return easily to slumber, she quietly left the bedroom and went down to the kitchen, where she made herself a cup of herbal tea and then sat down at the table.

Outside, the storm still raged and lightning flashed. Margo watched the pelting rain and felt completely secure in her solid house, out of reach of the wildness. She sipped her tea, savoring its warmth and sweetness.

When her eyelids began to feel heavy, she rose from the table, shut off the kitchen light, and felt her way carefully back up the stairs. Margo slipped into bed and nestled herself against the lean, strong body of the father of her child. She had her own man now, a man steady as a rock, and true. And a baby coming.

Drowsy, comforted by Steven's warmth, she drifted into sleep.

31

---

*T*wo weeks later, a deep layer of snow blanketed Margo's lawn and brisk winds buffeted the pine trees outside her kitchen window. Inside the house, Margo's dream was turning turbulent as it moved toward its finale. In the darkened ghetto street, a gang of hooligans was surrounding her, carrying a long hemp rope thick with many coils. Closing in on their prey, they wound it around her waist, then divided themselves into two groups. Each cluster of ruffians grasped one end of the rope and they began pulling in opposite directions, as in a tug of war. The rope pulled tighter and tighter, until she felt her guts crush into bruised pulp.

Margo's eyes opened suddenly. While darkness still surrounded her, there was no seamy street, no band of vicious children. Instead, she was lying in the warmth of her own bed with her husband by her side. Yet although the tormenting urchins had vanished, the hard, relentless squeezing still pressed into her belly. Gingerly, her hands moved to her waist, and documented that there definitely was no rope coiled there.

The pressure eased, the rigidity in her belly gave way.

She sighed with relief and wondered why nightmares kept going like this even after one's eyes were open. She closed her eyes again and nuzzled into the pillow, soothing herself with the feel of smooth percale grazing against her cheek. Her body softened and she started to drift back into sleep.

Then something began to pull at her again, lassoing and constricting her belly with a steady pressure. She wrenched herself out of drowsiness. This was not a dream. This was something violent actually gripping her belly.

Margo felt herself teetering, although she knew that her body was lying horizontal, and pressed firmly against the mattress. She jammed her fingernails into her palms, and her mind steadied. Don't dramatize. Don't exaggerate. It could be the flu. It could be nothing.

And in a moment, as if vanquished by her determination that it be nothing, the tightness in her abdomen dissolved. Her belly was as calm as a mountain lake unruffled by the slightest breath of wind. Wary, she stayed on the lookout for the slightest sign of turbulence. She relaxed her vigilance only after ten minutes had passed. Then the tightening began again: steady, slow, implacable. She turned to Steven instantly. "Wake up." Louder: "Wake up!" She jiggled his shoulder roughly.

"What?" he mumbled.

"Take me to the hospital. Something's wrong."

"What's wrong?" he said, sitting up, very awake now.

"Cramps. At least three of them already. They're low,

deep, and hard. I'm scared it's something bad. And it's not even twenty-three weeks yet."

Steven didn't wait for further clarification. He called the doctor.

The doctor's answering service put him through immediately. The doctor then answered, sounding as alert as if it were midday, no doubt conditioned by years of after-midnight awakenings.

Taking care to use Margo's exact words, Steven reported the situation to him. "Bring her to the Obstetrics Wing now," the doctor said. "I'll call the night nurse to have an examining room ready."

Steven hung up and turned to Margo. "He said it would be best to check you right now, and clarify exactly what, if anything, is going on. So let's get dressed." His voice sounded calm and steady.

"Should I bring something? Am I supposed to bring a suitcase?" she asked, the words fast and breathless.

"Let's not jump to any conclusions. Remember the spotting? Just a short visit to the hospital, then right back home."

THE NIGHT WAS FRIGID. BRIGHT LIGHTS ILLUMINATED the entrance door to the Emergency Room. Once inside, Steven explained that the doctor had told them to proceed directly to Obstetrics. A phone call was made for confirmation, and a wheelchair was provided for Steven to push through the halls. He did so quickly, and sometimes the wheels of the chair slid on the highly polished vinyl.

On the fourth floor, the receptionist at the front desk took their names and directed them to the nursing station nearby. There, the head nurse greeted them, motioned Steven to the small waiting area, and then steered Margo into an examining room, talking all the while. The nurse continued to speak as she helped Margo change into a hospital gown and sit on the examining table, and her steady stream of conversation and questions helped Margo keep her mind in gear.

"Okay, I'm going to check if the doctor's arrived yet," she said. "I'll be back in a minute."

Immediately, it was too quiet. Margo stared at the wall, trying to keep herself distracted. Its color was the same oyster gray that the hospital design team had selected for the entire hospital; she had always thought it a cold and dreary hue, and now, from the vantage point of a vulnerable patient, she found it even more forbidding. She noticed that a curious mix of odors permeated the room: a pungent sweetness that rose up from the floor—probably the disinfectant cleanser—while the smell of alcohol came from—never mind, she didn't want to think about where it came from, probably some bath for instruments of steel.

The nurse returned with Margo's doctor, who quickly asked his questions, and then they set her down flat on the examining table. She stared at the oyster-gray ceiling. Cold steel was in her now, stretching her so that the doctor would be able to see deeper. What exactly was he seeing? Clotted lumps of blood? Or a tiny arm hanging out?

Stop it, she thought. Stop it.

The doctor finished and came to stand at the side of the table. His face was serious. "The cervix is dilated. Not too much, but more than it should be. Let's get you into a bed where we can watch you carefully."

Panic began to flow through her with such velocity it was like water spilling over the edge of a waterfall. She was afraid it would overwhelm her. She jammed her fingernails deep into her palms. "Can't you do anything to stop it?"

"We have some drugs," the doctor said, resting his hand on her shoulder. "At times they are effective. I can't promise anything, but we'll do our best."

Steadier now, supported by the stinging in her palms, she let herself be soothed by his hand. He helped her slide off the table and led her to the wheelchair the nurse had brought in. "We're going to take you to the South Wing. You work here, so you are familiar with it, I suppose?" She nodded mutely. "Then you know we've got monitoring and treatment equipment as good as any in the state, and highly skilled personnel."

The nurse tucked an oven-warmed blanket around her and pushed the chair forward and out of the room. When they passed the waiting area, the doctor motioned Steven to join them, and as they walked down the hall, he summarized the situation. Margo held tightly to Steven's hand and heard the words only as a blur of sound, which was fine; she did not want to face the sharp edges of their meaning again so soon.

The tightening came again, this time more like a vise clamped around her abdomen. "I'm getting another one," she whispered.

The doctor looked at his watch. "It's ten after four. Let them know every time you have a contraction until we get the monitor on."

The nurse pushing the wheelchair picked up her speed. Clutching Steven's hand more tightly, Margo stuck her free hand atop her thigh under the blanket, hoping to stop its trembling.

32

———

*M*argo knew the South Wing well. It was steps from the Springer Perinatal Center, and she had often been the administration's representative on tours put on for visiting dignitaries who had come to see this frontier of medical science and technology. The Springer Center was a facility that provided special care for women with diabetes or other medical problems whose pregnancies were at high risk and needed careful observation. It was also one of Connecticut's centers for emergency treatment of newborn babies from around the state. The helicopter pad that served the ER and the Burn Unit was close by, and infants who were already in critical condition at the moment they entered the world were rushed here for intensive medical care. Miracles were wrought and babies were pulled back from the brink of death. Still, catastrophe also came calling here, and often. And Margo knew that.

They wheeled her past another nursing station, and brought her into a small room that was sparingly furnished with a hospital bed, one beige vinyl armchair, and a metal bedside table. Near the table stood the centerpiece of the room, a tall and elaborate electronic console with dials, display screens, push buttons, and lengths of paper tape dangling down its front. In a few minutes the doctor went to write orders, the nurse left to brief her counterparts on this unit, and Margo and Steven were alone.

While Margo lay quietly on the bed, Steven gazed around the room, observing the steel pole attached to his wife's bed, the panel of electrical and oxygen outlets above her pillow, the electronic console. Despite the fearfulness of this situation, he clearly seemed interested in the impressive electronic equipment, Margo noticed, and wondered if he found it reassuring or frightening.

Her body suddenly intruded on her thoughts. Margo's hand clutched Steven's, and his attention veered immediately from the impressive electronic console to his wife's face. "Press the call button, Steven," she said urgently, pointing to the white cord on the edge of the bed. "I'm having another one."

A new nurse came in, dressed in the shapeless blue hospital staff gown that bespoke delivery or operating room duties. "I was just coming to introduce myself. What do you need?"

"I'm supposed to tell someone every time I have a contraction."

The nurse nodded and came closer. She placed her hand on Margo's abdomen and pressed her fingers firmly into its boardlike solidity to keep track of the waxing and waning of the contraction, while her eyes fixed on her watch.

"All right. Over now," she said.

Margo nodded her head, gazing steadily into the nurse's eyes. There had been something strengthening in the way they had tracked the contraction together, even though only she could feel the bite of it.

"Okay. I'm Jenny. I'll try to be here as much as I can and as much as you'd like—or not, if you'd rather."

"As much as you can," Margo said.

Jenny nodded, as if a contract had been sealed. "And now, after that buildup, I have to leave. Just for a few minutes, to check the doctor's orders. Be right back."

As soon as Jenny left, Steven came out of the corner where he had retreated and clasped Margo's hand again, both of them needing the connection. No more than a few minutes later, Jenny returned, her arms laden with plastic bags filled with clear fluids and yards of plastic tubing. She deposited the paraphernalia on the bedside table, and began plunging tubing connections into the bags. The young resident doctor who accompanied her, also in operating room blues with a rubber tourniquet looped over his right hand, came over to the bedside. Steven let go of Margo's hand and backed away again to his corner.

"We're going to start you on intravenous medications now to try to stop the contractions. They'll also help you relax." He did not appear very relaxed himself.

Jenny had the bags hanging from the IV pole already. She checked the labels one more time. To the free end of the tubing, she attached a needle carefully covered with its sterile holder, and opened a packet containing an alcohol-

dampened square of cotton. The doctor twisted the tourniquet around Margo's upper arm.

Margo wasn't looking. Even the oyster-gray wall across
from her bed was better viewing, and she stared at it
intently until the poking and the puncturing and the taping
were all over with. Jenny was picking up after the doctor,
who was now adjusting the flow rate of medication to his
satisfaction. Steven was in his corner.

"One thing more, and then we'll let you get some rest,"
the resident doctor said. "We're going to attach a monitor
to a belt around your abdomen to record your contractions
and the baby's heartbeat. That way, we'll be able to track
what's going on. If you have any questions about it, Jenny
can explain the details to you." He strapped the strong
fabric belt around her and attached its wires to the electronic console.

Margo resolved to ask no questions at all. This was an
electronic sentinel and protector. That was all she needed
to know.

The medical pair left. Steven seated himself back in the
chair by her bed, visibly exhausted. By now it was almost
six in the morning. Margo drifted between alertness and
drowsiness, mesmerized at some moments by the clicks of
the electronic watchtower, intermittently startled by the
painful contractions in her belly, and sometimes slipping
into a torpor induced by the chemicals steadily dripping
into her vein.

Suddenly, a flood of warmth gushed between her thighs.
There was enough fluid to soak the mattress and leave a

puddle sopping under her buttocks. She jerked awake and reached for the call button, jabbing it over and over.

Was it water? Or blood? She dared not lift the sheet to look.

When Jenny came in, Margo yanked the sheet up while fixing her gaze on the nurse's face so as not to catch even a glimpse of whatever fluid was on the bed. "There's a lot of something wet between my legs," Margo said, feeling faint even as she said it, even though she was lying down.

"Your membranes have ruptured," Jenny explained in a flat voice. "I'm going to call your doctor and let him know."

"Tell me what that means. I can't remember what I read in the books."

"It means the sac of amniotic fluid surrounding the baby burst and the fluid came out. It's not anything abnormal for it to break open. It's a natural part of labor. What it means, though, is that the labor will continue now."

"But the medication was supposed to stop it," Margo wailed, her voice full of panic. "I'm just starting the twenty-second week!"

"Let me call your doctor, Margo. He'll come and explain. I'll be back as soon as I page him." The nurse turned toward the door.

"Please come back right away," Margo said plaintively. She felt insubstantial and fragile. Steven, in this place, was no more than a shadow hovering in the corner of the room. He could not help; he was as ignorant and impotent as she was. It was the doctors who had the knowledge and the power, and Jenny was their surrogate.

The nurse looked back over her shoulder. "I'll be back right away, that's a promise," she said.

When Jenny returned, she carried a small piece of blotting paper in her hand. "What's that for?" Margo asked.

"It's litmus paper. The doctor wants it as a check on my clinical opinion. It turns pink if it's amniotic fluid." She leaned down over the bed.

When Jenny straightened up again, Margo saw that the paper had turned pink. The meaning was clear: her baby's shield had broken. The liquid that had soothed its skin was now no more useful than dirty dishwater, and there was nothing she could do to create more again.

The nurse changed the sheet, taking away the remains of the baby's watery nest.

The resident doctor came in and disconnected the intravenous line from one of the bottles. "No pain medication," she told him firmly. There was little she could do, but she would do nothing to put her baby at any increased risk of harm.

The contractions came faster now, and harder. Margo gripped the edges of the mattress, and her knuckles went white. Jenny helped her breathe deeply, and deeper still, and ride out the contraction. In the chair again, Steven sat silently, his face drawn, the fingers of his right hand continuously rubbing his temples. His obvious fear and lack of composure were not as upsetting to Margo as she would have anticipated. She already knew he was powerless here, that it was Jenny and the doctors who were the baby's lifeline.

The contractions became her universe. With all her might, Margo willed them not to come, to stop and let her baby grow older and stronger, but they came nevertheless, traitors from her own interior core. Wave after wave, they came. She struggled hard against their coming, held her breath, pulled in her abdomen.

"It's best not to push against the pain," Jenny said.

So then, when each contraction began to unfurl itself from deep within, she hung on and let herself sail through black space and time with it. And in that darkness, as if from far away, she heard the voice of Jenny encouraging her to let go, to ride it out, to come back.

The resident doctor came and went, checking the electronic console, talking in a low voice to Jenny, to Steven. Margo paid him no mind; for now, there was only the sailing and the voice of her navigator-nurse. And the jumbled thoughts about the baby. Now that its watery cradle was gone, did it feel roughness against its skin? Was it being crushed by the grinding walls of her womb? God love it, God protect it. Her own baby, and she had been unable to keep it safe.

Her obstetrician came in, and at the sight of him, Steven jumped up at attention, his eyes searching the doctor's face. "Margo? Margo, can your hear me?" the doctor asked.

She'd closed her eyes for a moment and now here was the doctor, in his operating room blues, with all his skill and power. She mumbled an acknowledgement.

"You know that the amniotic fluid sac has ruptured,

and you are in advanced labor. We're going to take you into the delivery room now."

"But it isn't time," she wailed.

"It has to be now."

He must mean it was better for the baby to be born than to stay in her dry uterus. Poor baby, one danger worse than the other. Should she stop praying for the contractions to cease? Should she stop trying to slow them with the force of her will?

They began to wheel her out of the room.

33

It seemed to Margo that she had been transported into the midst of a science fiction movie, where oddly clad, robot-like figures moved among strange instruments in a cold, sterile landscape. Knowing that she was actually in one of the intensive-care delivery rooms of the West Unit did little to counteract the fearful effect of these surroundings.

She lay on a table beneath a huge, saucer-shaped lamp composed of a dozen powerful circlets of light rimmed in gray steel. Around the room were electronic consoles, some with blinking lights, some dark and dormant. Persons in blue pajamas, caps, and half-masks over their faces glided soundlessly across the floor in bootie-covered shoes. Only their eyes were visible.

White light poured continuously out of the overhead lamp. Metal tables and surfaces in the room reflected the intense beams of light, and there was glittering everywhere. The walls themselves were constructed of shiny steel, and as Margo looked at them, they buckled, like objects seen in very bright sunlight.

No. Walls didn't buckle. She would not permit her mind to start spinning out frightening perceptions, not when she and her baby needed discipline, endurance, and courage.

In her abdomen, the grinding started again. Inside it, a battering ram was pushing relentlessly outward. All her consciousness and thinking ceased, and she was gathered up into that huge knot of pain. She tried to breathe as Jenny had directed: "In"—belly rise high; "Out"—belly float down. It didn't seem to help.

"Good. Keep breathing in that slow and steady way," a male voice spoke from behind her head.

It wasn't Steven, for he was standing at her side, eyes widened and fixed on her face, and saying nothing at all. Someone else, someone she didn't know was there, observing her, assisting her. She breathed deeply again although she didn't actually need to, now that the contraction had passed. She wanted him to know she was acknowledging his presence, responding to his request, accepting their partnership. Keep watch; stay there for me, whoever you are.

A few moments of peace: no pain. And then another contraction came. She began the deep breathing in earnest now. The grinding in her belly eased a decibel—or however you measured roaring pain—and then drilled outward again. It ground against her with such force that surely, she thought, it would bore straight through her belly and crash into the belt still encircling her abdomen.

Then, mercifully, the contraction was over.

Two blue-suited persons came over on either side of her to bend her legs at the knees and stuff her feet into stirrups, and they readjusted the blue cloths draped across the lower half of Margo's body.

A tightness encircled her right arm. Margo turned her head and saw the cuff around her arm swelling with pumped air. "Your blood pressure's up," said the unseen anesthesiologist behind her. "Try to relax. Keep on with that deep breathing."

Relax? When they were poking at her bottom, swabbing her with cold liquids, and her baby was in deep trouble? But she forgave him that absurdity; right now, he was the only companion she had.

Another contraction assaulted her. Her body, now like a plane on automatic pilot, gave and received orders: lungs and abdomen expand in unison; slow, steady, deep, wide. "Much better," said the voice behind her. The contraction grew in strength. Would this relentless drilling in her belly continue until at last she burst open, spewing bits of skin and muscle and blood and bone all over the room? Then she sailed into the pain again, and all thinking stopped.

A little later, coming back on the receding edge of the contraction, Margo noticed the blue-clad people were looking toward the door. Her doctor had come into the room.

At her side, he spoke quietly. "You are twenty-two weeks pregnant, meaning the baby's fetal age is just twenty weeks. There is very little chance for a baby this immature to live—it's less than a five percent chance—but we are going to do everything we can. Now we can give you some anesthesia."

Margo grasped onto his words: very little chance meant *some* chance, didn't it?

So she resisted—not out of pride or masochism, but out of a protectiveness that surprised her with its strength. "No, it won't be good for the baby. I don't want anything."

"All right," the doctor replied. "It's your decision."

The grinding began again, crushing with such force that she was sure her belly must be on the verge of bursting open.

"I'm going to give you some oxygen through a mask on your face," said the voice behind her, "and I want you to breathe into it slowly and deeply."

Now she would have a mask like everyone else in the room, Margo thought, as she sailed away with the contraction.

A clear plastic mask, its shape smooth and curved, was lowered over her face and placed over her nose and mouth. It didn't press too tightly and so she didn't feel suffocated. But she could no longer talk. For a moment, stuffed into the stirrups, unable to move and muzzled by the mask pressed over her mouth, it seemed to her she was entombed.

The grinding again, joined now by another force deep within her belly that pressed her entrails down into her bottom. The insistent pressure demanded obedience. And without actually planning to, she was pushing down with it, grunting as she joined to it with all her might.

"All right, Margo, listen to me." It was her doctor's

voice coming up at her from the far end of the table. "Make that push smooth and steady."

Smooth and steady. She listened to his voice, but her body obeyed nothing but its own commands.

She spoke silently to her unborn child: "You can do it. You can make it."

And finally, with one long steady push, the pressure dissipated, the grinding ceased, and the baby was born.

"It's a girl," said the doctor, as he handed the baby to the waiting pediatricians.

At the far end of the delivery room, staff crowded around the table on which lay the tiny infant, warmed by a steady envelope of life-sustaining heat emitted by a bank of special lamps overhead. The child was so tiny that she seemed more a scale model of humanity than a living human being. If one were to look closely, though, one could see that her chest rose and her arms and legs moved, ever so slightly.

As the resident doctor attended to Margo, in a corner nearby, two nurses and Margo's doctor conferred in hushed tones.

"We should let them see the baby," said one nurse. The second nurse agreed, "It's always better to let the parents see the babies. Otherwise, the child is scarcely real to them. It helps them grieve better."

The doctor nodded. "The first thing, though, is for me to stress that the prognosis is close to hopeless, and the baby will probably die by the end of the day."

He glanced over at the neonatology section of the

room, where the tiny wisp of a baby was heaving her little chest to catch the few gasps of breath that would be the sole activity of her lifetime. Sighing deeply, he walked back to the delivery table.

As Steven held her hand tightly, Margo lay straining to catch a glimpse of the baby, oblivious to the cleansing and caring for her own body. Her ears strained to catch any hint of the baby's cries. Would the tiny voice sound like the rustling of the wind? But she heard no sound other than adult voices murmuring, and the low whine of machinery.

The doctor appeared at her side. Margo locked her eyes onto his, soundlessly appealing for information.

He began to speak. "Your little girl is lying under special warming lights that will keep her temperature up where it should be. When babies are that immature, they can't regulate their temperatures for themselves. She's had a breathing tube inserted because she was breathing with difficulty. That is expected, too."

He must have seen the hope that flared in her eyes, as he then got to the point more directly. "Margo, do you remember that we told you the chances of survival for a baby this premature were almost negligible?"

She nodded slowly. His manner warned that she might not wish to hear the remainder of this conversation, yet she knew she must not cover her ears or her mind.

"Sadly, that prognosis was correct. The baby weighs less than eleven ounces. Her basic life-sustaining processes are just not sufficiently developed."

Life sustaining . . . developed . . . It was as if he were

too far from the table, speaking in disconnected phrases. It was all becoming so fuzzy.

"Margo, listen to me carefully. We have your child in an incubator and will wheel her near so you can say hello to her. And then you both must start to say goodbye."

Steven tightened his grip on her hand. Hello. Goodbye. Those were titles of plays they put on at Summer Theater: *Hello, Dolly. The Goodbye Girl.* Hello, goodbye. How could it work that way? You didn't welcome a child into this life and then banish her away—to where?—with a cold farewell.

In the plastic and chrome box was a beautiful, tiny Thumbelina. Ten little fingers, ten little toes. Skin so transparent she could almost see through it. Skin that must be so soft, so smooth; oh, when would they let her touch it? Margo's mouth broadened with a smile of welcome, while at the same time her eyes brimmed over with tears.

Only when the box was wheeled away and out the door did the pain and horror grate against each other like shifting plates in the earth's crust, and the eruption cracked through to the surface.

She was unable to keep away the unendurable knowledge any longer. "Don't take the baby away," she shrieked. "Don't let her die."

The doctor steadied her shoulders as she tried to heave herself off from the table, her eyes glued to the door through which the incubator had been wheeled. "She's being taken to the intensive care nursery, where they know how to take care of her."

"Valium, 10 mg I.M.," he barked over his shoulder, and

a nurse nearby nodded her head in acknowledgement and soon gave the injection. He clasped Margo's free hand in his until the medication took hold and her shuddering dissolved into the torpor of sleep.

PART TWO

34

*T*his morning, Margo is seven days back from the hospital. Her sleep at night has been fitful, and she awoke much too early, before dawn broke. She has been lying in bed for hours now without moving. She feels her body heavy and immobile, as if it were a hunk of wax.

The glow of red digital numerals on the bedside clock signals that it is now well after twelve. Margo translates that into an instruction: time to get out of bed and try to have lunch. It is necessary to let her life be ordered by the clock now. Otherwise, she will simply stay in bed and let the day elapse, minute by turgid minute.

Margo swings her legs to the floor and stands up. I should probably go wash my face and brush my hair, she thinks. But it is too exhausting even to imagine pushing herself through all that movement, so she leaves the bedroom as she is, and walks slowly down the stairs.

In the kitchen she puts on water for tea. Fixing herself some toast, though, turns out to be a major dilemma. Should I have rye or white? The rye is staler and due for toasting, but the white would be less heavy in her morning-dry mouth. Rye? White? Rye?

Unable to decide, she reaches for whichever bag is closest to her hand in the breadbox, and removes a slice of the rye.

The toast is all Margo plans to consume for lunch. Her appetite has practically vanished. The function of the toast is not to assuage hunger but to make it possible for her to answer "yes" when Steven asks later if she ate anything. If she can answer "yes" convincingly, his mouth will not turn down at the corners, and he will not have to give that speech about nourishment in that pleading tone of voice.

The teakettle summons her with its whistle. She takes a cup and tea bag from the cabinet and pours the hot water. The liquid turns shades of gold and brown, but she has no interest in the colorings. She simply removes the tea bag and then slowly drinks the tea.

Margo eats a few bits of toast, and then gets up and moves to the living room. She slouches into the couch's cushions and rests again.

All about her, the air in the house hangs heavy and still. It is more than merely quiet. It is oppressively quiet, as if a thick fog of silence had seeped in under the door and spread through the house. She feels enveloped by yards and yards of silence.

"I love you, Mama."

The sweet words are quite clear. It is a little child's voice.

She doesn't know what, if anything, is happening, so she sits and waits.

"I love you, Mama."

This time she is sure she heard the words, and she knows absolutely that it is her child's voice—even though the baby hadn't grown old enough to speak.

"No," she says out loud. "This is impossible."

She looks everywhere in the room, under tables, behind the couch. And of course, as she knew all along, there is no one there at all.

"I love you, Mama."

It's unmistakable. The voice, sweet and pure, is calling out to her again.

"I'm going nuts," Margo says out loud.

She knows the baby is dead and buried. She forces herself to remember the horrors of the day she went with Steven to watch the small oak coffin lowered into the ground. She pictures the details that have seared themselves into her mind, even though she had staggered to the gravesite under heavy tranquilization.

Only a crazy person hears voices when no one is there, she thinks. Only a crackpot hears the voice of a dead child who never even learned to speak.

But oh, it feels so good to hear that voice.

THE NEXT DAY, THE CHILD CALLS OUT TO HER AGAIN. And this time, Margo is not frightened.

"I love you, too," she answers, realizing all the while that her mind must be playing some very bizarre game. "I love you, too."

The following day, the child calls yet again, and Margo answers with the same response.

She does not tell Steven about the little girl's voice. He will only tell the doctor, who will arrange for tranquilizers to try and silence the baby's voice.

As long as I know it's not real, Margo thinks, what's the harm?

She looks forward to the tiny voice that now visits with her daily. She goes down to the living room now without needing to check the time, so as to be ready for a visit in their usual spot.

But after three more weeks the child's voice disappears, without warning or farewell.

It stops on the day that Margo finds a few drops of blood in her underpants. It's not the flow of a period yet, but it washes away the child's voice that was all that remained of her existence.

And now, once again, Margo is enveloped by yards and yards of silence.

35

At eleven forty-five on a Thursday morning, ten weeks after the delivery, Margo is still in bed. She lies under the soft quilt in the bedroom, with the antique satin drapes still closed to keep out the morning light.

Being a lark, she has always been the one to arise early enough to hear the first chirps of the birds. But now she's still huddling in the big bed even though the sun is already high in the sky. I'm so tired, I just can't get up, she thinks. Used to feeling at full tilt early in the morning, she finds this bewildering. Several times in the past few weeks, she has taken her temperature to see if she's fallen victim to some undiagnosed illness, but it has always been normal.

She has permission to stay at home. Soon after the delivery, Rundell had called to offer condolences. "Take as much time to recuperate as you need," he'd said. "Mike volunteered to pick up your most urgent work, and we'll distribute the rest to the others." Likely Rundell never anticipated she'd take this long a leave, but it is impossible for her to even contemplate simply sitting at her desk.

More time passes by, and eventually Margo picks up the old pink bathrobe she had dropped last night in a heap at the foot of the bed. She slips it over her gown and slowly walks down the stairs.

After a few mouthfuls of toast and a glass of water, she walks to the living room, turns on the television, and waits for the familiar people in their familiar situations to appear.

The afternoon unfolds slowly; soap operas play out on the screen, saga following saga. Margo sits quietly in the lounge chair, her feet up on the hassock, paying little attention to the stories spinning themselves out before her. Instead, her mind wanders here and wanders there, awash like a boat loosened from its moorings.

Margo thinks of her mother's first call, her unexpected words. "I'm so sorry," she'd said, her voice at first shaky and then dissolving into quiet cries. That shared grief had brought her a rare moment of comfort.

Margo thinks of her mother-in-law's most recent call. "I know it's hard. They say that getting pregnant again as soon as possible is the best antidote." The words hit hard, and Margo gasped as if she'd been physically assaulted, even though she knew her mother-in-law meant no harm, and that the intention was to bring hope—to both of them.

She catches sight of the rip in the dining room drapes, caused by the misstep of a guest's high-heeled shoe. I need to take them in for repairs—someday, she thinks.

LATER IN THE AFTERNOON, THE AMUSING SHOWS ARE available, especially the courtroom shenanigans with impolite judges versus hapless defendants. But Margo cannot summon up a laugh feeling, or even a smile feeling. Pleasure seems to be a language she spoke once but has long since forgotten.

As the afternoon spins itself away, a turbulent mixture of desolation and rage begins to surface. It is unbearable, worse than the pain of the eardrum that once ruptured when she flew despite a bad cold, worse even than the cramps of her labor. She tries very hard to dispel it. She clasps her legs close to her body, buries her face on her knees, concentrates only on the flickering blackness underneath her closed lids until her breathing steadies, and the numbness and apathy creep over her again, and she is safely out of reach of the pain.

LATER, IN THE EVENING, STEVEN IS IN HIS OFFICE stuffing more papers into his already-full briefcase for the journey home. The other rooms in the office suite are already dark; secretaries and legal colleagues have long since left. He has valid reasons to be staying late, with a court case in the morning and his presentation still in need of polishing, although he could have worked on this at home.

While Steven is finally driving to the house—well under the speed limit, which obviously increases the length of time needed to get home—Margo is attending to his dinner. The completion of her last afternoon TV program signaled her next move: get up and go to the kitchen.

She removes her file of main-dish recipes from its place in the cupboard and spreads a few potential candidates out on the countertop, but cannot find merit in any of them. She deals out several more cards from the file, and then more, until the countertop is papered with recipes, row upon row.

She examines the cards that list instructions for stews laced with wine and herbs, for pot roasts rubbed with special seasonings and simmered in sauces redolent with garlic, but of course it is too late to start something requiring hours on the stove. In the end, she takes from the meat compartment the sirloin tip roast they bought together at the market and simply slices it into pieces of steak to slide under the grill when Steven comes home.

The front door slams. Margo takes the meat slices out of the refrigerator.

The door of the hall closet opens and closes as Steven puts away his jacket.

Margo turns the broiler on.

"Sorry I'm late," he calls from the front hall.

"It's all right," she answers, slipping the meat into the oven.

After he washes up and changes out of his suit into something more comfortable, he sits down at his place at the table. When the meat is ready, Margo cuts it into two uneven portions and places them on two plates, adds some of yesterday's tossed salad, and sits down opposite him.

Steven sprinkles salt and pepper onto his food. It is the third night this week that he is eating unseasoned steaks just tossed into the broiler.

"Did you have an okay day? Did you eat some lunch today?"

"Yes," Margo answers. "I ate."

"Tomorrow's Friday," he says. "And then we'll have the weekend. What would you like to do? Go to the movies? Or would you rather invite Kate and Walt over here for drinks?"

She can't bring herself to respond.

"No? What about a museum?"

"Whatever you like," she replies softly. "You're the one who's been working all week. You pick."

"I want it to be something *you'll* enjoy," he says.

"Any of those things sound all right, Steven."

"It's not good for you to stay at home all day. When you came home from the hospital, sure, you needed rest to get your strength back. But that was a very long time ago."

"I'd go back to work if I felt up to it," she says. "But I don't. Just doing routine things around the house takes so much effort—how could I possibly go to work?"

"I'm no doctor, but I think lying around this long can make you feel even more tired. You need something to get you going."

"Maybe you're right," she says.

Steven says nothing further as he clears the table and loads the dishwasher. He handles the plates and silverware roughly. He is clearly irritated by her verbal acquiescence in the absence of any agreement to change. Steven turns and looks at her, but likely all he notices is that her hair is clumped in bunches like sticky spaghetti. He says nothing more so as not to risk saying something harsh that might harm her.

Steven closets himself away in the study and occupies himself with the contents of his bricfcase, while Margo again spends the evening sitting impassively in front of the television screen.

At ten, Steven comes into the living room and looks for the remote so he can switch to the channel whose rendition of the evening news he favors. Margo squeezes her hands against the arms of her chair and pushes herself up slowly, like an arthritic old grandmother.

"I'm going to get ready for bed," she says quietly.

Steven nods his head, though he is likely wondering what is necessary to get ready, since yesterday's nightgown is still peeking out from underneath her robe and the bedspread was never put on the bed.

Upstairs, Margo takes off her robe and sinks into the bed.

As she waits for Steven, she worries that despite working so long, he is still not exhausted enough to lack enthusiasm for sex. For a month now, it's been medically permissible for them to engage in sex and they have, but she finds no pleasure in it and wishes only to be left alone.

Out of guilt, though, when he does come to bed, she makes no protest and lets Steven do it, although she wonders how he finds pleasure in making love to a limp puppet.

36

One month later, Margo is still at home, still dragging herself through despondent days. At night, she awakens every two or three hours from the light nap that now passes for deep sleep. She has given up hope that the little voice will ever come again to break the deep silence that surrounds her.

Rundell called several days ago to check in on her. "Of course the most important thing is for you to get strong, but it's been a long while," he said. "Can you give me an estimate of when you'll be back? How about part-time?"

"I'll think about it," Margo said, although she could not imagine even part-time work, with her mind so dull and unfocused.

It is Saturday morning, and time for her to clean herself with water and soap. Steven is home and will expect it of her. She draws water into the tub and sprinkles in the bath flakes, although the fragrant suds no longer bring any special pleasure. It is just simpler to continue to put them in, as is her custom, than to think about making a change in her standard routine. Margo slips out of her nightgown, sinks into the hot water, reclines enough so her neck is almost submerged, and lies like that for a long time, letting the heat seep into her aching muscles and pull her into a semi-sleep that helps the minutes go by. Her mind welcomes the opportunity to be empty of thoughts.

When the water cools too much for comfort, she pulls herself up and steps out of the tub onto the bathmat, careful not to let too much water drip on the bathroom floor. Steven will be upset if he steps in a puddle. He has become more impatient and more irritable.

Margo reaches for the towel. It's the one Steven used earlier this morning, and it's still damp, but it's simply too much effort to open the cabinet and pick a fresh one. She dries her neck, blots the towel down past her breasts. That is when she sees it—a newly increased fullness in her abdomen.

She looks down at the gently rounded shape, puzzled. She stands there and inspects it, measuring it with her eyes while water continues to drip down her legs.

What is this? she wonders. I can't be getting fat, because I'm eating less and my weight is dropping.

Margo turns sideways and peers at her profile in the mirror. She sees it again: the very slight swell of her belly is definitely there.

She counts the weeks. My period should have come weeks ago, she realizes, according to the seven-week average they told me to expect.

Comprehension comes quickly and with complete certainty: it's a miracle, but she is pregnant again. Perhaps it's still too early for much of a new protuberance, but then again, she thinks, probably her trained uterus is already responding with growth. And she won't need to buy a pregnancy test kit because now that she's aware of what is going on, she definitely recognizes the signs.

Margo finishes toweling herself off. She puts on jeans and a T-shirt. She plumps up the pillows, straightens the quilt, and takes a seat on the bedroom's upholstered chair. She lets the discovery flow through her mind, and it is as if a stream of fresh water has opened in the desert.

Downstairs, the doorbell rings. It's Kate, coming for one of her regular visits. Kate has been like a visiting nurse, coming to Margo's home regularly since the birth. She has tolerated Margo's inertia and one-word answers with no signs of impatience or disapproval.

Steven lets her in, and Kate soon sweeps into the bedroom. Margo is enveloped in a warm hug.

"I made you a vat of chicken soup and matzo balls. It's guaranteed to cure whatever ails you."

Margo smiles.

"Hey, that amuses you!"

Despite Kate's efforts to entertain her and lighten her burden, this is the first time Margo has been in any way responsive.

"You're wondering why an Irish colleen like me makes matzo balls? And excellent ones, I might add? My childhood next-door neighbor, Mrs. Margolis, liked to cook and my mother didn't. So she took me under her wing, and I learned to make a complete traditional Sabbath dinner.

"I can teach you how—chicken soup, brisket, kugel, the works. Want me to? Next weekend, maybe?"

Surprisingly to them both, Margo nods and means it. It's so great, she thinks, to feel alive again.

❧

OVER THE NEXT FEW DAYS, MARGO FEELS INTERMITTENT spurts of energy, a marked change from the months of unremitting lassitude. She sends an e-mail to Sylvia: "I'm still tired, but it's time for me to try a half day at work. I'll be in tomorrow."

Once in her office, after an enthusiastic welcome from Sylvia, Margo powers up her computer and updates herself on the status of projects in her portfolio of responsibilities that her colleagues have shouldered during her absence. She works eagerly, and steadily.

By the end of the week, Margo notifies Rundell's administrative assistant that she will be starting back at work full time.

The following Monday, by midmorning, computer printouts are spread all across Margo's desk. She examines them one by one, cross-checking figures between them. If you knew where to look, in some unassuming column, you could find the clue that explained pages of discrepant results: an incorrect command entered, a single error in a decimal place, or one missing entry could sabotage an entire data analysis.

As a child, she had watched her mother mending. Her

mother's fingers had moved so nimbly, and Margo had been in awe of that skill, because she had no manual dexterity— then or now. But mending numbers: that she could do, and well.

❦

AT LUNCHTIME MARGO AND KATE WALK TO THE DINER down the street. It's still a bit cool, but daffodils are blooming, adding to the festive mood of the day. Kate has insisted on celebrating Margo's return to full-time work with something a bit more special than the tuna fish salad plate in the hospital cafeteria.

When they're seated, Kate proposes a toast, and they salute the end of Margo's convalescence with clinks of glasses of ginger ale.

"It's good to be back," Margo says. "I didn't realize how much I missed being at work."

They munch on tacos smothered in melted cheese and salsa, and Kate happily brings Margo up to date on happenings in the hospital and other news.

Margo's own news she keeps to herself. She has resolved to keep that private for a while. Except for Steven, of course; she will tell him soon. No need to visit her obstetrician yet, since she already knows to take her vitamins and get her rest, and he'll probably scold her about becoming pregnant again too soon.

The reasons for not saying anything to anyone are good ones, Margo thinks. She will be calmer and more confident if she avoids the overconcern and solicitousness she can expect from Steven, Kate, her doctor, her mother, her mother-in-law, Sylvia, everyone.

This time, it has nothing whatsoever to do with the Evil Eye.

37

---

*M*id-June, Margo visits her doctor for her first prenatal checkup. Only Steven's firm insistence has induced her to go, since she feels well enough to be sure that there's no harm in putting it off a bit longer. The first visit would remind her of the sad days, so she'd rather wait longer if possible.

But Steven would not hear of a further delay, which led Margo to wonder if she should have waited longer before telling him about the pregnancy.

At first, the doctor is all smiles, although he chides her over her tardiness in letting him know the good news and for not coming to see him earlier. He feels her enlarged belly and peers at her cervix. Then he turns solemn.

He informs her that he does not think she is pregnant. "We'll run a double set of pregnancy tests to be absolutely certain."

"No, that has to be a mistake," she insists. How else to explain the missed periods? The fullness of her breasts and the nipples sometimes wet with secretions? His diagnosis must be wrong. How else to explain the feathery flutterings in her belly? "Wait till you get the results of the tests," she says, startling him with her firm disagreement.

He calls her as soon as he has the results. "They're negative. You definitely are not pregnant."

"Sometimes lab tests aren't correct, isn't that right?" She knows that from what she's learned at the hospital, and surely he knows that, too.

"Come in this week for another visit," he says.

She is glad to comply.

Again, the doctor questions her carefully about the movements she feels. Again, she describes to him how they feel.

"Probably you are misperceiving gas bubbling through your intestines," he declares.

Margo finds his tone arrogant and insulting. How can he, who has never felt life as she previously has, proclaim that she is misperceiving these unmistakably unique feathery movements?

Margo shakes her head in disagreement. To deny the soft flutterings the baby is making would be like bearing false witness.

The doctor sets up another meeting and asks Margo to bring Steven along.

When they both are seated in his office, and with the preliminary greetings over, the doctor repeats his diagnosis. "I know how much you want to be pregnant, but this isn't it."

Once more, Margo disagrees.

Worried looks pass between the two men.

Margo keeps her equanimity. In this, she thinks, she

should have the last word over these males. She is the one with the innate feminine intuition.

The doctor sighs. "I'll schedule an ultrasound. The sound waves will show what's in your abdomen. You'll be able to see that there definitely is no baby there."

"Sure," Margo says.

The doctor seems taken aback by her easy acquiescence, as if he has been girding himself for an extended debate.

But Margo is happy to agree. She knows an ultrasound is the only way to convince him that she is pregnant.

38

_____

*I*n a waiting room at the hospital, the nurse brings Margo a third glass of water to drink. "Just this one more glass," the nurse promises. "Your bladder has to be absolutely full if we are to get a good exam."

In a few minutes, the nurse returns for her. Steven squeezes her hand as she gets up. He has taken the afternoon off from work at the doctor's recommendation. She knows Steven has felt confused because of the doctor's opinion, and she's glad this exam will finally eliminate his uncertainty. The nurse escorts Margo to an examination room and instructs her to disrobe and put on a hospital gown. She returns to help Margo climb onto the table and pulls a white sheet over Margo's protuberant abdomen.

The sonographer arrives. Margo's doctor has requested a radiologist rather than a technician to do the procedure, hoping to ensure Margo has no grounds to challenge the competence of the examiner. The doctor introduces himself and explains the procedure.

Margo knows all about it from her previous pregnancy,

of course, but graciously lets him run through his entire presentation without interruption, and nods agreeably to indicate she understands.

He applies a good amount of gel and then presses the paddle that emits the sound waves into her lower abdomen. "All right, there's the bladder, now we're in business," he says, almost to himself.

The doctor passes the paddle back and forth across her abdomen, shoving it deeply now in one spot, then in another, looking at the monitor while he slides the paddle to and fro.

When he is satisfied with his examination, he reduces the pressure of the paddle on her abdomen. "Everything looks quite normal."

He pushes the monitor to a slightly different position so that Margo can better see the screen. "Now I'm going to show you the inside of your abdomen," he says.

"See this large area here? That's the bladder. We can use it to orient ourselves. And here, up higher, is the left kidney. Here are the intestines. A lot of gas in there, more than usual."

Margo is attentive, but she is not interested in intestines and kidneys. She wants him to show her the baby.

"Now," he continues, "using the bladder as a landmark, we come to the uterus. There it is—that black area. It is a normal size for a nonpregnant uterus. There is nothing in it: no tumor, no baby, nothing. Can you see that?"

Margo doesn't answer.

"Your doctor wants to be sure you see clearly, Mrs.

Kerber. You can see that, can't you? That the uterus is small and it is empty?"

Margo is too busy searching to pay much attention to what he is saying. "There!" she says. "There's a little area that looks exactly like a little hand." If she were more experienced at this, she thinks, she could probably make out the five bony fingers as well.

"Mrs. Kerber, I need to be certain you understand me. There is no baby there. You definitely are not pregnant. There's no question about it."

Why does he have to raise his voice? It's reverberating inside her head: No baby there, no baby.

Now it is *her* voice that is loud in the room: "No baby, no baby."

She can hear it bouncing off the walls. She is wailing and creating sound waves that smash against the ceiling, the machine, the doctor. Steven bends down and embraces her as she lies on the table. She sobs horrible, groaning sobs, her chest heaving against his.

39

It takes two doses of tranquilizers simply to stop the sobbing. Margo lies on the examining table staring at the wall, refusing to talk to Steven, or the radiologist, or the psychiatric consultant whom the radiologist has summoned.

Four hours pass before Margo settles down enough for the psychiatrist to recommend that Steven take her home. "You think she's ready?" Steven asks doubtfully. "We don't know what will happen when the medicine wears off."

"I'll give you a few extra doses in case she needs them. But the best thing is for her to be in familiar surroundings. That's what will help calm her down."

"I'm not so sure about that."

The psychiatrist provides Steven with additional support and encouragement: "Here's my card. Call me at any time if you have any questions at all." Reluctantly, Steven accedes to the doctor's decision.

"We need to go home now," he says to Margo, and slips his arm under her shoulders to guide her up from the table.

She moves as his arms direct, docile and obedient.

Steven looks greatly relieved; despite the tranquilizers, he has fearfully anticipated a great deal of physical resistance.

⁓

THEY DRIVE HOME IN SILENCE. MARGO STARES OUT the windshield. Steven, too, says nothing, likely unwilling to risk provoking her with the wrong remark.

Margo allows Steven to help her up the stairs, undress her, and pull the nightgown over her head. He pleads with her to "eat a little something," but she touches nothing he brings. Neither does she pay any attention to the magazines he puts in bed next to her.

When midnight chimes on the grandfather clock in the downstairs foyer, Steven climbs into bed and lies at her side. He does not close his eyes but remains alert, because the woman beside him is the same woman who had been in such a fierce frenzy only hours before.

Neither sleeps, neither reaches out to the other for comfort.

Sometime close to 3:00 a.m., Steven is breathing deeply, fatigue finally having triumphed over fear. Margo, however, remains fully awake.

She places her hand on her nightgown and rubs her hand over her abdomen in widening, concentric circles. She can feel her abdomen shriveling from its protuberant state, the skin caving in over the emptiness of her womb, like dirt settling over a new grave. The pit of her stomach churns. Her scalp feels too tight for her skull, like a bathing cap one size too small. Her teeth clench, and the bones of her jaw grate one against the other.

Inside her head, behind the temples, a scream is being born. Whirling in ever-expanding spirals, it forces her jaws open and bursts out of the confines of her body.

"Aaaaaaaahhhh."

Steven jumps up and rushes to turn on every lamp. Light floods the room. He returns to the bed, kneels beside Margo, and smoothes her hair, caresses her neck, whispers comforting sounds.

In a while, her screams change into quieter moans. In part, that is because her vocal cords have hoarsened from the day's abuse; in part, it is because she is almost emptied of feelings.

After a few hours, daylight seeps in past the edges of the draperies. Steven quickly pulls them open, as if grateful to be out of the night at last. Even so, he keeps all the lamps on.

To Margo, the daylight makes no difference. Her womb is empty, and sunlight is neither solution nor relief. She simply lies there, staring at the ceiling.

Steven tries hard to engage her attention. He offers food again, strokes her hair, lifts her head to straighten the pillow.

Margo ignores him completely. Her eyes are closed, and with the palm of one hand she touches her belly, circling and circling over it.

"I'm going downstairs to make some tea and toast," Steven says.

He rushes down the steps and then walks quickly to the kitchen phone.

40

———

espite the hour, the consulting psychiatrist sounds alert as he responds to Steven's terse summary of what has happened. "Given the several months of grieving with these additional complicating symptoms, her continuing withdrawn behavior now is worrisome. The safest course, I think, would be to bring her into the hospital. At least for observation. And maybe treatment."

These are precisely the words Steven hoped to hear.

"Bring her to the Emergency Room. We'll have the psychiatrist on duty evaluate her. I'll call ahead to brief them on the case and let them know to expect her. They'll provide some treatment. And if she doesn't improve, they'll try to have her sign the voluntary admission form and then she'll be brought straight up to the Psychiatry Unit."

Steven thanks the doctor and then rushes up the stairs. He has read plenty of newspaper accounts of tragedies initiated by distraught human beings. The little bits of information he has gathered through the years concerning the suicide of Margo's father flash through his mind, and he takes the stairs two at a time.

Margo is lying in the exact position she was in when he left her. Softly, Steven tells her that he has been alarmed by her shrieking and her withdrawal, and that he has called the psychiatrist.

Margo's lips move. She wants to say never mind the psychiatrist, just let me shrivel up entirely, like my womb already has. But no sounds come from her mouth.

In a calm, even voice, Steven tells her that the psychiatrist suggested the best thing for her now would be a brief hospitalization, and that he will take her there.

It is almost like bringing the dead to life. The dormant Margo springs up with the energy of an unloosed jack-in-the-box.

"You bastard!" she yells. "Because I don't give you babies, you want to be rid of me entirely?"

Steven's face goes white. Quietly, firmly, he explains that he is just repeating the doctor's recommendations, that it's in her own best interest to do what the doctor advises, that it's the surest way for her to feel better.

Over and over he repeats the phrases while stroking her arm, as if to hypnotize her into acceptance.

After a time, although she appears not to hear him or feel his caresses, her body slackens and she falls back upon the bed. The expression on her face melts from anger to despondency. She seems to be contracting in upon herself.

Steven seizes the opportunity. He packs the small suitcase stored at the bottom of her closet. He puts in underwear, a few pairs of jeans, and several T-shirts. He steps into the hallway, calls Kate, and asks her to meet them at the Emergency Room; he is deploying his forces in the event there will be trouble with Margo once they arrive.

Steven returns to Margo's side, slips his arm under her shoulders, and draws her toward him and out of the bed.

She offers no resistance.

He moves her toward her closet. "Let's get you into this dress. It looks comfortable and it's easy to put on."

He steers Margo down the stairs and out the door to the car, all the while touching her arm very carefully as if it too, like her mind, might crack into tiny pieces.

41

$\mathcal{I}$n front of the nursing station of the Psychiatry Unit,
Margo stands completely still and mute, refusing to
bid Steven goodbye, refusing to beg him to take her home.

For the last ten minutes, Steven has been doing all the
talking: "That's what the doctor recommends. . . . Please
tell me you understand." Gradually, Steven has inched
closer so there is barely any separation between them, as if
he hopes the sheer physical impact of his body might coax
some words from her mouth.

But Margo's lips remain pursed shut. Only her eyes
speak to him, with a chilly accusation he likely understands
all too well. He sighs, shrugs his shoulders, and becomes
silent too.

The unit's command center behind them is the very
opposite of quiet. The clerk, a rotund middle-aged black
woman with a round shiny face, is listening good-naturedly
to a young woman earnestly informing her of a devious
CIA plot devised for this very place. In a glass-enclosed
staff room, nurses and doctors are discussing patients and
entering notes and orders into computers. Near the clerk's

desk, a small group of patient care workers—called PCWs by everyone on the unit—are having an animated conversation, gesticulating as they speak. Dressed informally in jeans and T-shirts, they could be mistaken for patients but for the identifying badges around their necks.

"Kate will stay a little longer after I leave," Steven is saying. "Right, Kate?" The desperation is clear in the expression on his face.

Kate is startled to attention when she hears her name. She has been standing at Margo's side, observing but not attempting to intervene in this sad non-conversation.

She quickly replies, "Of course I will," though it means calling her own unit and convincing the nurse whom she'd hastily begged to cover for her patients to continue doing so for a bit longer.

Steven plants a kiss on Margo's cheek and receives no response of any sort. He draws away, but continues to stand in front of her, making no move to leave.

Kate gives him a little shove to get him started. It is indeed better for him to leave as quickly as possible, since his continued presence only keeps fueling Margo's resentment and increasing his own guilt.

Steven walks down the corridor, turning to wave goodbye. The clerk at her desk pushes the button to unlock the steel door that is the only entrance and exit for the unit, and Steven is gone.

"Come on, let's explore a little," Kate says to Margo. "This place was remodeled last year, remember? Now you can check if the money was well spent. Why don't we start with the dining room first, so we can have some juice or whatever they have for snacks?"

Margo lets herself be led and lets herself be seated. She watches as Kate brings over two containers of apple juice and some straws. As soon as Kate settles herself into her chair, Margo begins to speak.

"He put me here. He made me sign the so-called voluntary admission form. He said it's for my own good, but the real reason is that he thinks I'm too much trouble for him. I could've stayed home. I made it through the days after the baby died, didn't I? But no, he's sick and tired of me. Maybe he wants to bring another woman into the house."

Kate covers Margo's clenched first with her hand. "Maybe it feels like that right now, but you know that isn't true. I'm not saying this to defend him. I'm saying it because he's only doing what the doctors recommended. He knows you need more care than he can give you."

Margo looks over at her. "Kate, you're being naïve," she says, in a loud and agitated voice.

"I know what you've lost," Kate replies gently, "and it's enough to make anyone want to tear the world apart. Steven may be the nearest target, but he's going through a hard time, too."

"Because he has to deal with his mother's disappointment that he's not going to provide her with the Kerber grandson he promised her? It's not the same for him—how can you even say that? He hasn't felt life in his body and then had it ripped away."

Kate realizes it is pointless to try and reason with Margo just now. She knows that suffering people sometimes lock themselves in irrational hopes or rages, and at times they are better not tampered with, since who knows how much despair and chaos lay behind them?

"All right, Margo, we won't talk about it anymore. I can see how it upsets you." Kate says nothing more, but watches carefully with her nurse's eyes.

At first Margo stares down at her untouched juice box. Soon, though, her shoulders droop and her face crumples like melting wax. The belligerence in her eyes dies away and is replaced by a spiritless gaze like that of a broken animal.

This seems to Kate even worse than the rage. She knows she is out of her depth, that she lacks sufficient training to know what to say. Better to leave psychotherapy to the psychotherapists, she thinks.

"You look absolutely exhausted. Probably we should let them settle you into your room so you can get some rest."

Margo makes no move to rise.

"Can somebody show Mrs. Kerber her room and get her settled in?" Kate calls to a PCW walking by outside in the corridor.

He comes into the dining room. "We can do it right now." His manner is much more professional than his appearance suggests.

"Well, then," Kate says brightly, to no one in particular. She gives Margo a hug. "I'll be back every break I get. Promise."

Margo glances at Kate for a fraction of a second, then casts her eyes down and stares at the table. Shielded again by anesthetizing apathy, Margo allows herself to be led to her quarters by the young man. Her room surprises her, for it looks nothing like the padded cell she has been imagining. It is painted a soothing cream color, and the floor and furniture are made of pale oak wood. What Margo does not notice is that the room is carefully designed to prevent anything in it from being used as ammunition should some destructive impulse suddenly overtake the room's occupant.

At the PCW's instruction, Margo begins to unpack the suitcase that someone has already placed in her room. Where should I put this? she thinks, as she picks up each item in turn.

The PCW takes over for her impaired executive function and suggests where in the cubbies of the shelves she might place each item. Although Steven hasn't packed much, it takes close to fifteen minutes for her to empty the little that is in the suitcase, so hesitant is she, so slowly does she move.

The young man reminds her to check all the zippered sections in the suitcase, and her fingers find three hundred-dollar bills; some coins; a forgotten, for-travel-use credit card; and old hotel receipts. All of these she simply stuffs into the pocket of her dress.

Once the suitcase is unloaded, the PCW picks it up in order to put it in storage: as a loose object, it is potentially dangerous. "Good job," he says. "Getting your things on the shelves helps the room look more friendly, doesn't it?"

Margo gives no answer.

"And now it's lunchtime. That's good—everyone will be in the dining room, so you can meet some of the other patients and the staff."

Margo doesn't want to go. She wants only to fade into the room, disappear into a cubby like her more fortunate underwear. But she does not have the energy to resist, so she simply lets him lead her back to the dining room.

42

---

ou can usually choose where you'd like to sit, Margo,"
says the PCW, "but today, why don't you let me find
you a place?" He leads her to a table for four, pulls out the
one empty chair, and nods reassuringly.

She sits down, and her eyes follow him enviously as he
disappears into the corridor.

The young man seated next to her turns and smiles at
her in welcome. At least Margo thinks it's a smile; she finds
it difficult to tell what his lips are actually doing, since
they're covered by a beard below and a floppy mustache
above.

"I'm Greg, one of the PCWs on the day shift. This is
Karen"—he points directly across from himself—"and
that's Peter," he says, motioning to the young man across
from Margo.

Karen looks to be in her early twenties, lost in her own
thoughts. Rapidly and rhythmically, she shakes her head
back and forth, sending her straggly, sandy-brown hair in
quick trips across her cheeks in a motion that only empha-
sizes the frightened look in her eyes.

Peter is eagerly tearing through his meal, shoveling food into his mouth without regard to appearances or manners. Between swallows, he grins at Margo, says "Welcome," then resumes his intense eating.

Margo isn't interested in eating, and the plate of macaroni and cheese Greg brought for her sits untouched.

When Peter's plate is clean, he turns his energy to conversation in a spitfire soliloquy. "Relax, Karen. There's nothing to be scared of. In the two weeks I've been here, I haven't seen a beating, a ghost, or a devil, like you're always talking about. No bullshit. Greg, isn't that right? You read the twenty-four-hour staff reports, and they never mention demons or any of those other things being here, right?"

"Yes, that's right," says Greg.

"Bet those reports tell about my nightlife, though. Yes, I'm up all night, but it's because of all the coffee I've been drinking. It's not speed, honest. They tell me it's decaf, but I figure my energy has got to be coming from the coffee. Coffee, toffee," he rhymes with a smile. Without interrupting his chatter, he turns to Margo. "The coffee's real good here. The food stinks, but the coffee's real good. Here in the 'hood, it's good."

A grating moan emerges from Karen's mouth. Her eyes are blinking fast. "If the devil kills me, he'll contaminate me, and then it's hell for sure. Burn in hell. Please, nooooo."

Greg reaches over and puts a hand on her shoulder. "Karen, there's no devil here. It's all right, it's safe here."

"No, it's not. The devil's laughing at me. He kills with his devil touch. Watch out!"

"No, Karen, there's no devil here. You're having a scary thought. An imagining. It's your voice in your head, not the devil here. I'm going to ask your doctor to prescribe some extra medicine to help you not have these scary thoughts. And we're going to stick with constant one-to-one observation with you today, so you can feel safer."

"You think you can protect me from the devil?" Karen asks, scorn in her voice, her head shaking faster, her hair whipping back and forth. "I have to kill myself before the devil can get me. Keep pure, keep clean, keep pure."

As rapidly as she'd begun her frenzied speech, Karen lapses back again into silence, although her chest still heaves with rapid and shallow breaths.

"Crazee," says Peter. "It's gals like her that give this place a bad reputation."

The desserts are brought in. Peter jumps up joyfully and returns with four portions for the entire table, the plates perched precariously between his fingers. He proffers a portion to Margo. "The cake is usually dry, but the frosting is pretty good," he says to her solemnly, like a battle-tested soldier orienting the raw recruit.

As Peter stretches his hand toward her, one of the plates slips from his fingers.

Margo watches it clatter onto the table, bounce off, and shatter on the floor. White frosting spatters across green vinyl tiles. The sound of shattering china reverberates inside Margo's skull and augments the echoes of Karen's psychotic ramblings and Peter's frenetic monologue. Margo can't contain the tide any longer. She begins to wail.

Greg is assigned to watch over Karen and can't leave her. He calls out to a PCW seated at a table nearby, "Get Margo back to her room."

Tears trickle down Margo's face as she lets herself be led through the well-illuminated corridor. The tears blur her eyes, refracting the bright light into beams that jar her retinas. Barely seeing where she's going, she shuffles her feet on the flat industrial carpeting as she moves closer to the silent emptiness of her new room.

43

---

*O*utside Margo's window, dusk is falling. There's a knock, and Margo turns to see a PCW standing in the frame of the doorway. "Time for dinner," he announces.

Is eating the main therapy they have around here? The hours in her room since lunch have helped her feel calmer, and the numbness that helps protect her from panic is back in place. She dreads venturing out again, but protest requires energy she doesn't have, and protest requires shattering the apathy that shields her. There is nothing to do but walk wherever they choose to send her.

In the dining room, Margo scans the tables so as to avoid both Karen and Peter. Over by the window, a slight, middle-aged woman is sitting alone. She seems to Margo subdued and mild, and perhaps less distressing to be near.

Margo walks over to the table, wondering what the protocol here is: Should she ask the woman for permission to join her? Can she simply claim any empty seat? She looks questioningly at the woman for some signal by which to guide herself.

"Please, sit down," the woman says, tapping the chair

beside her. "My name is Sarah. You're the new one, aren't you?"

Margo nods.

"Are you depressed?" Sarah asks nonchalantly. In this setting, this is not regarded as an intrusive question.

Margo nods again.

"Me, too. I've been here almost three weeks already. I'm better now, thank God for that. When I came here, it didn't matter to me where I was. I didn't care what they did to me, didn't care if I was alive or dead. I thought the pain would never end, that just a once-every-two-days minute of relief was all I was ever going to get.

"The thing is, I was positive my whole family was going to starve. My husband's job wasn't paying that much, but he did bring home a steady paycheck every week. Didn't matter, I was convinced we were almost in total poverty. I imagined my kids with those bony faces and big eyes like you see in those pictures of the starving children in Africa. I felt so guilty, because a good mother should be able to protect her family from that, shouldn't she? I saw it coming, and I knew there wasn't anything I could do to stop it."

The woman becomes silent for a moment and seems to be reconnecting with a private grief. Then her face softens and she becomes animated again.

"But you don't want to hear all that stuff. Listen, what I want to tell you is that the depression will get better. It really will. When you're in the middle of it, you're sure it'll never pass. You know for sure the life you had is gone forever. And you think you've uncovered a terrible flaw in yourself that can never be repaired. You're sure you can never be whole, or right, or good ever again."

Margo is staring at her. That's how I feel, she thinks. That's exactly how I feel.

"I see you know what I'm talking about," Sarah says.

Sarah looks earnestly into Margo's face. It seems important to her to be able to give comfort to another person.

"Look, when the doctors told me these feelings and thoughts would pass when I got better, I wouldn't believe it. I couldn't believe it. But it's true. Please try and remember that when it's really bad."

Maybe for you, Margo thinks. Maybe it's true for you. I'll never feel better, because I don't deserve to.

Sarah sees that Margo hasn't yet picked up her fork or started on the plate of food a PCW has unobtrusively placed before her. "Even if you're not hungry, try to eat a little anyway. Just to keep your strength up."

Margo takes a forkful of carrots. Again, it is easier to obey than to protest. The vegetables are tasteless; they seem to swell in her mouth until she feels she will choke.

The dining room is now completely full, and food is on plates everywhere. It reminds Margo of the hospital cafeteria, which in turn reminds her that she *is*, in fact, in her very own hospital. And that is a bit reassuring: it makes this place to which she had been exiled a little less foreign.

Suddenly, a chair screeches against the floor. Margo hears running feet pounding the floor tiles. She sees Karen, running fast, her one-to-one keeper yards behind. Karen runs past the doorway, and then she is gone.

A cracking noise, a scream, and sounds of chaos in the corridor.

Margo sits rooted to her chair, her mouth agape. Sarah mutters: "What now? What now?" Peter, who is sitting at a table near the door, is unable to contain himself. He dashes out into the corridor.

The PCWs in the dining room stay in their seats, knowing there will be other staff in the hall and that their own responsibilities at this moment are to comfort and support the frightened patients right here in the dining room.

The senior PCW stands up and takes charge. Despite her embroidered ethnic blouse and jeans, her manner is one of authority. "Everyone, stay calm. There is nothing to be afraid of. The nurses and PCWs outside are taking care of whatever it is. Soon they'll let us know what's going on."

Peter rushes back in, his eyes wide. "Jesus, Karen sliced her arm open, gashed it across the inside part of the elbow. She took a fluorescent tube from the bathroom ceiling, smashed it against the wall, and used the cut end to slice her arm open. She's still screaming, something about how she won't go to hell now because the devil didn't do it to her, she did. Jesus, all that blood."

A nurse comes into the dining room. Her expression is grim, but she softens it when she sees how frightened all the patients look. "Karen is all right," she says. "She cut her arm badly, but we put a tourniquet on right away, put her in a wheelchair, and took her over to the emergency room. It's being fixed now. She's all right."

THE CORRIDOR IS QUIET NOW—NO MORE SCREAMS, NO agitated whispers. Lights are dimmed all through the unit; only the nurses' station is aglow. Even though it's still early in the evening, the patients are in their rooms, huddled away and hiding. Most are trying to sleep, and most are unsuccessful.

Margo lies in bed. It seems very chilly, so cold that the air seems to quiver. She pulls the covers up close to her chin, but that doesn't help her feel much warmer.

Over by her window, bits of light from the lamps illuminating the outside of the hospital creep through the blinds sandwiched between two layers of glass. As she watches, the fragments of light seem to gather into a flickering image, a kind of hologram against the dark. At first, it looks as if a tribe of lightning bugs has gathered. But then, the fragments coalesce and transform themselves into a single image. An image of a dead bird hanging lifeless in midair.

Margo knows there is nothing really there—no lightning bugs, no bird. She knows it's all just an illusion. Still, though, she can see the vivid image of the bird stamped into the dark space of her room. And there's something familiar about it, the way its wings are spread wide and limp, the way its head hangs crookedly to one side. But what is it?

Her mind comes alive. She searches for any similarities, any likenesses, any bits of memories. And slowly they come: wisps of recollection, picture joining picture.

She had been five years old when she'd found the bird lying across the dirt path at the edge of their woods. Its skin was splayed open, and its innards hung over the poor useless body. She slid off her tricycle, walked nearer, stooped over the carcass to get a better view. Inspecting it carefully, she saw stained and matted feathers, and, beneath them, raw flesh flecked with clots of blood. A tiger could have done it, she had thought. She pictured a tiger's teeth, and then rivulets of blood. And she'd wondered: Could *I* do that? Could I pick up a rock and hit the bird until its blood squirted out and tangled up the feathers?

Although she knows it isn't real, just as the lightning bugs and the bird are not real, Margo thinks she smells a stench all around her.

Nausea sweeps over her, and Margo clutches at her heaving stomach. "Oh God, I *am* going crazy," she whispers into the darkness.

44

---

*W*oodchester Hospital's Psychiatry Unit has—as most modern psychiatric facilities do—an impressive array of sophisticated diagnostic and treatment techniques at their disposal. Medication carts carry potent tranquilizers and antidepressants formulated to repair the faulty concentrations of neurochemicals that disrupt normal thinking and feeling. In the neuromodulation section, the electroshock treatment room—for patients who meet the rigid criteria for eligibility—has full facilities for pretreatment anesthesia and muscle relaxant therapy to permit the administration of effective voltage doses to the brain while sparing the patient from awareness or muscle spasms other than a barely observable movement of the big toe. Transcranial magnetic stimulation, a simpler procedure, is also available.

The majority of patients on this acute treatment unit, however, have little contact with these advances of modern psychiatry. Their days are spent not in the electronics-filled treatment rooms, but in patient dayrooms filled with ordinary sofas and chairs. Or in occupational therapy rooms,

where watercolor paints stand ready at the easel and, yes—
in keeping with caricatures of mental hospitals—long strips
of straw can be woven into slightly wobbly baskets. And
sometimes, they spend time in the simplest of spaces: the
corridor, which can serve many purposes, social or solitary.

The following morning, Margo seeks out the corridor
as the only place to remain solitary. Back and forth she
walks, staying close to the wall. Back and forth, no destination other than the opposite end, like a swimmer doing
lap after interminable lap in a pool.

I don't recognize myself, she thinks as she walks. What's
happened to my mind? Her mind has become foreign to
her. Gone are the lively conversations she once had with
herself, replaced now by thoughts that are either slow and
ponderous or unruly and wild. And I'm getting worse here,
she thinks, because the sick people are making me sicker.

There is no place other than this corridor I can safely
go, she thinks. The patient lounge is unacceptable. Sitting
there would only make her fair game for manic patients like
Peter who chatter at anyone within reach. The medical
students doing their required month's rotation also come to
the lounge. Slightly embarrassed and slightly frightened,
they try hard to engage with the patients sitting there, and
she doesn't want to be one of their targets.

She can't seek refuge in her room because she's locked
out. The door isn't actually bolted shut, but she's expected
to stay outside. Rules of the unit: patients aren't allowed to
vegetate in their beds all day, unless the staff agrees they
need major protection from overstimulation. This was

carefully explained to Margo soon after her arrival, as it is to all newcomers. The policy is designed to support two important functions: to forestall regression into helplessness, and to facilitate participation in the Milieu.

The Milieu was explained to her in a tone that implied it deserved respect. Certainly, psychopharmacology is used and medications prescribed when indicated, and of course, group and individual psychotherapies are administered. Yet also important is the therapeutic force of the Milieu. That is, the staff believes human interactions in real day-to-day living situations are healing when structured by professionals, and patients can find there opportunities to expand their coping skills and regain self-esteem.

Whatever the Milieu means to the staff, to Margo the implication is plain: she is not allowed to escape others by retreating to her room. So where else but the corridor can she go?

As she walks, Margo regularly passes by the clerk's desk, which is not solitary at all, especially on the hour, when patients are in transit between scheduled activities. Here, there is always a changing cast of characters: now a patient with yet another sudden panic attack, worried her heart will stop dead in her chest; now a young drug abuser who leans against the desk slinging put-downs at the good-natured, unflappable clerk, who skillfully and cheerfully fends them off. The clerk is probably part of the Milieu, Margo thinks as she passes by.

At ten fifteen this morning, the corridor is relatively deserted, and Margo has the lanes to herself. Once the doctors have seen them on rounds, patients go off to occupational therapy, music or dance therapy, sports. Margo is counting on having the corridor to herself for at least half an hour more before the patients come into it again. She slips into a slow rhythm, partly because she's getting a little tired and partly because, after all, she is going nowhere.

Suddenly, a door opens. A sockless foot clad in a dirty canvas sneaker steps out, followed by another leg, a torso, and a head topped by matted strands of sandy-brown hair. Karen. Without looking left or right, Karen shuffles into the corridor and begins moving in Margo's direction, followed closely by her one-to-one attendant like some gangster trailed by a hawkeyed bodyguard.

Margo stares at Karen's right arm. It's wrapped from wrist to shoulder in layers of white gauze, like a frankfurter encased in a floury bun. The bandage is white, but Margo pictures the raw wound underneath, red drops seeping from around the sutured skin, drops that could seep through the gauze and drip onto the corridor's carpeting.

They're making me sicker, Margo agonizes. Or maybe being here is a punishment. But for what? Because the baby was born too early? Because of the mangled dead bird?

She turns and flees in the opposite direction, to get away from Karen, away from the violence, away from the red.

45

*M*edical students at teaching hospitals sometimes feel they are second in vulnerability only to the patients themselves. As students, they are deficient in the very commodities most valued at a medical center: knowledge and experience. Much like underclassmen at military academies, they are sometimes subjected to verbal put-downs from residents in the ranks above them, and since their careers are hanging in the balance, they are powerless to do much but accept any indignities that come their way.

Jim Monroe, the student currently assigned to the Psychiatry Unit at Woodchester for his one-month psychiatry clinical clerkship, is sitting in the small conference room and congratulating himself on his good fortune. He has been lucky this month: the usual random assignment method linked him to a smart and generous-spirited resident.

Jim is sitting at the rectangular oak table that, with the twelve chairs wedged around it, takes up almost all the space in the unit's conference room. Seated next to him is Dr. Claire Eaton, his resident, chatting with her colleagues about things residents care about: the next month's night call schedule, the numbers of patients per resident.

Dr. Paul Steinberg, for whom they have been waiting, enters the room. Although the residents' work is supervised daily by the attending psychiatrists of the inpatient unit, every week they have a much anticipated special conference with this respected teacher. Lean, midfifties, and sporting a vivid paisley bowtie, he walks quickly to the chair left empty for him at the head of the table. "Sorry to be delayed," he apologizes. "Why don't we get right to the case for today. Who's presenting?"

"I am," says Dr. Ron Jacobs, one of the psychiatry residents on the unit this month. Two years junior to Claire, he seems a little nervous as he flips through his pages of notes before beginning.

"Today we're presenting Margo Kerber. She's a forty-year-old Caucasian woman admitted a week ago. Much of the history was obtained from her husband. She herself doesn't say much spontaneously, but she did respond to my direct questions with brief answers, and I think her answers are reliable.

"She is the oldest of five children, raised in a small town in Ohio. The major trauma of her childhood was the death of her father when she was twelve. He committed suicide by hanging himself during a depressive episode, and she caught a glimpse of the scene. She said he'd been depressed at least twice before that, both sounding pretty serious with social withdrawal, poor appetite, and inability to work. No prior suicide attempts that she is aware of, though of course there may have been others kept secret from the children."

"Any history of manic behavior in the father?" asks Dr. Steinberg.

"She denied witnessing any episodes of euphoria, money-spending sprees, grandiose schemes, or anything like that."

Claire Eaton whispers quietly to Jim: "Recurrent depressive episodes are classified as unipolar, if all the patient's periods of abnormal mood are depressions. Bipolar—that's the same as manic-depressive—means that depressions alternate with spells of mania."

"The patient took his death very hard," continues Dr. Jacobs. "She's been told that at the funeral she tried to get into his casket, but has no memory of it. Afterward, she continued to attend school regularly and kept her grades up. She'd always been a good student, and this had meant a lot to the father.

"She went on to college, which was something unusual in her family and community. Hospital administration seemed to her a good way to combine her math skills with doing meaningful work. Most recently, she's been a successful middle-level administrator here at this hospital.

"She's been married for seven years, and her husband told me it's been a good marriage. He is nine years older than she is. When I asked her about previous relationships, she said she'd had a relationship while a teenager in high school, also with a man considerably older, and married as well. This would have been just a few years after her father died.

"The major difficulty in the marriage has been long-standing infertility, with many failed attempts to treat her ovulation problems. Then, very unexpectedly, she conceived.

The pregnancy went well and was complicated only by one early and relatively minor episode of bleeding. But then she went into labor, with the fetal age barely twenty weeks. The baby died shortly after birth.

"She then plunged into what sounds like a major depressive episode. She meets all the criteria: depressed mood, crying every day, no appetite, poor sleep with early morning wakening, complete loss of interest in sex, careless about her appearance, apathetic, unable to feel pleasure in anything. And the episode lasted for several months. An alternate diagnosis could be an intense grief reaction, but it seems much more serious than that.

"A striking thing about it"—and here Dr. Jacobs pauses for emphasis—"is that for a period of many days, she hallucinated the baby's voice talking to her. It wasn't just a thought. She actually heard the voice coming from somewhere in the room."

"That's an important distinction," Claire Eaton whispers to Jim. "Lots of people hear their thoughts spoken inside their heads. In a real hallucination, the words seem spoken from somewhere outside the person's head."

"And while she welcomed the voice, at the same time she realized it was impossible. She knew the baby was dead and buried and could not return, and it obviously hadn't learned to speak before it died."

Claire whispers to her pupil: "Also an important diagnostic point. People with psychoses, like schizophrenia for example, don't question the reality of the voices they hear around them."

"And then she saw a bit of blood in her panties, and the voice suddenly and permanently disappeared."

"Did she ever hear voices of any sort before or since?" Dr. Steinberg asks.

"No."

Dr. Jacobs continues. "Weeks later she noticed that she hadn't had a real period, her belly started enlarging, and she was sure she was pregnant again. Her mood improved, she told her husband the good news, and she went back to work. But she delayed going to the doctor, and her husband said she finally went only because he insisted.

"The obstetrician found that her belly was enlarged and she had some secretions from her breasts. But the pelvic exam revealed a nonpregnant uterus."

Here, Dr. Jacobs pauses for emphasis, the faces of his audience members already registering surprise.

"She refused to believe the obstetrician's diagnosis. He had to schedule an ultrasound to show and convince her that the uterus was empty. After that, she started sobbing and writhing on the table. There was no way she could deny the evidence of the ultrasound, and she lost control."

"No, that's not quite accurate," says Dr. Steinberg. "She *could* have denied it. Her acceptance and distress indicates that her reality testing was intact enough to keep her from that degree of denial."

"Okay," says Dr. Jacobs.

Claire Eaton whispers to Jim again. "Another important diagnostic point. One of the distinguishing features of psychosis is that the person insists on denying reality."

Dr. Jacobs continues. "Once home, she again became agitated and then withdrawn. Her husband called the psychiatric consultant who had seen her right after the sonography, and he recommended bringing her to the emergency room. She did not resist, but she is bitter about being admitted and doesn't really want to be here.

"So, in summary, we think she has a major depressive disorder. She's had episodes of agitation by history, and she has displayed some psychomotor excitation here manifested by pacing, so we are leaning toward a diagnosis that is consonant with an agitated depression subtype."

Dr. Jacobs has reached the last page of his notes. "That's it," he says, and settles back in his chair.

His eyes—and all eyes—turn to Dr. Steinberg, who seems to gather his thoughts in a moment of silence.

"Now he'll put it all together," Claire whispers to Jim, pride for her mentor in her voice.

"Good presentation, Ron," Dr. Steinberg says. "You set out clearly the relevant data we need to know."

Ron Jacobs smiles, clearly both relieved and pleased.

"Patients with false pregnancy—pseudocyesis is its formal name—have been described throughout the centuries. Hippocrates described several cases as far back as 400 BC. The most famous case was probably Mary Tudor, Queen of England, who twice had false pregnancies lasting nine months each. Some common threads have been identified, but let's not fit the patient to the pattern. Let's stick to the clinical data we have here.

"Biology first. There's the family history suggesting an

underlying genetic predisposition for major depressive disorder. She's also postpartum, and postpartum depression is relatively common. I don't mean the "baby blues," the short-lived episode of crying and sudden mood shifts that comes on two or three days after delivery in fifty percent of women. That can be considered a normal response to the sudden changes in hormone levels. What I mean is a persistent depression starting within months after delivery.

"The breast secretions and abdominal distension are interesting. The literature does report endocrine changes in pseudocyesis, and the abdominal distension is caused by retention of large amounts of intestinal gas, which is expelled quickly once the patient accepts she is not pregnant.

"Now the psychological level. She suffered a grievous loss. How does this event intersect with prior life events, her personality, and her conflicts?"

It's a rhetorical question. The psychiatric residents know this is his typical teaching style, and so they say nothing. The medical students also stay silent because they feel too ignorant to even consider responding.

"Separation and the loss of loved ones have clearly been very difficult for her in the past. Because of the history of her behavior of trying to get into her father's coffin, we already know she has a low tolerance for loss, as well as some impulsivity.

"The late miscarriage was even more than the tragic loss of an infant. She lost not just a child but also the opportunities a child always presents, such as a chance to nurture another, a kind of immortality, and a source of unconditional love. Given her history of parental suicide, the baby could also have represented someone who would not abandon her, who would love her reliably. Also, in her case, the additional inability to carry a child to term after such a long period of infertility was also a severe blow to her self-esteem as a woman.

"So how does she deal with this severe stressor, the loss of her baby? From her repertoire of psychological defenses, which does she call into play?

"Some rather primitive ones: hallucinating the baby's voice and then a fantasied pregnancy. Recall again the impulsive rush into her father's casket, the wish to be reunited with him and the acting out of that wish in behavior. See the pattern? Hallucinating the voice of the baby reunites her with it, and the false pregnancy brings her in physical proximity with it.

"Here's a good opportunity for us to give some thought to the psychoanalytic perspective. We don't often do that much around here, and whether or not you buy into these ideas, it's worth a look.

"For example, her childlessness could be experienced as an oedipal defeat in competition with her mother and other women, who succeed in getting babies from men while she does not. The loss of the baby could be seen as another humiliating confirmation—at the phallic level—that her re-productive organs are deficient. With the fantasies, she tried to fend off unendurable oral-level feelings of deprivation and rage that threatened to overwhelm her."

Jim has a puzzled look, as if he finds this manner of

thinking quite foreign. Claire notices, and whispers: "There's a certain logic to it, don't you think?"

"Now, let's look at the patient's strengths," says Dr. Steinberg. "We need to assess the inner resources she possesses and how to help her access them.

"We know she has intelligence and self-discipline and used them to study and achieve professional training. She has a responsible job and has functioned effectively in it. She is able to make and keep close friends, and has a stable long-term relationship with her husband. These strengths make one optimistic about her treatability and long-term prognosis.

"So," Dr. Steinberg says, "let's move on to treatment. What are the immediate and short-term risks? What goals do you have for the acute treatment while she's in the hospital? Dr. Jacobs?"

Dr. Jacobs draws himself up. "She is very depressed, but we don't think she is acutely suicidal right now. However, given the family history of suicide and her reliance on fantasies which may get crushed, there is still some suicide risk until she recovers from the depression."

"Right," Dr. Steinberg says.

"We've put her on an antidepressant. We've also added an antipsychotic for now, because of the pacing and the outside chance the false pregnancy indicates a depression with psychotic features. As for psychotherapy, I'm not sure."

"A supportive treatment is best right now," says Dr. Steinberg. "You want to communicate you understand how depressed she is. You want to communicate hope that the medication will help, and with treatment she *will* emerge from what she now feels as an endless pain she'll be in permanently. And you want to help her try and access her strengths. The more intensive psychotherapy is for outpatient work later. Agree?"

Dr. Jacobs nods his head.

In the few minutes that remain, the residents review the progress of patients they've discussed together in previous conferences, enjoying a lively discussion comparing Dr. Steinberg's clinical predictions with the actual clinical course that followed.

Dr. Steinberg then leaves the room and the unit, while the residents and students head back to work.

Jim Monroe exits the conference room and walks down the corridor toward the nursing station. He is passed by a few patients making their way to their next scheduled activity. Halfway down the corridor, he nears Margo Kerber, clad in the same gray dress she wears most every day, and trudging along her usual back-and-forth route.

Jim smiles at her warmly. In the span of an hour, she has become someone he knows much better, and someone he has begun to care about.

But she does not return his smile. Instead, she turns her head to the wall and slips quickly away from him.

46

$\mathcal{E}$ight days later, Margo receives a "promotion." Her official status designation on the unit has been upgraded to Level 2. This means she is now able to leave for brief trips into the hospital to places such as the Gift Shop, although only in the presence of a reliable supervisor. To the unit staff, Steven counts as such a one. They know him well: he has been making daily visits to Margo and has been a willing provider of information for just about anything they ask him about her or about himself.

Margo has not always been as pleased as the staff with Steven's visits. The first few days she mainly stared at the floor when he sat with her, filled with hopelessness and certainty that he cared nothing for her or for anything she might say, and had just come out of guilt or simple curiosity. When he kept coming despite her silences, though, she loosened her self-protective barrier and allowed herself to notice something entirely unexpected about him: his concern. He *does* care about me, she thought with surprise. She began to speak to him about her days, her endlessly long and unfulfilling days. "I want to go home," she told him every time he visited. "I want to lie in my own bed in my own room and get rest. That's what I really need, a good rest, and I can't get it here." He listened, but his response was always the same: "I understand, but being here is what will help you get better." She didn't have the energy to protest or argue with him about it.

Today, Steven has decided to take her to the hospital cafeteria. He asks if she would like that, and she easily acquiesces. Without telling her the reason, he timed their outing so they would be there in the late afternoon, when her administrative colleagues would be wrapping up their day's work, eager to get home and unlikely to appear in the cafeteria for a break. While Margo is not thinking into the future, Steven is, and wants to reduce any embarrassment or hesitation on her part once she improves and can return to work.

Margo sits across from him at the small table, wearing her gray dress. She looks around the familiar room. Most of the people here look to be visitors, as they wear no employee identification cards. Some are chatting easily with table partners, but many sit quietly with serious looks on their faces. They have reason to look serious, Margo thinks. At this time of day, they'd either be awaiting their last consultation or test of the day, or a meeting about results that might indicate much difficulty lies ahead. Here are patients and families with concern and grief etched on their faces. Perhaps they are here to settle themselves before attempting a heavyhearted drive home.

They are troubled, like she is. Yet here they are sitting

with quiet dignity, dealing with their problems without allowing bitterness and anguish to disintegrate into violence and agitation. That's more what I need, Margo thinks. What I don't need is the chaos and agitation upstairs, being surrounded by people even less put together than me. But is there any use trying to convince Steven of that?

The only thing she can do is to leave on her own. Trying to undo the voluntary admission she had signed would take days, as they explained when she was first admitted, and she knows it would entail many difficulties. If she simply left, Margo thinks, as she picks at a raisin stuck tightly to the muffin cake surrounding it, if she left for some safe place where she could get away from all of this, from the gloom of the hospital to the healing blue sky and sun, to the fragrant summer breeze.

She could manage it; as always, she had in her dress pocket the money and credit card from her suitcase, since with the door of her room unlocked and wide open, who knew what patient might go in and rifle through her things?

Steven's people-watching is limited to his own table. He watches Margo as she picks at the raisins in her muffin, watches her fork scratch at the little cake and clean carefully around each raisin until it tumbles out. She eats neither the raisins nor the muffin left behind. She has already lost two more pounds since she entered the hospital, he's been told.

Margo frees a raisin from the muffin surrounding it. She watches it plop to the plate and decides to do it: to run fast, to run free.

"Steven," she says, "I don't like the raisin taste of the muffin. Could you please buy me a plain bran one, or some other kind?"

"Sure. That's the way—figure out what you most want to eat."

"Thanks," she says, smiling faintly.

He gets up and walks toward the cafeteria counter and cashier. Partway there, he glances backward over his shoulder, as if he isn't sure he is doing the right thing in leaving her at the table unattended.

Margo sees him pass the water fountain and then move out of sight. Which means she is out of sight to him.

Now!

Margo jumps up with more energy than she realized she possessed. She quickly strides to the cafeteria exit, jogs down the long corridor to the doors of the main hospital entrance, and pushes through them into bright daylight.

47

---

*W*arm fresh air caresses her face, and she runs into it. She runs faster and faster, away from the hospital, a whole block away now, not yet safe but free, untethered from people's stares, from the condescending smiles, from the pity.

She's a whole block away, now two, three, a turn to the right.

At the far end of the next block, there's a bus stop. Here she has to stop and wait while her heart continues to race, pounding an incantation: come on bus, hurry, please, come faster than they come for me.

It's getting close to the afternoon rush hour, when the bus runs are accelerated, and the bus arrives quite soon. Margo bounces up the steps, crams the coins from the pocket of her dress into the fare box, and rushes past the driver for fear he'll ask her for exact change.

She takes an empty seat toward the back, across from a young man bent over his reading who pays her no heed. The bus lurches forward. To stabilize herself, Margo clutches the seat in front of her. Although the bus soon settles into a smooth riding rhythm, her hands don't relax their grip.

Fortunately, few passengers on the bus need to get off, and fewer still wait on the streets for a ride, so the bus lopes along in long stretches of uninterrupted traveling. Soon, they are a good distance from the hospital, and Margo sees no cop car in pursuit. The tension in the tiny muscles encircling her eyes eases, and she begins to gaze with interest rather than vigilance out the bus window.

They have already gone well toward the center of Woodchester. The shops they pass are quite familiar to her. There's the one that sells sports clothes, and across the street the jewelry boutique that displays its wares on little sculptures. What delightful afternoons she had spent browsing among the clothes and baubles, fingering soft woven wool shawls and metals fashioned into marvelously shaped necklaces. The lighthearted shopping trips had been the closest thing to play in her adult life, except for sex.

No. Just don't think about all that, she tells herself. Forget that, those days are gone forever.

The bus moves on, and through its windows, Margo spies a few more familiar shops, but now she regards them simply as archeological artifacts from an era long since vanished.

After a while, the bus turns into unfamiliar streets in a neighborhood she doesn't recognize. Margo thinks that "lower middle class" would be the label assigned to it by sociologists, or whoever's job it is to know these things. The brick buildings here are so dusty with soot that the original colors have gone gray, and the concrete pavement is cracked and chipped. Spots of color are provided by plastic flowers in plastic pots that decorate storefront windows, flowers so similarly artificial that they look as if they'd all been purchased at some neighborhood store's liquidation sale.

Immediately past a movie house marquee, a neon sign flickers "Hotel" over a building with clean windows and a slightly shabby awning out front. Here, Margo decides, and pulls the cord to let the driver know.

The driver stops the bus, but only after he has driven four additional blocks to the next designated stop. Margo doesn't mind; the walk back to the hotel will be an opportunity to familiarize herself with her new neighborhood.

First, she comes upon a Chinese laundry, where she stops to watch a woman working a sewing machine, stitching seams on some dark but unidentifiable garment. A few more steps, and she's in front of an outpatient medical clinic. It's small and quiet, without any bustle of activity. Of one thing she is certain: she has no use for doctors, nurses, or medical facilities now.

A drugstore is next, not surprisingly; hospitals and clinics always seem to be surrounded by the accessories of illness. Yet Margo is pleased to see hairbrushes, combs, and umbrellas displayed in the window, a refrigerator case visible inside with milk, cheese, and beer. A place for medications, she thinks, but also the basic essentials of normal life. It's a good sign, and she feels the first awakening of a hopefulness she hasn't felt in a very long time.

A few more blocks, and she has arrived at the hotel.

48

*M*argo enters a dark lobby that is neat and simple, with vinyl sofas on a worn carpet that looks like it had once been fine.

She approaches the front desk and speaks to the wiry, oldish man that sits there. "I'd like a quiet room please," she says. "I'm not sure how long I'll be staying." The clerk seems surprised—most of his customers probably don't make room requests—and, in turn, he requests a night's deposit.

She reaches into her pocket, pulls out money, and proffers her credit card, which he inspects carefully and accepts.

The clerk, who doubles as the bellman, offers to show her to her room. He looks about to take her bag, but seems not terribly surprised to find she has none. Many of this hotel's clientele likely travel light.

Out of the elevator: floor number two. She follows him down a corridor whose ceiling is punctuated by low-wattage fixtures that shed little light. In front of the door next to the last, he hands her a room key and leaves without a word.

She opens the door and enters a room that neither

welcomes nor repels. The carpet is a faded floral, with pinkish blossoms still visible on the beige background. The double bed is covered by a nondescript beige bedspread. It seems clean, and the bed is surprisingly firm. Near the bed stands a dresser of knotty pine, and near the bathroom a small refrigerator—unexpected luxury—whines steadily. By the window, which is draped with a striped cotton fabric whose colors match nothing in the room, stands a pine kneehole desk with a Bible on top. Plastic flowers sprout stiffly in a plastic pot on the sill.

Margo walks slowly around the room and touches each object in turn: bed, dresser, desk, sagging pink velvet armchair. These things belong to her now, at least for a time. It feels good to have belongings after being in the hospital. "This is your room," they had said on the unit. But it really was their room, and they had placed her in it and tended her as if she were a rare plant of theirs.

She walks for a second time around the room, feeling the furniture against her fingertips; she is their owner now, and they are her possessions. She uproots the flowerpot from its place on the windowsill and places it on the desktop, a small demonstration of her ownership.

She's feeling better, and she has more energy. She is more in command of herself now, no longer like the leaf blown here and there at the whim of the wind. Perhaps the medications they gave her have helped after all.

Humans aren't meant to be that vulnerable, she thinks. Isn't that what the Bible says? Hadn't Mrs. Byne taught in Sunday school that God's gift to Adam and all his descendants was dominion over the earth and everything on it? It's a sacred trust and a duty, she'd said. Of course, almost everything Mrs. Byne had ever mentioned was a duty.

Margo picks up the Bible and begins to search through its crisp, relatively untouched pages for the phrase. She starts with the first sentence of Genesis: "In the beginning . . ." A bit farther on, she finds it. "Let man have dominion over the flesh, the fowl, the cattle, over all the earth, over every creeping thing."

Captivated by the phrases, she reads further, on to Eve and the subtle serpent. Margo has not read these Bible stories since she sat in Sunday school, scared of old Mrs. Byne, who warned of unimaginable punishments for sinners like inattentive pupils. Her chilly voice spoke of sin and damnation as though she herself would personally see to it that each child got every shovelful of pitch and brimstone that was coming to him or her. Mrs. Byne had seized on the snake as a symbol of the temptations that lurked everywhere. The rest of Eden Mrs. Byne glossed over. Margo, though, had been fascinated by those very sections. She imagined a grown man and woman running naked, and in broad daylight. She imagined them laughing together as they chased through lacy ferns or splashed among colored fish in clear pools. She pictured breasts bobbing, penis swinging, and it got very exciting. It wasn't possible that Mrs. Byne could read her thoughts, was it?

Margo reads further now, of Father Abraham, and God's grace and comfort that came to shine on Sarah and brought the miraculous gift of a child to an old woman hopeless in her infertility. Mrs. Byne had skipped over that part too, not one to linger any longer than absolutely necessary over the mysteries of reproduction.

Dusk falls, and Margo keeps on reading. The stories are familiar, yet suddenly they sparkle with new meaning.

After a time she stops and leaves the room to buy something for dinner at the drugstore: a chocolate bar, a yogurt, a loaf of bread.

Night comes. She reads until the saga of Genesis ends with Joseph comforting his remorseful brothers, telling them that through their evil deed against him, God's hand had worked to save tens of thousands from starvation; it was a transmutation of Evil into Good.

Only when Genesis ends and she closes the book does Margo notice the deep weariness in her body. She pulls open the bedspread, takes off her clothes, heaps them into a pile on the pink armchair, and slips between the worn-soft sheets. The sturdy mattress presses up against her back and supports her. With the sheets tucked tightly around her, like swaddling blankets, she feels secure.

Thoughts begin to tumble lightly through her mind. Adam and Eve. First humankind pair, at least in Western stories. Eastern cultures have their own pairs, she knows. She's seen statues of Krishna and Devi in the museums, the graceful, multi-limbed arms and fingers undulating in the air.

Mothers and infants are pairs, too. Sarah and Isaac, who was wrenched from his mother's care in order to be almost slain on a sacrificial stone. The baby Moses, his mother trying to save him from death by fashioning a basket so he could float in marshy waters. Mary and the baby Jesus, unaware of what was in store for them both.

Margo's mind conjures up images of children prematurely torn away by death from grieving mothers. She sees them float up in their gossamer shrouds, through the serene streets of heaven. She sees them sitting in God's lap as He wipes away their tears and tells them that quite soon their mothers will also come and nestle them close again, and they'll feel kisses on their cheeks, kisses soft as clouds.

God is gracious. Doesn't the Bible say so? God had sent a powerful princess to discover the baby Moses and let the mother become the wet nurse, so that the babe was soon suckling from familiar breasts brimming with warm milk. God turned Evil into Good. Even old Mrs. Byne, with all her tales of retribution and wrath, had said so.

God is gracious. Margo repeats the phrase in her mind like a mantra, until her thoughts turn into filmy fragments that drift into nothingness, and she falls asleep.

49

Morning sunlight shines through the thinly textured drapes hung at the window, awakening Margo to walls striped with color. For several minutes she lies watching the patterns surrounding her; it seems as if she's inside a kaleidoscope.

The growling of her stomach surprises her. How long has it been since she's felt the slightest indication that her physical appetites still exist?

She showers in the tiny bathroom, glad to wash away the remnants of confinement and the grubby sweat of her escape. Margo puts her same underwear on again, followed by the gray dress. The cash in her pocket will subsidize a healthy breakfast.

In the dim hallway, she hears no sound or movement anywhere. Am I the only person on this floor? she wonders. Once this would have frightened her, to have no one within earshot in unfamiliar surroundings. Now, unpopulated rooms are a gift and the empty corridor a welcome breathing space, even though its air is stale and smells of mold.

Out on the street the bright sunshine warms Margo's skin, and she tilts up her face for a moment to receive more rays of light. She looks around, but there's no restaurant, cafeteria, or fast food enterprise in sight. So she picks a direction without agonizing over the choice, and sets out to seek her breakfast.

Down the sidewalk she walks, peering into pawnshop windows crammed with watches, guns, faded beribboned medals, and tarnished candlesticks: sad signs of past glory and affluence, now abandoned and forgotten. Farther down the street, she sees a small baseball diamond with dirt paths rubbed smooth by thousands of runners' feet. A few more blocks, and she comes upon what seems to be a main shopping area of the neighborhood.

There is a supermarket here, and she goes in to check out the wares. A produce section on her right, the fruits and vegetables not particularly fresh-looking but not browned or blighted, either. Next is meat, and then a fresh fish section, with fish heads piled on one side. "Good for soup," says the sign near them, an economical choice for those with limited means who likely live somewhere nearby.

Margo stops and stares, fascinated by the fish heads staring back. So many eyes stare unseeingly from the pile; no matter where she places herself, some dull eye is fixed in her direction. What have those eyes seen deep in the ocean, she wonders. Suppose all the images could be played back, like a movie. Would the screen show soft-colored coral and green seaweed that gently sways in the water's currents? Or frantic schools of fish swooping here and there to avoid nets and predators nearby? No, Margo whispers to herself. No more sharks, birds, and blood. I'm better now.

She walks quickly out of the supermarket and back onto the sidewalk.

Next, a clothing shop: "Sale, Sale, Sale," and finally, a diner.

Except for an old man dressed in baggy pants frayed at the cuffs who sits at the counter nursing a cup of coffee, she has the place to herself. She chooses a seat at one of the booths. The waitress—a heavyset young woman with a coffee stain on her dress—comes over with a menu. Surprisingly, much of it seems appealing. I have an appetite, Margo thinks with pleased surprise. She orders herself the Super Special: a short stack of blueberry pancakes, scrambled eggs, bacon, and cinnamon coffee cake.

When the waitress returns and places the plates before her, Margo finds the sizable amount of food less appealing. Still, she has some appetite: she eats a few forkfuls of the eggs, a slice of bacon, half a pancake, and a sliver of cake.

Back on the street, she walks yet farther, and watches the shopkeepers preparing for the business day. They roll up black protective grilles from storefronts, spray glass windows with blue cleaning fluid, and all the while call out morning greetings to each other. Probably they're relieved not to have found evidence of nighttime theft or destruction, Margo thinks.

It's early in the morning still, and there aren't yet any shoppers to be seen. Likely the homemakers who are the stores' clientele aren't yet out, are still enjoying a cup of coffee in peace, Margo thinks, after husbands and children have been launched to work and school. How lucky those women are. How lucky, even though they probably don't give what they have a second thought.

She keeps walking and eventually finds herself in a better neighborhood—large stores instead of small ones, a midsize shopping center, with parking lots for the more affluent living a few miles away from the Walmart and Kmart. On the next block there's a Target, one of her favorite chains for both browsing and buying.

I'll go in there, Margo thinks. It will be familiar; it might even be fun. I am the provider of my own therapy now, she decides with some satisfaction.

50

Now, Steven is the one racked with anxiety. He seeks out medical help quickly, not able to function anywhere near his necessary level at work. His primary care physician prescribes some clonazepam "just for the short term, or it will be hard to get off it." Although Steven has always prided himself on being someone with no need for the "crutch" of pills, he rushes right out to the pharmacy once the doctor gives him the prescription and swallows down the allowable dose of tranquilizer as soon as he gets home.

The pills do help, but jarring thoughts still fill his mind. He calls for more assistance: "Kate, can you please come over tonight? Just you?"

Kate comes, bringing a box of chocolate chip cookies from her pantry. She prepares tea from Margo's stash in the kitchen cabinet, and they sit down at the table.

"They gave me the responsibility of watching her, and I failed. Now Margo's wandering the streets like a homeless person." The volume of his voice and the anxiety in it escalate. "Where *is* she? What's happened to her? What *could* happen to her?"

Kate takes Steven's hands in hers. "The police are looking everywhere. Try and concentrate on the fact that Margo was thinking clearly enough to figure out a plan to get away. It was a good plan, a plan that worked, so she's not without the resourcefulness to take care of herself, wherever she went."

"How could I have been so stupid?" he groans. "How could I have left her sitting alone like that?"

"Think of it this way: Margo set you up. She knew your concern about her not eating would be the one way to get herself out of your sight. Stop beating yourself up with guilt, Steven. You don't deserve it."

51

Walking through the aisles of Target, Margo is indeed finding comfort in the familiar brands and displays. She feels altogether more secure, and even a bit confident. Isn't this proof, she thinks, that I made a very good decision to put my treatment into my own hands?

Margo stops and inspects the items in one of her favorite sections in a Target store: the picture frames aisle. The frames sit on the shelves in all their variety, from austere, simple silver to decoratively painted ceramic. She turns to pick up one with an interesting, copper-colored braid pattern, and from the corner of her eye, Margo notices a charming baby carriage across the center aisle. It is a warm tomato-red color, with wheels of an unusually ornate and large circumference.

I'd like to look inside, she thinks. I'm ready to have a look at a sweet baby.

EARLIER THAT MORNING, RENEE LAMARATO HAD BEEN
tending to her firstborn child, rocking, cooing, and planting
many kisses on top of his sweet-smelling little head. She
and her husband, Tony, live in a starter home not far from
the older center of Woodchester, a nondescript Cape Cod
that is still sparely landscaped; this way, they had obtained
three bedrooms for the same price that two bedrooms closer
to the newer parts of town commanded. During her pregnancy, they had made do with the few pieces of furniture
they'd had from their former apartment, so as to spend
what remained of their post-down-payment savings on
furnishings for the nursery.

Renee and the baby had been sitting in a comfortable
nursing chair, near the crib with its white canopy and blue-
and-white gingham-checked quilt. On the walls are colorful
pictures of nursery rhyme characters, all smiles and good
cheer. Tomorrow, however, Renee's in-laws would be
arriving for a visit, and as she sat she considered again that
the room set aside for guests wasn't yet ready to receive
them. Its walls were already painted a creamy butter yellow,
and pale yellow sheets and blankets were stretched over the
twin beds, but it still lacked the bedspreads and throw
pillows she needed to complete a welcoming décor.

So, taking advantage of a lull in the baby's feeding
demands, she'd settled him into his car seat, folded up the
beautiful, extravagantly expensive carriage bought by her
ecstatic parents, and set off for Target.

Once there, Renee immediately seeks out the pillow
section. She peeks into the carriage once more to assure

herself that Timothy is still fast asleep. Yes, it seems from his blissfully sleeping face that his tummy is still full of the milk she gave him shortly before she left, so she sets the brake and turns her attention to the merchandise on the shelves.

The selection of throw pillows and shams is good. Here is one with creamy yellow flowers on an ivory background, and here another lovely one: silky with subtle stripes, in yellow and gold. With one pillow in each arm, she goes around the end of the pillow aisle to the bedspread aisle, and begins to scan the selection to find the spread that would be loveliest in combination with one of the pillows she is carrying. This poses a difficult choice, she soon discovers—the stock of suitable bedspreads is as robust as that of the pillows.

AT THE SAME TIME THAT RENEE IS SCRUTINIZING THE spreads, Margo crosses over from the picture frame aisle and approaches the colorful carriage.

She peeks inside.

This baby is so very tiny, she thinks. She looks at the little hands, smooth and round, the fingers delicately curved. She slips her index finger into the palm, and the baby's fingers fasten tightly around it, so tightly that she can scarcely draw her finger away.

Margo looks at the long fringes of eyelashes, and the tiny, rose-colored mouth. Something seems so very familiar about this baby; yet, at the same time, it is clearly not any child she has ever actually seen before.

The baby has begun to squirm under the cotton blanket and its head moves from side to side. Perhaps gas bubbles are disturbing its rest.

Margo bends down, reaches into the carriage, and lifts the child out to cuddle and soothe it in her arms. The infant immediately becomes quiet and still, and as its warm, delicate solidity presses against her dress, the baby seems to be attaching itself to her body.

As if it belongs there.

So she makes yet another decision. It is sudden, more an impulse than a decision, but she feels quite sure; she feels quite confident.

She reaches into the carriage and takes out the blanket to wrap the child and shield it from the dirt in the streets they will have to traverse to reach the hotel. Then, awkwardly with her one free hand, she slips the diaper bag off the carriage handles, for she will need the supplies stocked inside until she can make a purchase of her own.

Holding the child firmly in her arms, Margo is soon out the door.

52
---

*R*enee has found a bedspread that is the perfect color: dark creamy yellow saturated with a tinge of orange. She places each pillow in turn on the spread, stepping back as far as she can in the narrow aisle for a better view. After some consideration, she chooses the silky striped one, the one that brings out the apricot overtones of the spread.

She plucks the matching spread from the shelf, and now holds a tower of spreads and pillows that come up to her chin. Carefully, so as not to spill the stack, she rounds the far end of the bedspread aisle, turns once again into the pillow aisle, and exchanges the rejected pillow for a second one of the chosen pattern.

Approaching the carriage now from the hooded side, she stuffs one bedspread and two pillows onto the rack under the body of the baby carriage, and settles the other bedspread under one arm. Then she looks into the carriage to make sure the blanket is still in place around the sleeping baby.

But the blanket isn't here.

And neither is Timothy. Neither is Timothy!

Renee flies into the next aisle and then the next. She flies through each of the many aisles, flies around the perimeter of the store. She runs outside, up and down the sidewalk—he is not there, either.

Renee rushes back into Target, grabs the nearest customer service representative, and, gasping for air, says impossible words: "My baby's gone, he's gone! He was in the pillow aisle, and now he's gone."

Her face turns white, and she buckles to the floor.

53

Swiftly, Margo walks toward the hotel. Carefully avoiding cracks in the crumbling sidewalks, empty water bottles, and other litter, her good sense of direction guides her through the streets.

She wants to get the baby to the clean and quiet of the hotel room as soon as possible. But first, she picks up a package of disposable diapers, some milk, and a jar of peanut butter to sustain herself so she can be completely at the baby's beck and call, with no need to go out for meals.

As she walks, Margo hears faint rumblings of protest in her mind. Take another woman's child? A child she made and bore in pain? But other thoughts joust like knights against the protest. The woman left the child alone. I'll never do that. I can assist this child, nurture it, protect it better than its mother can.

Cuddling the baby even closer to her body, she walks quickly to the end of the block, turns the corner, and vanishes into the warren of side streets. Almost there, Margo hears a siren wail. It is not far away, but not near, either. Perhaps it's firemen come to put out a blaze, she thinks, or an ambulance rushing to help an old man who has fainted on the street. I can't think about it, she tells herself. I have responsibilities now. Let someone else tend the other needy of the world.

54

The big pink armchair is comfortable, and Margo lets herself be enveloped by it. The baby lies in her arms fast asleep in that deeply unconscious way of young infants. Sitting so, with the baby snuggled close against her, Margo feels, at last, at peace.

In a while, the baby begins to stir and whimper. Margo is instantly alert to its tiny movements, and begins to rock herself with a firm, steady beat. The child sighs, relaxes its grimacing face, and settles back again into heavy, motionless slumber.

Even after the baby becomes quiet, Margo continues her rocking to and fro. There is something intoxicating about her ability to bring comfort to the child. It is so very long that she has been waiting for something so affirming.

She looks more closely at this tiny person, so small yet with such power to send her spirits soaring. The head is so tiny she can cradle it in the palm of her hand; the little nails on each finger are hardly bigger than a grain of rice. She still has no idea of the child's sex, since the clothing gives no clue: the child is dressed in a pale yellow stretch suit and white sweater. When it wakes, when she undresses it and changes its diaper, then she'll know that secret.

Her rocking slows and her thoughts turn to the practical details of care. First, she will need a bed for the child. She can make a respectable one from one of the dresser drawers, she thinks. She will take it out, scour it thoroughly, pad it well with fresh towels, and line it with a clean pillowcase from her bed. Since the baby is such a tiny thing, he or she (oh, who exactly are you, love?) will have plenty of room to stretch out in the sturdy wooden box.

Second, feeding. Just milk for now, she thinks. Nature's perfect food. She would begin to nurse the baby as soon as it woke. Long ago, long before the infertility cast its pall on her plans for childrearing, long before her first pregnancy, she had resolved to nurse her infants at the breast. She had never understood why some women chose to use artificial milk in bottles topped with stiff, plastic nipples; it seemed so impersonal and mechanical, more like fueling up a car than feeding a baby.

It is entirely possible for her to breastfeed this child, she is sure. When she was pregnant, she'd read a section entitled "How I Nursed My Adopted Child" in one of her child-care books. The doctor who was the author of the book explained that although breast milk was usually initiated by the hormone changes of pregnancy and delivery, lactation could be initiated in other ways as well. One effective way was by the stimulus of an infant sucking steadily at the breasts. The book quoted the anthropologist Margaret Mead, who reported that in some societies nonparturient women—women who had not recently borne a child—commonly served as wet nurses.

Now Margo sits and rocks, the to-and-fro motion lulling and hypnotic, like watching surf spreading and receding on a sandy ocean shore. She thinks how miraculous it is: how milk comes almost magically, like manna from heaven, brought forth not from the skies but from one human body responding to the desperate need of another.

The baby stirs. Eyelids flutter open and Margo sees blue eyes, unfocused at first. The eyelashes match the golden fringe of hair wrapping around the back of the baby's head —like a monk's, she thinks. She smiles, amused that this tiny mewling creature might have something in common with such a spiritual and serious person.

Margo moves quickly into action. She places the baby on the clean towel she has put on the bedspread, then searches inside the well-stocked baby bag and pulls out a disposable diaper. Gently, she unsnaps the little suit and, with a growing sense of excitement, pulls off a sopping wet diaper.

"It's a boy," she whispers.

She stares down at the tiny genitals. They remind her of a flower, an iris perhaps, so delicately shaped and still partly unfurled. She covers him quickly with the diaper; she knows from caring for several younger brothers that if she isn't fast enough she could get sprayed with a squirt of urine.

Lucky little guy, Margo thinks, he will never know the humiliation of squatting outdoors and feeling urine trickle down his leg to soak his socks and shoes. She finishes attaching the diaper tabs to each other, and snaps the little onesie back on to keep him warm.

The baby stiffens and begins to punch the air with his arms and legs. Now he looks like a miniature boxer. His little face grows red, his cheeks puff, eyes pinch shut. Then he begins to cry, and his cry is desperate and demanding, the cry of hungry infants everywhere. Margo feels impelled by the insistence of his cry—just as nature intends, she thinks. She quickly unbuttons the front of her dress and unhooks her bra, pushing it up so that her breasts are bare. She scoops up the shrieking child and rushes back to the armchair, sinks down, and lifts his head to her breast.

The baby's nose bobs across her chest. She laughs with excited delight at the bobbing of his dear little head. He seeks her nipple blindly, frantically. Dear little thing, she croons to him as she watches and awaits the moment when he will come upon it.

The baby finds her and begins to suck ferociously. His eyes are open wide now, blazing with determination. The pressure of his lips kneading against her nipple is not gentle, and it gives a strangely bittersweet blend of pleasure and pain. "Ooh," she says, a little startled by his wildness.

Just as she is beginning to adjust herself to it, the kneading suddenly ceases. The baby's arms begin to churn, and his little feet thrust into her stomach. His nose begins to bob across her breasts again, in a manner that is even more disorganized and frantic.

Margo tries to help him. She steers her nipple toward

his mouth. Again, he fastens on tightly and begins kneading it with his lips. This time, though, he stops sucking very soon and wrenches his mouth away.

Margo takes charge again with loving pity. She firmly presses his lips against her nipple. But this time his mouth refuses to even open. He jerks his head away, and as he does, his tiny hand scrapes against her chest. Margo sees and feels his distress, and she is disconcerted by it. Maybe I can't do this, she thinks. Maybe my milk's no good, and that's why he doesn't want it.

No, she thinks, I can't allow myself to become agitated. I'm the adult here; it's my responsibility to stay calm.

"All right," she says out loud, taking herself in hand. "It probably takes time for the milk to form. The body needs time to react to the baby's demands." She tries to remember the book chapter, but the fine detail hadn't registered enough to be readily summoned from her memory.

"We will have to rely on nature," she says to the child. "The two of us will learn together."

The baby's whimpering turns to shrieks. Margo searches through the diaper bag and yes, here is a bottle of water, with a white plastic cap to keep it clean.

The baby accepts the water. He drinks in huge gulps, guzzling the fluid down. Halfway through the bottle, though, he wrenches his head away. She nuzzles the nipple against his lips, but he refuses and wrenches away again.

Gently, Margo places the baby over her shoulder and pats his back. Soon, he belches, quite emphatically for such a tiny person, and she settles him in the makeshift bassinet she has hastily assembled. He whimpers softly, and his little fists push against the sides of the box. Margo watches, willing him to quiet down: rest, relax, sleep now, little one.

And, finally, he does.

Margo feels content now, with the baby deeply asleep by her side. She gazes at him lovingly and begins to consider what to name him. She tries out biblical names— Noah, Jacob, Luke—but they seem so austere for such a sweet and tiny thing. She murmurs melodic names—Oliver, Anthony—but they seem too sophisticated for this innocent child. Robert, maybe? Robbie now; Bob when an assertive, masculine name will be best.

Little Robbie, she says out loud, and likes the sound of it.

Now her thoughts turn to where they'll live. A studio apartment would do fine. She'd scrub and disinfect it top to bottom, and get a real crib with a stimulating mobile to hang over his head. She'd work from home doing telemarketing while Robbie napped. And when he woke, she'd be right there to feed him, snuggle him, and tell him little stories.

What could be better?

55

———

While her baby sleeps loose-limbed and uncon-
cerned, Renee Lamarato sits on the sofa in her
living room in a heap, as if her head and thorax have
collapsed into her abdomen. It is two hours since she has
returned to her home, though it feels like a year. Detective
George Marshaw sits nearby, his large body overflowing the
narrow dining room chair brought over for him. Renee's
husband, Tony, sits on the floor beside her, his cheek
pressed against her thigh, his arm encircling her lower leg.

The detective observes her closely as he talks to her in
as gentle a voice as his baritone can produce. "While my
team is out on the trail, you and I are going to work just as
hard here. You're going to go over every minute of the day.
We're going to discuss every friend, every acquaintance you
two have ever had. You're going to try and remember every
person who ever praised your baby. You're going to think of
anyone who might feel you disrespected them, anyone who
might be envious of you."

Since the squad car delivered them to her home,
Detective Marshaw has kept from Renee the details of the

updates he has received from his team so far: that they are examining the baby carriage for fingerprints, which will be checked against all databases, and hairs, which will be sent to the lab for DNA testing. He decides on a case-by-case basis how much information to share with people: some need to know every minute detail, while others only want the reassurance that he is competent and taking care of everything. Whether specific information will reassure or frighten Renee Lamarato further he will not know until he has listened to some of her questions and observed her responses to his comments.

"While you and I work on this, my team is doing everything they can," he says in a quiet voice, "and will keep on doing it through the night."

Renee flinches, as if the words came from a high-volume boom box held close to her ear. She seems to be even more alarmed—if such a thing is possible.

"What's everything?" Tony asks.

The detective explains about checking the carriage, scanning the store's security video, questioning every employee and customer in the store when the 911 call was placed by the Target manager.

Renee slumps further into the sofa, and then slides off onto her knees on the floor. Her hands are clasped tightly against her lips. "Sweet Jesus. Mary, Mother of God, help!"

56

Dusk falls.

Margo is not hungry, but she reminds herself that it's important for her to eat and drink. She heaps two slices of bread with peanut butter and takes some milk from the carton she had placed in the small refrigerator. And then she drinks more milk, enough to start her own milk flowing well, she hopes.

While she is still nibbling at the sandwich, the baby wakes and cries. Putting her food down, Margo walks quickly to him, unbuttoning her dress as she goes, and presses him to her breast.

He mashes his lips around her nipple, then spits it out and screams, his head bobbing wildly. She takes the half-full bottle of water and presses it into his mouth. He gulps twice, then spits the nipple out. He screams and screams again, not stopping for breath.

For lack of anything else to do, Margo presses her finger into his mouth. The toothless gums clamp immediately around the finger with amazing strength, and he starts sucking; it is like putting a finger into a vacuum cleaner, she thinks.

But soon, he spits the finger out, and then spits out breast and water bottle when she offers each again in turn.

She tries to stay calm. All babies scream, she tells herself. She paces the floor with the baby dangling over her shoulder. "Babies scream to let out their tension," she advises herself out loud. "They can't jog or play racquetball, so what else can they do?" She listens attentively to her own lecture, as if it were Dr. Spock himself addressing her.

She walks and walks across the room and still the baby squirms and screams. Her dress is soaked with the saliva that drools from his mouth as he pecks against her shoulder.

The door slams in a room nearby. She begins to worry about the crying. Is a hotel guest coming to protest the disturbance of the peace? She waits, and thankfully, no one comes to bang on her door. She is relieved—but for just a second: perhaps the guest had simply rushed by and gone directly to the front desk clerk to complain. Perhaps from now on she should turn on the TV loud enough to mask Robbie's crying.

For now, no one comes, and his cries are also diminished in intensity. Finally, long after her back has begun to ache, he drops asleep. His forehead is damp with perspiration.

Carefully, she places him in his sleeping drawer, and then collapses into the armchair. She wipes back her sweat-dampened hair, too tired to turn off the lights, too tired to walk to the bed. Just let me rest right here, she thinks.

It seems to her only minutes in the quietness before the baby is awake and shrieking.

Margo drags herself up out of the chair, checks on him, and then changes his diaper. With little confidence, she puts his still-screaming mouth to her breast. He pecks and bobs, fastens and spits. He spits out the water bottle after a few sips, too.

Now she is the helpless one. Why is he so defiant?

The baby screams continuously. She turns on the TV. At last, exhaustion forces his mouth to slacken and his eyes to close. Again, she places him back in his box.

The scene repeats itself through the night: the baby wakens, refuses breast and bottle, and shrieks.

"Please suck!" she begs him, as the baby spits out her nipple yet another time. "You have to make it come—it's you that makes it come!"

She walks and walks with him atop her shoulder, tracing miles across the faded carpet.

After a while, Margo puts the baby, who is still crying, into his box. The place on her abdomen where his little feet pounded feels raw, although when she inspects the spot, there is no mark to be seen.

It is difficult for her to look at the baby now. She goes to sit in the faded pink chair, staring at the furniture. Her confidence in herself as a caregiver is crumbling. Angry feelings come, angry thoughts: Maybe I should just take you back. Maybe you're not the one. She recoils from what her brain is proposing.

Toward dawn, the child's cries weaken. After he has

been silent for a time, Margo walks to the bed and sinks down upon it in total exhaustion.

Atop the bedspread she lies, half asleep, half awake. Images of fish eyes float in front of her, and it seems as if she is swimming in the sea with them. The fish and the fowl: Genesis. Exodus comes next: plagues, the life-giving Nile water fouled, the firstborn terminally cold in the night.

Finally, she falls into restless, troubled sleep.

*O*nly a few hours later, an early morning delivery truck lumbers along the street beneath Margo's window. It bounces in potholes, it squeaks as the driver brakes for the red light, and its motor whines as it accelerates when the light turns green again. Like most people who live in suburbia, Margo is accustomed to sleeping on a quiet street in a house insulated by thick windows that effectively shut out the little noise there is. The sounds of this truck easily rouse her from her light sleep.

Margo awakens in a state of disorientation. Groping to establish where she is, she peers into the room. The walls are alight with stripes as morning sunlight streams through the drapes, and on a desk near the window stands the plastic flowerpot. That visual fingerprint identifies the room absolutely.

Margo's thoughts fly to the baby. Is he really there? Or has he been yet another fantasy?

She hurries to the box. He is there. Her eyes fasten on the familiar, monk-like hair; the tender, tiny nails. His little body is solid and real, no figment of her imagination.

But something is odd. His eyes are open but they are devoid of sparkle, as if the light source illuminating them from within has dimmed. Though he is awake, the torpor in the baby's body is like that of someone drunkenly asleep, or drugged. When he moves, it is only to drag a hand or foot listlessly across the sheet. His lips are slack, and tiny cracks crease their surface.

Margo is startled by his appearance. When she touches his cheek, the skin feels rough and dry, like a crumpled piece of paper. "You're sick," she whispers to him, her voice cracking with fear.

Don't panic, Margo warns herself. She instructs her brain to summon up the diagnostic possibilities. Very soon, a clutch of ideas begins to press for consideration, and she rushes to the desk to search for writing material to catch and keep the thoughts.

She yanks on the sticky center drawer until it gives way and jerkily opens. Inside, there are paper sheets with slightly yellowed edges and a ballpoint pen that she has to scratch back and forth across the paper several times before the recalcitrant blue ink begins to flow.

Her mind stays calm and clear, not clouding over or shriveling into a useless, quivering thing. She labels a sheet of paper "Possible Diagnoses" and begins to sort into organized columns her thoughts of disorders she has learned about from hospital conferences and computer printouts. She ignores the trembling of her fingers as she writes.

Margo concentrates hard on the first diagnosis she has listed. She runs her forefinger over the word, as if an electric eye in its tip might help her see things more clearly: Infection. Babies came to the hospital limp with meningitis or pneumonia, their fragile bodies colonized by deadly bacteria with beautiful names like Hemophilus. Her baby has been carried through dirty streets where germs could have infiltrated the air, or hidden in thick grime. Or perhaps dirty silt had seeped through cracked pipes into the hotel's water system, and the water she has washed him with, that flowed from the faucet with seeming innocence, had ferried germs onto his delicate skin.

For Diagnosis II, Margo writes: Poisons. Chemical toxins were the contemporary scourge of children, and every baby book she'd read had warned against them. Her baby was much too little to have guzzled bleach or munched on aspirin tablets. But, she thinks, the drawer he lay in could have been tinged with lead-containing paint, which could have stuck onto his tiny fists as they brushed across its sides. Metallic fragments in the old plumbing could have leached into the water she washed him with, letting unseen particles infiltrate his soft and unresisting skin.

She comes to Diagnosis III: Dehydration and Malnutrition. As her eyes reread the words she has just written, a chill streaks across her skin, as if she has been suddenly dropped into ice water. This is the one, and it was entirely caused by her own doing.

Margo forces herself to think about it. Using her fingers as an abacus, she begins to add up the hours that have elapsed. Almost twenty-four hours have passed since the child began to subsist on whatever meager drops he could wrest from her breasts. And when he refused the water bottle too, she reasons, his body began to suffer from insufficient fluid intake. Such dehydration could cause his entire metabolic rhythm to falter. And in such a tiny body, error would compound error, shifting the delicate chemistry further and further out of balance.

The chill returns full force. This time, it spreads implacably throughout her body, speeding through her limbs, coursing into her torso.

Margo fights to stave off the rising panic. "No!" she exclaims out loud. "I have to continue reasoning this out. It's my duty, and there's nobody else here to do it."

Her mind steadies, and the chill recedes.

Margo resumes her thinking about Diagnosis III. As time passes with no fluid intake, she reasons, the delicate chemistry would shift further and further out of balance, until the metabolic errors reached the point where their deterioration was irreversible—and no longer compatible with life.

The diagnostician in her struggles to maintain control, but her composure begins to shrivel, like a balloon leaking air. With this last conclusion, she cannot stem the icy tide of panic. Thoughts glitter as they flash by. It feels as if ice crystals are forming throughout her body, shimmering in unison. She feels so terribly, terribly cold.

I am changing into the Snow Queen, she thinks. The Snow Queen, who wickedly lures children to her frozen kingdom, where they experience loneliness and desolation instead of warmth and love. It has always been a terrifying tale. But now it is she who is being transformed into the glacial woman.

Margo stares at the skin of her arms. Will sharp icicles poke through to the surface? Will her defectiveness finally become incarnate for herself and all the world to see?

She feels herself perilously close to the edge of an icy pool, about to drop into the deep and watery darkness.

"I'm not like that," she pleads to some unseen judge—herself, perhaps—trying to move back from the edge of the darkness. "It wasn't on purpose. I never want to hurt or destroy. I only want to love."

But what about the dead bird? The dead bird, remember? The ice crystals within her seem to hiss the accusation in unison: you thought about smashing, you thought about hurting, you thought about destroying.

The chill penetrates deeper, into muscle fibers and bones. Margo's body shakes in long swells of shivering. In her mind's eye she sees her childhood book's picture of the Snow Queen in her ermine mantle: the elegant, unnatural woman who lured innocent children away from their mothers.

With a last huge burst of effort, Margo rebuts the identification. "I'm not like that!" she exclaims. "I'm not!" She digs her nails deep into her palms. The sharp sting helps to steady her. "I'm not like that!" she says again.

When the fainty feeling recedes enough, Margo rises from the desk to dress herself. She buttons in such haste that the buttons and buttonholes don't match up correctly and the dress hangs crookedly. No matter, she has no time or interest in fixing it.

Margo hurries to the baby's box. She kneels by his side and smoothes the sheet under his head so that it will be free of disturbing wrinkles. Taking oil and cotton from the well-stocked diaper bag, she gently cleans his little bottom and puts on a fresh diaper. Over his yellow stretch suit she gently pulls on his little white cardigan.

The baby lies still. His face has a yellowish tinge, she notices, and his breathing is irregular with little rushes of panting. She moves around the room getting ready for their departure, all the while whispering soft words of encouragement: "It'll be fine. You're going to be all right."

When everything is ready, she picks him up, wraps his blanket securely around him, and walks out the door, diaper bag on her arm. Margo clasps the child closer to her body, and rocks him gently to comfort him.

In the lobby, the clerk sits at his desk. He looks up as Margo passes with her bundle. He appears annoyed; perhaps he is realizing that she has smuggled another person, albeit a tiny one that doesn't qualify as a customer, into his hotel without his knowledge.

"Hey lady," he calls out.

But she ignores him and pushes her shoulder against the hotel's front door.

58

------

*O*utside, the sun is bright. Margo begins walking steadily, distracted neither by the light nor the city noises nor the child who scampers across her path to retrieve a ball from the street. Two blocks, three, four; her steps lengthen and her walking rhythm quickens as she draws closer to her destination.

"We're almost there," she whispers to the child.

The building she seeks is just ahead. Its beige bricks are surprisingly clean, a testament to its relatively young age, by neighborhood standards. She locates the main entrance and turns into the short entrance walk that leads to it.

At the door, she slows her steps for the first time since leaving the hotel. Kisses for the baby now, first on one tiny eyelid, then the other. Her lips graze across his forehead, lingering, as if to commit the shape of his brow to memory, and press into his skin the invisible and enduring imprint of her lips.

Inside the outpatient clinic door, a signboard lists the specialty clinics and their locations. Midway down, after Orthopedics, she finds Pediatrics. Following arrows marking the way, she walks down a short corridor, then up one flight and to the right.

Except for a solitary clerk sitting at a small desk, the clinic waiting room is empty. The clerk is engrossed in her work. She finally looks up to see a woman in a gray dress in front of her. "Hope you haven't been standing there long," she says. "I wasn't expecting anyone yet. The clinic doesn't open for another half hour, you know."

"Isn't this a walk-in clinic? Should I have gone to an emergency room instead?" Margo asks, upset.

"It *should* be a walk-in clinic, but we don't have the staff or the patient flow to keep it open all day," the woman explains. "But since you're already here, let me see if I can find a doctor."

Her experienced eyes have taken note of the mother's pinched, anxious face, and she has heard the raspy, irregular breathing of the baby. With a calm yet commanding tone, the woman picks up the phone and contacts the operator. "Page Dr. Bromley and ask him to come to the Pediatrics Clinic as soon as he can."

Margo is satisfied. "Excuse me, miss," she says to the clerk, "but I left my purse with the Blue Cross card in it in the car. I'm just too nervous to think straight. Could I just leave the baby here for a minute with you while I run and get it?"

"No problem. Just give me a minute so I can get a crib from the other room for . . . him?" she asks tentatively. Margo nods her assent to both the minute and the baby's gender.

The clerk leaves and soon returns with a small wooden crib that she places beside her desk.

"Could I leave the diaper bag, too, up here on the desk?"

The woman smiles. "Sure."

Margo sets the bag on the desk and the baby in the crib. As she tucks the blanket around him, her hands lovingly caress each curve of his still body. Then she turns and walks from the room.

The clerk turns her attention back to her desktop. Blue and yellow papers are spread across it, unsorted sheets that had been stacked in an unattended heap in the far corner of the staff room. She sleuths and she sorts, continuing to put them in some semblance of order.

After a time, she looks up and notices that the baby's mother has not yet returned. She checks her watch. Something seems wrong to her, because that kind of mother, so attached to the child, who rocked him and smoothed his hair as she stood and talked, that kind of mother should have flown right back to him.

The clerk sorts another few pages, and still the mother has not returned. From the crib at her side, the baby's breathing seems even more labored. He lies motionless, eyes half closed, skin pasty and unhealthy-looking, mouth slack and working aimlessly. Every so often he tries to complain, but his weak cries fade out at the end, as if smothered before their time.

The clerk pulls the diaper bag over, exasperated now at the delays of both the doctor and the mother. "I hope she's got a bottle in here," the clerk mutters as her hand gropes blindly in the bag, but her hand encounters nothing except its cool plastic lining.

She opens the bag as widely as she can and circum-navigates the interior carefully with her hand. She finds an unsealed envelope with a sheet of paper folded inside.

The message is written in blue ink that seems to have stuttered out of the pen. Although the letters are imper-fectly inked, the meaning of the words they spell out is startlingly clear.

"I found this baby yesterday in the Target store," it reads. "I tried to love him and care for him, I tried to nurse him, but I failed. So he has had practically no fluids for over twenty-four hours and . . ."

The clerk reads no further. She grabs for the phone. "Paging? This is Pediatrics Clinic. Get Dr. Bromley here. Immediately. Do you understand?"

After that, she phones the police.

59

Before returning to the hotel, Margo shops at two drugstores. The incredible variety of medications on the well-stocked shelves is overwhelming. How could she know which sleeping pills would interact dangerously with the others?

To avoid raising suspicion, she decides to purchase several different brands at different drugstores. She goes about it in the way of someone who is diversifying a stock portfolio: one selection, at least, should be a stellar performer. In the end, she purchases four different brands of sleeping pills. The cost is quite modest. Death does not have to be very expensive, she thinks.

Now the brands are all mixed together in her stomach, a veritable melting pot of pills. The bed feels as if it is turning into a cocoon, and Margo lets the soft warmth wrap itself around her. The extra blanket she has found on the top shelf of the closet and piled on top of the bedspread adds weight as well as heat, and she feels comforted by the gentle pressure of the bedding, like a child secure in tight swaddling blankets.

While she lies there, her mind begins to drift, now receiving new sensations signaled from inside her body, now spinning a thought or coming upon a memory.

How unfair of God to portion out parental joy so unevenly, she thinks. The fortunate rejoiced daily in moist kisses and fragrant hugs with happy, healthy children they could watch grow to adulthood. To others was given pain, agonizing over healthy infants ripped from their arms to be tossed into Nazi ovens; sorrowing over once-healthy children as leukemic cells took over their blood. No, God is not gracious. The Bible and Mrs. Byne lied.

How unfair of God to measure out mental and physical health so unjustly. How unfair that she'd lacked the emotional strength to mother Janie in her time of need. How unfair to have been given a body so naïve in the ways of womanhood that it had stumbled, as if by chance, into conception. How unfair to be cursed with a body so faulty it had expelled, before its time, the baby that had finally grown within it. How unfair to have been unable to nourish the thirsty child that had at first suckled expectantly.

Humiliation heaped upon humiliation. It is impossible to tolerate any longer.

The cocoon becomes warmer and warmer. Heat radiates down from the blankets and penetrates deeply into her muscles and bones. Heat radiates outward, as well, from her pill-stocked stomach, as from a country stove.

Margo is suspended between these crosscurrents of warmth, rocked by them, drifting back and forth, back and forth. She senses ice crystals in her body melting, their crystalline-sharp edges softening and blurring as warm currents flow around them.

Margo's eyes droop shut. Against the orangey membranous lining of her eyelids, she sees a cloud of babies with honeyed skin and rosy cheeks. Waving gaily and excitedly, they drift loose and free. The babies surround her and laughingly pull her from the bed. Together they all rise up, higher and higher, wafted along by warm streams of air, floating effortlessly, ascending together closer, ever closer, to the brightly shining sun.

Everything is dissolving. Only wisps of feelings and filaments of thoughts remain.

And soon, the last bits of consciousness slip away.

60

———

The tube they have threaded through Margo's nostril down into her stomach is rubbing against the back of her throat like a rough wooden stick. The muscles of her arm begin throbbing from the ceaseless tightenings and loosenings of the blood pressure cuff.

The swooshing sounds she is hearing are ceaseless and regular. What are they? Lapping ocean waves? Strong river currents?

As her mind becomes clearer, she realizes what it is: someone is flushing water back and forth into and out of her body. Someone is washing out the contents of her stomach, retrieving the pills she has so diligently stored there.

Stop! she wants to say. All I want is to escape the overwhelming pain and humiliation. Can't you see how cruel it is not to let me? Stop!

But only a croak emerges from her bruised throat, and water continues to be pushed relentlessly in and out, sucking away the pills she has buried there. Margo tries again to protest, and only whispery words come out. This time, a nurse bends over to listen, but seems unable to make any sense of her mumbles.

After shaking her head with a smile, the nurse wheels away and turns her attention back to the readout from the blood pressure cuff.

IN A SMALL FAMILY ROOM NEARBY, A YOUNG DOCTOR, who has broken away momentarily from the urgent pace in the ER bays, is briefing Steven. "We're pretty sure she will be all right," he says. "There's always the danger of aspiration—that she might breathe the vomitus down her airway —but the tube we have in place in her stomach should prevent most of that.

"I don't think she'll go much deeper—get less conscious, I mean. They got to her soon enough. And we pulled a lot of drugs out of her stomach before they dissolved and passed into her bloodstream."

"How did they find her so fast?" Steven asks, vaguely aware that he has already asked this question of someone else and it has already been answered.

"The note in the baby's diaper bag was written on the hotel's stationery. When the pediatrics clerk called the police and read them the name and address, the police went there to check it out. And the hotel desk clerk knew which guest had brought a baby into the hotel.

"The police found your wife in a stupor, with empty sleeping pill bottles scattered around the bed. They called for an ambulance immediately. Pretty lucky, wouldn't you say?"

Steven can't answer this question, since "lucky" isn't a word he would use to describe either Margo or himself.

"Any other questions?" the doctor asks, already out of his chair.

"No. At least, not now."

"Okay. Take a seat in the main waiting room, and we'll call you when we're ready to move her to the floor."

In the waiting room, Steven looks blankly at the other people there. Many, like himself, are trying hard to get hold of themselves. In the seat nearby, a tall, thin woman sits with her arms around herself, silently rocking. Some sit with dazed faces and pursed lips; others are talking to themselves. They look shell-shocked, he thinks, like the patients in the psychiatric unit upstairs, where Margo too was a patient before she escaped.

Steven calls the main Woodchester Hospital number, which he stored in his phone in the event he needed to reach Margo at work should her cell phone not be operative. He asks the answering operator to call Kate's unit and leave a message for her to call his cell phone as soon as possible.

It rings almost immediately. "They found her. Three hours ago. She took sleeping pills. We're down here in the emergency room."

A sharp intake of breath from Kate. "How bad is it?"

"They told me she'll be all right."

"I'm coming right down."

Steven gets up and stations himself at the door of the waiting room where Kate will be coming in.

In a few moments she is there. She embraces him and lightly rubs his back. "She's still all right?" Kate asks.

"No one's said anything different."

A deep, long sigh from Kate. "What happened?"

Steven takes her to a place he spied in the waiting room where there are two seats together and tells her everything, exactly as he has been told it.

"And the baby?"

"After the clerk found the note, he was brought right over to pediatric intensive care. They tell me the baby is doing very well."

"Thank God!"

Kate rubs Steven's hand. "Will Margo have to go to jail?"

"I don't know. It all depends on whether the chief prosecutor decides to prosecute or not."

"So there might not be a trial?"

"Maybe not. If the CP is persuaded there was diminished responsibility, and if the baby is all right, then maybe not."

Steven's face begins to quiver.

He, the dispassionate one, the stoic, is going to cry, and in front of all these people in the waiting room. He tries to blink away the first tears that moisten his eyes, but the sadness expands too quickly and more tears come, faster than he can blink them away.

Unsure how to ask for comfort, he sits as if paralyzed. But when Kate puts her arm around him, he leans his weight against her and lets sobs shake his body as they will.

61

Margo's throat feels raw, as if it has been gouged with nails. Nausea washes over her in green waves. Since they had washed her stomach to their satisfaction, and she became more alert, they took out the horrible tube and left her to retch into a blue plastic disposable basin.

Is this to be my punishment? Margo thinks. Purgation and purification, instead of the searing fires of hell that Mrs. Byne warned about in Sunday school?

A rustling sound nearby. What are they going to do to me now? she wonders.

"I could have lost you forever."

She recognizes Steven's voice, even though it sounds gravelly and it wavers as he speaks the words. She pushes open her still-heavy eyelids.

Margo sees that his eyes are watery, although she knows he almost never cries. And when he buries his face in her hair, she can feel warm tears trickling into her ear. What does it all mean?

A white-coat-wearing person bends over Steven and says something to him.

Steven straightens up and moves away, but not too far, not enough to stop him from keeping his hand on her head and stroking her hair.

"Look at me," the white-clothed person orders.

Margo obeys and looks up.

"Very good. You're all right now, Margo. We're going to move you out of here to a room on the Medicine Unit. You're out of the woods, but you need to be followed for a while longer."

The cart squeals as they wheel her out.

All right? How can I be all right? she thinks. Have they done some new kind of surgery to repair her useless body? Have they cut away all traces of how she harmed a dear sweet baby? Has she done the proper amount of penance, suffered enough to satisfy even old Mrs. Byne?

What do they mean, all right?

62

At Dr. Taynor's office, a long day of seeing patients is over. However, the phone has rung several times during her last session, so she checks to see if any messages have been left. She finds two: each from Woodchester Hospital, from someone who identifies himself as a psychiatry resident.

"Margo Kerber was admitted to the hospital after a suicide attempt. She eloped from our unit after depression resulting from an ultrasound challenge to her false pregnancy brought her in. Then she took a baby from his carriage in a store, and about twenty-four hours later brought him to a medical facility for care. Then, she overdosed on pills.

"Her husband told the ER team you'd seen her previously, so we got his written consent for you to discuss her case with us. Could you call? We have information from her recent admission, but we need some additional background. Also, would you be willing to take her as an outpatient when she's ready for discharge? The baby's fine, by the way."

Dr. Taynor quickly dials the paging number the

resident left and enters her phone number when prompted. As she waits for the return call, she unlocks the patient file drawer and extracts the file on Mrs. Kerber in order to refresh her memory and be as accurate as possible with the details.

When the call comes, Dr. Taynor answers the questions the resident asks and lets him know she would be happy to accept the referral for outpatient treatment. "I'm also willing to make a brief visit to the inpatient unit in a few days when you think she's ready, just to reestablish contact, if you think this would be useful," she adds.

The resident expresses his gratitude profusely—in this age of heightened scrutiny about the length of a patient's stay, pressure on the residents and social workers for disposition planning means they must begin to make discharge arrangements as soon as patients are admitted, and this one has turned out to be easier than most.

After Dr. Taynor finishes the call, she starts thinking the thoughts that invariably come to her when she hears that a person—in treatment or not—has made a suicide attempt. If the patient was in treatment, could the doctor have done better? Had the desperation of the patient been minimized or rationalized away? And the deeper question: Why had the need for suicide been so strong in that person, the pain so great and so relentless that death seemed the only escape?

Dr. Taynor becomes aware of a pressing need to write. She needs to grapple with these questions on the page as a way of arriving at answers for herself and for the benefit of her patients.

She walks to the cabinet where she stores her writings, the fantasies in which she can set her imagination loose and let her free associations roam. Dr. Taynor finds and removes the folder with her current work-in-progress, and takes it to her desk.

It is a fanciful meeting of long-dead intellectual giants of psychoanalysis. She has allowed each to state his or her key concepts, and then put her own ideas into their mouths. It's been enlightening to come to her own conclusions, and fun to express them on an equal footing with these icons.

Before beginning to write today, Dr. Taynor reads through what she has already written.

It is the sector of space-time where the dead geniuses congregate after their deaths, above puffy clouds enveloping the Earth, past the rings of Saturn, and far beyond the Milky Way. They communicate through variations in the frequency and amplitude of their energy pulsations, indulging in continuous uninterrupted intellectual discussion since there is no need anymore for their restless minds to shut down every eighteen hours for sleep.

"Sigmund, you were right to champion the importance of guilt and anxiety—especially oedipal anxiety—in human psychology. But you were wrong to neglect the importance of self-esteem and shame," says Heinz Kohut.

"Not so. I wrote about envy. And envy is the by-product of shame," says Sigmund Freud.

"What you wrote about, Sigmund, was penis envy," says Melanie Klein. "You always made penises so impor-

tant. Did you know your critics said your theories gave permission to analysts, including yourself, to think about penises all day long?"

"Please don't forget the point of those writings, Melanie. Penis envy results from a major misconception. The little girl has a secret shame: that little boys and grown men have a wonderful appendage she doesn't have. Her sense of body incompleteness is unconscious and incorrect, but it is nevertheless real. And the unconscious solution to repair this perceived body flaw is to bear a child."

"No, that cannot be considered the central feature of female psychology," says Karen Horney. "Like men, women need to feel self-esteem and have self-respect. That does not require a filled womb, Sigmund. They can achieve that self-esteem in multiple ways, not just in one."

"Then consider that behavior stems from biology," says Sigmund Freud. "At the root of human psychology is biology: the drives for food, sex, and reproduction, as well as the primal emotions like rage. Those of you arguing that self-esteem is the central motivator of psychological life must explain why that is. Otherwise, the idea is just bullshit."

Sigmund emits an energy pulse of pleasure as he uses his favorite expletive, the one he has learned from the younger colleagues who have more recently arrived here. He greatly loves this word bullshit; it is so explosively anal.

Now Dr. Taynor picks up her pen. The words flow quickly, thought to pen, pen to paper.

In their sector of space-time, the dead psychiatric geniuses are still deeply engrossed in their discussion. Alfred Adler is speaking.

"Sigmund, a person's maturation to reach their real *self is a psychic journey. Psychological health is not just about developing healthier defenses to psychic conflicts over aggressive and sex drives. It's also about dealing with shame. And where does this shame come from?*

"All children have an idealized image of themselves, which is partly conscious and partly unconscious," continues Alfred, answering his own question. "You know this, Sigmund. You even gave it a beautiful name: ego-ideal.

"But problems come because people judge themselves by how well they measure up to these expectations they have. To be psychologically healthy, the self needs to come to a healthy compromise with these unrealistic aspirations."

"Yes," says Sigmund, "I do agree with that."

"In the best situation, simple and mild neurotic distortions are enough to deal with the shame of not measuring up. But sometimes they're not enough. And then what?"

Alfred realizes he has the full attention of the group: he can sense the increased intensity of vibrations emanating from his audience.

"When the most vulnerable people fail to measure up to these ego-ideals," he continues, "their self-esteem splinters deeply. Self-hatred becomes strong. Then, the repairs the psyche has to make to hide from shame must be major. They may be imaginative, even very creative, but they come at a

great price—the world must be severely distorted, and reality must be pulled out of shape.

"What does it take for a person to perform massive self-deception?" asks Alfred. "Can anyone do it? Falsify reality if the threat is sufficiently great?"

Silence, as all the psychoanalysts reflect on the question.

At moments like these, Freud very much misses not having his earthly beard for stroking as he thinks things through. "That, my friends, is indeed a complicated question, and we all may have different viewpoints about it," he finally says.

"But one thing we do know: that psychotherapy helps people explore their self-deceptions. It helps them extricate themselves from their self-created webs. So that they can become free to unfold and become who they really are.

"We can all agree on that, can't we?"

63

In her hospital bed on the General Medicine Unit, Margo dozes fitfully. Half asleep, half awake, images and thoughts float in and out of her awareness, barely perceived, barely heeded.

Because she has made a suicide attempt, there is always a sitter in her room, although when Steven comes the sitter leaves and waits outside in the hallway until his departure. At first, as Margo dozes, the sitters attend mainly to their laptops or their books. As time passes, Margo's eyes remain open and she gazes out the window or around the room. When she looks at them directly, they introduce themselves to her and make a few attempts at conversation. Margo acknowledges their greetings with a nod and looks away. I don't want to talk with them, she thinks, and the sitters thankfully let her be.

Twenty-four hours of observation pass. Margo steadily becomes less drowsy, and her meals are moved up from full liquids to a regular diet; she has a small appetite and samples what's on her trays. As her mind is better able to focus, she begins to sort through a welter of memories of the recent past. She remembers running, a bus ride, fish heads, and plastic flowers. Wild and weird, were those images from a nightmare? she wonders. Then comes the memory of a stick put down her throat, doctors in blue scrub suits, the whoosh of water. My throat does feel raw, so that probably is something that really happened, she thinks.

And then she remembers more. A baby in a carriage. A baby she picks up, holds in her arms, brings to a hotel room. A baby boy, who sickens and becomes very, very ill. With certainty, she knows. That, too, really happened.

Oh God! she thinks, and a swell of nausea washes over her.

Her mind fastens on one anxiety-laden thought: The baby, how is he? She jabs the call button, and more than once.

With this sudden burst of activity from her charge, the sitter comes to attention and her gaze focuses steadily on Margo.

The nurse soon appears at the door, and Margo blurts out her dread-fueled question: "The baby, is he all right?"

"I'll tell your doctor you need to talk to him."

This noncommittal reply makes Margo even more frightened. If the baby is all right, she thinks, wouldn't the nurse just tell me that straight out?

When the doctor comes, he asks the sitter to leave and then reassures Margo immediately: "The nurse told me you're asking about the baby. No need to worry—he's fine. They'll send him home tomorrow."

The doctor soon departs, and the sitter returns. Margo lies quietly and reflects on the momentous good news she's just received. Thank God, thank God, she whispers to herself, and the tension in her muscles releases.

But in a moment a tight knot clamps itself into her abdomen. How *could* I? she thinks. And the next question she asks herself sears just as deeply: Who *am* I?

⟡

THE NEXT MORNING, MARGO IS ALERT ENOUGH TO PASS their cognitive testing: she knows the month and the year; she can subtract the number seven serially backward from one hundred; five minutes after being told to remember three unrelated words, she can recall them; she can name the current US president as well as several before him.

The medical staff concludes that although she is still weak, Margo is medically stable and can safely be transferred to Psychiatry. They waste little time, and do so early that afternoon.

⟡

MARGO RIDES IN A WHEELCHAIR TO THE PSYCHIATRY Unit. There, the clerk and the PCWs in the corridor greet her with friendly Hi's, and she nods a greeting back to each of them. They assign her to a room different from the one she'd occupied before, in a different corridor as well, and she is grateful. I wouldn't want the room where my mind went off the tracks, she thinks, the room where I saw the dead bird.

Margo settles in and, to her surprise, feels reassured to be here. The staff and the rhythms of the day comfort her. They probably figured I'd be better off in a different room than last time, she thinks. They know what they're doing, she thinks.

After work, Steven comes to visit. He brings clothes for her to wear, and tells her the events of the day at his office. She's glad to see him, and tries to concentrate on what he's saying, so that she can nod at the appropriate times. He kisses her cheek when he leaves, and she grasps his hand.

That night, she finally gets a solid four hours of sleep before the awakenings begin. The following morning, Margo walks shakily to the dining room for breakfast, a PCW's hand at her elbow. None of the patients are familiar, and she is not surprised by that; as a hospital administrator, she knows the average length of stay on the unit is less than two weeks. The PCW brings her to a small table for two. The young woman already there smiles wanly at her and then looks down at her plate. Margo says hello in return and then stays quiet, not wanting to try and start a conversation that neither of them seems motivated enough to have.

After she's done nibbling at some toast and sipping some orange juice, Margo walks back to her room, where she is allowed to stay with the nurse's blessing. Earlier, she'd vigorously brushed her teeth and combed her hair, but the trips back and forth to the dining room have sapped the little energy she'd woken with. She sinks onto her bed and, for the next half hour, sleeps.

When Margo awakens, she finds Kate sitting close to the side of the bed. Margo grasps Kate's hand, and the two sit quietly with no need for words to enhance—or risk diminishing—the closeness between them.

Three soft knocks on the partially open door break the silence. Margo turns to look, and sees Dr. Taynor standing in the doorway.

Kate rises from her chair. "I'll come back later," she says, and blows Margo a kiss as she leaves.

Margo sits up on the side of the bed and glances with surprise at her visitor. Is Dr. Taynor a member of the psychiatrist staff here when she's not in her private office? Margo wonders. She's also a bit embarrassed, because they'd never scheduled the second appointment that had been so strongly recommended.

"Your doctors asked me to consult and come see you. Is that all right with you?"

Margo nods.

Dr. Taynor sits down in the chair Kate has vacated. She briefly summarizes what she's been told and what she's read in the hospital notes.

Margo is listening closely for it, but she hears not a trace of disapproval—or judgment—in Dr. Taynor's words. Instead, she hears what she thinks is compassion.

"How are you feeling now?"

"Horrified."

"Is there anything you'd like to ask or tell me?"

"How could I do that? Was that really me? I wanted a baby so much—too much," Margo confides softly.

Dr. Taynor nods. "I know."

"I really don't know why I wanted one that badly."

"If we worked together, once you're out of the hospital, I think you could find that out."

Margo sits very still, her brow furrowed, as she concentrates on Dr. Taynor's words. She circles round and round the idea as a child appraises a high tree she is considering climbing, cautiously at first, then approaching it more boldly.

"Could I?" Margo asks, wonder and doubt in her voice. "Could I really?" The question is meant for both the doctor and herself.

THAT NIGHT, WRAPPED SNUGLY IN HER HOSPITAL BED, Margo dreams of the salty sea and of herself floating atop the buoyant surface, supported by its saline richness. Steadily, she paddles toward the shore, where, on the fine, pale sand, a small group of people stand watching and waiting for her. And although a soft, hazy mist blurs their features, the tall, stalwart one, the one who stands well forward of the rest, reminds her so of Steven.

64

_____

The next evening, Cecilia places a call to Kate.

First, she oversees the toothbrushing and other bedtime rituals, and dims the lights. Then, from the locked file drawer in her room, Cecilia pulls out the prior year's daily activity log, which includes a brief summary of how each day had gone, as well as the volunteers that had assisted. She also pulls out her diary to reread any entries that included Margo's name.

Cecilia examines the documents closely, looking at each entry to see if some minor observation might now be seen in hindsight as a veiled clue. Despite all those hours conversing together while spooning food onto plates or supervising gluing at the arts and crafts table, she had noted nothing that was in any way a harbinger of what had happened to Margo. Despite a psychic pain so deep it eventually unmoored her, Margo was experienced by Cecilia only as a dedicated, competent, and stable volunteer.

Cecilia is puzzled and disturbed by this. How is it that someone who could become so unraveled by psychic pain always appeared to be so normal? Or did the problem lie with the observer, who hadn't the skill and intuition to notice?

She reaches for her phone and makes the call to Kate.

"I'd like to come over and talk with you tomorrow at the hospital," she says, "whenever you've got a few minutes to spare. If you tell me the approximate time, I'll hang around until you're free. Okay?"

After Kate agrees, Cecilia calls a colleague about to have a day off.

"Sorry for the bother and for asking, but could you please trade some time and cover Share House for a couple of hours tomorrow around noon?"

IN THE HOSPITAL CAFETERIA, KATE AND CECILIA SIT together at a table in a far corner where they are unlikely to be overheard. Each, in turn, engages in self-recrimination.

"I should have noticed something," says Cecilia. "I'm usually a good observer, and I'm trained for it. So why didn't I notice anything? And why didn't I try to help when things got bad?"

"Well," says Kate, "my problem is that I found it so much easier to be Florence Nightingale to a stranger than to Margo. I had plenty of empathy for Mrs. Patient-For-A-Week on my unit, but with my best friend—" Her voice trails off. "I have to be honest—I got tired of Margo never responding to me when I made visits after the baby died."

It's Cecilia who finds a way out of their thicket of remorse. Getting stuck in guilt isn't very productive, and so she thinks about something she's learned from observing her young people at Share House. Despite their cognitive limitations, they know, instinctively, the powers of reparation. Break someone's crayon? Then give them yours. Such is their way. Cecilia realizes that from their wisdom can come some relief for the two of them now. Relief will come not from more breast-beating, but from concrete positive action.

"Okay, so you weren't Florence Nightingale and I wasn't Mother Teresa," Cecilia says. "But we can still have another turn at bat."

65

___

*M*argo has settled into the routines and timetables of the Psychiatry Unit. She looks forward to the morning stretching sessions, when her body feels it is awakening and leaving behind its heaviness and torpor. When the events scheduled for the day are presented in the daily morning community meeting, she listens closely and then works with one of the PCWs to set out her individual goals for the day. She participates in occupational therapy even though art is not one of her talents, and engages actively in the music therapy sessions that surprisingly bring her moments of pleasure. She pays attention at the coping skills sessions presented by the social workers. As each day's activities are accomplished successfully, she becomes more and more confident in her ability to function again.

It is one and a half weeks since she's arrived on the unit, and Margo is sitting this morning, together with four other patients and a therapist, in the group therapy room. They are seated on comfortable chairs arrayed in a wide circle with just the right amount of distance between them to foster a sense of community while providing a generous amount of personal space. Two of the patients are staring at the floor, and Margo feels a surge of sympathy for them; she remembers and understands their desperate need to keep silent and avoid meeting the eyes of the others.

What she doesn't understand so well is her intention to speak frankly, because not only is she willing to speak openly, she feels a desire to do so. Maybe because it felt good to talk to Dr. Taynor, she thinks, without the effort of having to keep all my faults and doubts from getting exposed.

When the therapist gently invites them to participate, Margo responds first.

"I'm here because I've been very depressed for a long while and I need help."

That wasn't so hard, she thinks. Maybe it's also the antidepressant medication taking hold?

"I got so depressed that I even made a suicide attempt," she continues.

Two of the group members look intently at her. She notices that their mouths are not pinched in judgment, and they look curious rather than shocked. She feels no embarrassment, only a sense of anticipation that perhaps her disclosures will encourage the others to speak openly. It feels good, she thinks, to be able to function, and maybe even to help.

Talking about taking the baby, though, she cannot do, for she is not yet ready to confront this enormity even in her own thoughts.

RENEE LAMARATO HAS NO TROUBLE TALKING ABOUT anything and has plenty to say on any number of topics. She calls the chief prosecutor's office almost daily, demanding to know when he is going to start the case against Margo. On the occasions his assistant puts her through to him, she gives him quite an earful.

Now, she stares at the two women standing like missionaries on her front porch. She switches on the porch lamp as a searchlight over their heads, even though there is still plenty of daylight at this time in the late afternoon. Through the intercom newly installed at her front door, she quizzes the women thoroughly. Through the new panel of unbreakable glass adjacent to the door, she examines their identification and affiliation cards. Then she opens the door slightly on its chain to look them directly in the face.

Renee stands stolidly at the threshold, as if ready to prevent the two from crossing over into her home, should they try. Behind her, the tiny foyer and adjoining living room are fully illuminated in bright light, every table lamp and ceiling fixture turned on, although it is not yet dark. In the living room is the portable crib she now wheels from room to room as she cooks and vacuums. From the crib's attached mobile of dangling spheres, a new, blue-beaded rosary hangs over the baby's head.

There's a bitter, slightly irritating smell in the outside air, as if all the marigolds planted throughout the subdivision have sent their pungent odor directly onto the front porch. It's clear to Kate and Cecilia that this is as far as they are going to be allowed to get near Mrs. Lamarato and her baby. The women begin to speak, in turn, the words they have carefully prepared. They express sincere sympathy for the anguish she's experienced. They apologize for intruding on her today. They explain how ill Margo has been. They ask her to please not press for prosecution.

"We know this is asking a lot of you, after all you went through," says Kate. "We can't even imagine what it was like. We're certainly not here to ask you to forgive."

Renee tightens her lips.

"What we're asking is for your understanding," says Cecilia. "Margo's basically a very good person. We're hoping you'll try to understand how she went off the tracks when she lost probably the only pregnancy she'll ever have. Yes, she did something wrong and cruel. But that was her behavior, not her intention—she meant only to love and care for the child.

"And she did that. In the end, Mrs. Lamarato, that's just what she did. No matter what it cost her, she protected your child. That should count for something."

"It counts for nothing!" Renee bursts out. "She's a criminal! She should be punished."

"She *is* being punished," Kate says, with feeling. "She feels so bad that she tried to kill herself. Please, if you could just search your heart, so if you meet with the chief prosecutor . . ."

Renee leans against the door, as if she suddenly feels

faint, but soon straightens up again and looks her visitors in the eyes.

"You have the nerve to ask me to lobby the prosecutor not to prosecute Margo Kerber? You say she's suffering? Well, what about *my* suffering, *my* nightmares? The ones where I'm on my knees begging God to bring the baby back and take me instead? The ones that make me scream and wake my husband up?

"No!" yells Renee. "She should be locked away for a hundred years. And then she should burn in hell!"

66

———

A few days later, Margo is sent home, deemed safe to be discharged with the proviso that she attend regular therapy sessions with Dr. Taynor. Since this requirement was in no way unwelcome to Margo, she agreed to it readily.

Now, Margo is sitting in the comfortably upholstered patient chair across from Dr. Taynor and the ivy plants at the window. Steven is sitting out in the waiting room. He's taken a few weeks off from work in order to give Margo support as well as to reassure himself that she is safe. Actually, he's not really comfortable unless she's directly in his line of sight, even though the hospital doctor assured him she was ready for discharge.

Margo has come today out of a sense of duty, to Steven even more than to herself.

This is the second time she's come, and, as in the previous visit, Dr. Taynor begins with a review of the status of her depressive symptoms.

"How's your concentration?"

"Maybe a little better, but my mind still wanders when I try to read a book."

"How's your sleep?"

"A little better. I sleep better through the night, but I still get up too early and can't fall asleep again."

"Your appetite?"

"Not great, but I eat a little more than before."

"What's happening with your weight?"

"I haven't lost any since the last time I was here."

"Sounds like things are going in the right direction," Dr. Taynor says, "which tells us the medication is taking hold. How about your mood?"

"That's not much different. I still feel depressed almost all the time."

"Not surprising, since the other symptoms of depression usually improve before mood does. So let's check for any suicide potential. Do you have any plans or wish to kill yourself?"

"No."

"Any fleeting thoughts of suicide, even if you have no intention of acting on them?"

"None at all."

"And you will call me anytime, day or night, if that changes in any way?"

"Yes, I will."

Once this important contract between them has been clearly established, Dr. Taynor shifts to another topic.

"Our work here is to help you understand yourself better, so you understand *why* what happened, happened. It will take time, but we'll have many sessions together and we'll always go at whatever pace feels right to you."

Margo solemnly nods.

"This time is yours, so please begin wherever you'd like to."

Wherever I'd like to begin? That's a whole lot harder than being given a question to answer, Margo thinks. Perhaps she should start where everything began—but she hasn't the slightest idea where that really was.

She starts by talking about her hospitalizations, a topic she thinks will be of interest to Dr. Taynor and one not too uncomfortable to recall.

"When I was in the Psychiatry Unit the first time, I felt so bad about being there. Because it meant there was nothing right about me at all, because it meant that my mind was as messed up as my body." Margo shakes her head, and is silent for a moment.

"But the second time was different. The patients were different from before, quieter, so it didn't seem like such a weird place. But I don't think that was all of it. Maybe it was that I was different, too. I went to the group sessions, and this time I was one of the people who talked. I'm not sure why, but maybe talking to you a little bit in the hospital started me off. I didn't tell them all that much, but even that helped me, because it was kind of a relief to say things out loud instead of having them bottled up in my head."

Dr. Taynor smiles. While all that is true, Margo is also telling her, indirectly, that she has positive feelings about therapy, is forming the all-important working alliance with her therapist, and is ready to begin work.

6 7

———

Several days later, Margo is nestled into the cushions of her living room sofa sipping from a mug of Earl Grey tea and surrounded by the books and magazines Kate has bought and brought over to her. For the past half hour she has been savoring a respite from the tension that regularly twists her stomach into knots and amplifies the anxieties in her mind. The tea brings a pleasant internal warmth, and the lively articles in the magazines capture her interest. This feels so good, she thinks, even though it's just for now. She has no illusion about this and knows that this respite is temporary, that sad and worrisome thoughts will soon again hold sway over her mind and her body.

One unpleasant thought she will not have to contend with—because she has no knowledge of it—is that in the County Justice Center, two men are discussing her fate.

❧

UP ON THE SECOND FLOOR, NEAR THE COURTROOMS and one floor below the chief prosecutor's office, the four assistant prosecuting attorneys have their offices. The coffeepot in the hallway niche is always the site of much activity, as the overworked assistant prosecutors come regularly for doses of caffeine to keep their mental energy high and their physical endurance from flagging.

One of these young prosecutors, James Claight, sits now in his small office. This being a county government office, the furnishings are not luxurious, but the fluorescent lighting is very good, and the desk surface is large enough to accommodate the paper files and computer printouts that cover it. Now three years past his law school graduation, he is in his third year as an assistant prosecutor. After two years doing routine boring cases, he has become a seasoned prosecutor and so is freed from days dealing with civil infraction tickets under the state motor vehicle code, preparing and reviewing search warrants, reviewing applications for concealed weapon permits, and prosecuting trespassing and petty thefts. Now he prosecutes car thefts and burglaries by himself and participates in trials for robbery and rape. The complaint against Margo Kerber is clearly the most complex and challenging case he has been assigned to work on. Even more to his liking, it testifies to his seniority and favored status among the assistant prosecutors.

So far, he has analyzed the issues raised by the case and determined the parties to be interviewed in order to obtain the data needed by his boss, the chief prosecutor. The one thing he has not added to the spreadsheets and files— cognizant that everything on the computer could be admissible as evidence—is the category of Political Impact. That would clearly be important for his boss to consider, given the upcoming elections. The local newspaper and cable TV station have jumped on this case, and it has received continuous and emotional coverage. Approval or disapproval of his decision to prosecute—and his performance should he prosecute—will be brought into the voting booth and help determine his boss's longevity in the job.

Jim Claight is pleased to be working closely with his boss on this case; in addition to the learning experience it provides, it will help when he needs a letter of recommendation to the private firm he hopes to join as a criminal defense attorney. Jim lives in a miniscule one-bedroom apartment in a renovated Queen Anne Victorian, filled with hand-me-down furniture from relatives and housewares from Ikea, and he is looking forward to the day his salary will soar in private practice well beyond that of any civil servant.

He has worked this case vigorously and thoroughly. Huddled over his computer keyboard for hours scouring legal research websites, he has kept precise and comprehensive notes on what he's found. The CP himself kept a close eye on the results of his interviews as they occurred, which was an opportunity for Jim to show off his investigative abilities; the case is complex enough—and potentially incendiary enough—that regular supervision by the boss is needed.

The wall clock notifies Jim it's almost time for the final review preceding the CP's decision. He clicks the print command, and as he watches the pages emerge, he eats one of the Snickers bars he keeps in his office for extra energy and washes it down with a Coke. He runs his fingers through his hair to smooth any strands gone astray, pulls from its hook the navy two-button jacket that is the office's unofficial uniform (together with camel-colored pants), and adjusts the knot in his tie. He picks up the two printout copies and the folders of relevant files, and is on his way.

Charles Annison, the CP, welcomes him with a brisk nod and a smile. Jim shuts the door behind him and strides over to the round worktable where his boss already sits. He takes the chair across from his boss and sits at attention. At moments like these, he is still awed by the power residing in a chief prosecutor. Supreme Court Justice Jackson once said that the prosecutor had more control over life, liberty, and reputation than any other person in America.

"All right, Jim—you've finished your last interviews, so we're ready for the final review and my determination." He stretches out his arm. "Let's have the updated summary sheets." The CP peruses them closely, turning page after page without pause or question until he is done.

"All right, summarize the key findings from these investigative interviews and statements one more time. By the way," the CP says, "I like the way you've done this written summary by posing questions and grouping the interview results to answer them."

"Thanks, much appreciated," Jim says, satisfaction in his voice. The CP is fair, gives criticism that is constructive and not corrosive, but he dispenses praise rarely.

Jim knows from prior experience that in this meeting he will be asked to summarize verbally the facts in the written summary. He therefore has practiced his presentation twice in the last twelve hours and is well prepared.

"First question: Was the arrest appropriate? The police were called by the clinic staff. They were shown Margo Kerber's letter, and they interviewed the staff that had interacted with her. They checked with their station for the names of the parents who had reported the kidnapping; they interviewed the parents at the hospital after giving them an hour to be with their baby and pull themselves together. So yes, they had the information that met the criteria for probable cause to arrest.

"Second question: Was the arrest appropriately handled? The police then submitted a sworn statement setting out the basis for the arrest, and obtained a valid arrest warrant from the magistrate. The next day, once Mrs. Kerber had been moved to a medical unit for continuing observation and treatment of the overdose, and prior to her transfer to the psychiatric unit, they arrested her. There are notes from the doctors that she was fully conscious at the time and documentation indicating that she had her constitutional rights read to her. So yes, the arrest was both appropriate and appropriately handled.

"Next question: Are the follow-up data consistent with the complaint filed with our office by the police? Yes, the interviews with the mother, the clerk at Target, and the nurse who received the baby corroborate the information on the police complaints.

"Next question: Does the act meet the criteria of the appropriate state statute regarding kidnapping? Yes. The child was taken and confined without legal authority, in this case without the consent of the parents.

"Next question: Does the act meet the criteria of the statute regarding intent and harm? The intent was clear: to take the child. How that intent developed, whether it was planned or not premeditated, is unclear. The patient fled during a hospital cafeteria visit with her husband, a well-respected attorney. Had she planned that in order to go kidnap a child? The treating psychiatrists believe not. They say her action was likely spontaneous once she set eyes on the child. Certainly, she had made no statements to them giving any hint of such a wish, much less intent. With regard to harm, certainly there was pain and suffering for the parents. Was there harm to the child? Likely not, although the baby was dehydrated when examined at the hospital. And with respect to intent to cause harm, it is just the opposite—once Mrs. Kerber realized the child was not doing well, she took action to keep the child from harm.

"Next question: Is there evidence for prior criminal behavior or predisposition to such behavior, or for socially problematic behavior? A state police and FBI search revealed no criminal history or records of any sort. As for socially problematic behavior, certainly nothing deviant. However, we did uncover an episode that occurred in the newborn nursery of the hospital where she is employed. She was not authorized to enter the newborn nursery, but she did. Since she was not actively psychiatrically ill at the time, this might reveal some propensity to be close to babies, and to disregard rules in order to do so. But interviews with the nurses who witnessed this showed no evidence that abduction was the intent of this intrusion."

Here, the CP interrupts, wanting specifics of the interview with the nursing personnel. This was the last interview Jim did, and since he has not yet reviewed it with the boss, Jim has brought along the relevant file. He reads slowly and distinctly the questions he posed and the answers he was given: in particular, that Margo Kerber simply stood looking at the babies and had not taken any of them in her arms, much less tried to run out with one.

"All right, continue with the rest."

"Next question: Does her state of mind meet the statutory criteria? Did she understand that what she did was wrong? There are enough facts and opinions to think she likely did. In particular, the psychiatrists stated there were no cognitive deficits or indication that she could not reason or that she was incompetent. Although some of them thought she was delusional enough about motherhood and mothering to interfere with her reasoning ability limited to that particular area.

"And lastly, could she control her behavior, supposing she did understand that what she contemplated doing was wrong? Mrs. Kerber carried the diagnosis of major depressive disorder, moderate to severe, with psychotic features. Mental illness can weaken control of behavior, and psychiatric experts often point out that many mentally ill persons, especially severely ill ones, cannot control their behavior. In this case, however, most of the psychiatrists stated that the act was specifically in that sector of the patient's thinking that was a cause and a consequence of her illness: the intensifying desire to be a mother at all costs. They pointed out that she had had a false pregnancy, in which her fantasies outweighed her reason. They concurred that her belief that she could nurse a baby was irrational."

With that, Jim puts down his notes. At first there is silence from across the table—but Charles Annison soon speaks. "That is all consistent with my own thinking. So I have reached my decision."

This is not the usual course of events. After a presentation of the final summary, the CP typically asks his assistant prosecutors for their own opinion about the case; he usually regards this as a teaching opportunity.

"We must operate under our guiding principles," the CP says, his manner formal, as if he were educating an invisible jury and not just his student. "We prosecute the law vigorously, and we do so justly. Our client is the public."

Jim considers that public. Given the many interviews offered freely by the victim-mother, the photographs of her with the returned baby, the minimal information about Mrs. Kerber given by doctors and nurses constrained from commenting because of confidentiality, and the outpouring of sympathy and support for the parents from so many, public opinion would seem to be quite clear.

"Mrs. Kerber is part of the public we serve," says Charles Annison. "She is entitled to a just application of the law. And my determination is that I will not prosecute."

Jim's face registers surprise. Given the thrust of public opinion, it would seem extremely risky to choose not to prosecute. And the CP is standing for reelection next November.

"Does this decision seem illogical to you?" the CP asks. "Do you think this decision will seem to the general public incorrect? Then consider this. Once the full evidence is in front of the jury, once the psychiatrist and expert witnesses have testified about Mrs. Kerber's acute psychiatric illness, and once the judge has instructed them on the legal definition of guilt required to be met for conviction—we will lose the case.

"So ask yourself this: How would that sit with the public?"

Left unsaid is the fact that the voting public would certainly be less than enthusiastic to reelect a chief prosecutor so demonstrably ineffective with a case that they believed in.

"And what about Renee Lamarato?" Jim asks.

"You know our office prides itself on service to our constituents. Renee Lamarato, as a mother traumatized by her child's kidnapping, deserves our every consideration. I've met with her twice and taken her daily calls with their demands for full justice. I will meet with her again and explain that a 'not guilty by reason of insanity' defense would, with almost absolute certainty, prevail with the jury. And then Margo Kerber would be remanded to a psychiatric hospital or to outpatient treatment. Which is exactly what she is receiving now."

Left unsaid is what they both know: that even with the most compassionate hand-holding, there is no way Renee Lamarato will accept this decision with simple resignation.

68

Dr. Taynor welcomes Steven into her office and motions him to a seat.

"Mrs. Kerber told me you wanted a consultation, and gave me permission to say anything about my work with her that I thought might be helpful to you."

"Thanks for agreeing to see me," he says, soberly. "I didn't expect to have to talk to you, but I do. It's the memories of Margo, how she was, what she did. They're so strong, and they jump into my mind out of the blue, anywhere: home, work, in the car."

Dr. Taynor nods and waits for Steven to continue.

"I love Margo dearly, but having seen her become a different person than the one I thought I knew . . . thinking of her being that psychologically unstable . . . it has shaken me up."

"It's good you can recognize and acknowledge that," says Dr. Taynor.

"It's very hard. It's scary."

"It is," she says. "And that kind of reaction is not

unusual. Let me give you an example that shows how frequent it is that family members have these kinds of fears.

"In every medical hospital, a common problem is that patients develop a delirium. It can be caused by any one of a number of etiologies: for example, a urinary tract infection, a pneumonia that limits oxygen getting to the brain, or a narcotic given for pain. But no matter the cause, the psychiatric picture is the same: disorientation, irritability, hearing and seeing things that are not there, developing fears and suspicions not only of hospital staff but of family. Once the underlying medical condition is treated, the patient returns to their normal mental state.

"I tell you this because once the patient is ready to go home, it is the family that becomes fearful. They're afraid this person, whom they have previously considered mentally stable, has now revealed themselves as mentally unstable. They fear this person is now always at risk of becoming bizarre or psychotic, and so they need to be constantly on guard for that reappearing.

"And that is not necessarily the case. Unless the same combination of physiologic abnormalities happens, or something similar goes wrong in the person's body, the disorientation and psychosis is highly unlikely to just re-appear."

"But Margo's situation is different from the medical patients," Steven says, "and nothing has changed in her underlying problems."

"Yes, certainly it's different, and I meant that as an example of family reactions. But some things *have* already changed. She is no longer being assaulted by multiple severe stressors, one after another. And physiologically, the antidepressants are already altering the biochemistry and neural signaling in her brain.

"Let me explain it this way. For all of us, our psychological state at any given moment is a balance between the severity of stressors active in our lives and our repertoire of coping mechanisms. Some defenses and coping mechanisms are healthy and useful, while others are not so healthy: they can diminish psychological pain to some degree, but at a heavy cost in successful coping. You know the stressors your wife faced, especially the chronic infertility and the tragic late miscarriage of the baby. There were also internal blows, such as the resulting loss of self-esteem, on top of long-standing psychological vulnerabilities that acted together to reduce her ability to cope."

"But that's it, she has these psychological vulnerabilities."

"The human mind is an amazing thing, Mr. Kerber. It has an ability to change, to learn. It can grow new neurons. It can remodel old circuits. Psychotherapy can help us recognize and understand how our less healthy defenses get in our way, and help us develop and strengthen healthier ones."

"I'm glad to hear you say that," Steven says.

"From the reports I have of your wife's most recent inpatient stay, she already showed some positive changes there. In therapy here, I won't go into details, but she is working hard and well. So there is every reason to think that the balance for her will be much different should a major stressor come into her life again."

"It's such a relief to hear that," says Steven. "I've been so concerned that I might say the wrong thing to her, or something will happen at work when she goes back to it, or who knows what, and boom, change her into *that* again."

"You, too, Mr. Kerber, are a person who has been under great stress from all that's happened."

Steven looks intently at Dr. Taynor. "It's been so hard, all this worry about Margo. I haven't been the same person either. I fly off the handle at work. I'm not always hungry at mealtime. My sleep isn't so great."

"The stress you've experienced hasn't been only Margo's illness. It's also the stress of the chronic infertility situation for *you*. And your own feelings about the late miscarriage. You, too, have lost your child, and lost your dreams for that child, for the future you envisioned with that child."

"I don't think about it that much. I try not to think about it."

"That trying not to also takes a toll on you. Because it's all still in there, all that pain and grief."

Steven's eyes fill with tears.

"So your irritability, your trouble concentrating, they're understandable."

"It might help you to have a few sessions where you can focus on yourself. I can give you the name of a colleague to see, if you'd like."

Steven sighs deeply, nodding his head. "I would," he says. "I surely would."

69

Charles Annison is not having an easy time of it. He invited Renee Lamarato to his office, and steeled himself as he ushered her in, but he isn't prepared for the blasts of criticism and hostility that come his way.

"You what? Did I hear you right? You're not going to prosecute that bitch? Since when is being fucked up an excuse for kidnapping? Is any kidnapper *not* fucked up?"

"There's a difference between being mentally ill and behaving in a criminal fashion without having a mental illness," the CP says.

"What are you talking about? They're all sick, but they get prosecuted and tried anyway."

"Not always."

"How do you know she's not faking mental illness? That this wasn't her plan all along? What do they call it in the crime TV shows—premeditated? Thought out all along."

"Mrs. Lamarato, if you knew her personal and medical history as I do, you'd see that there is no doubt she was mentally ill when she took your child."

"So that means that once she is 'cured' of this so-called mental illness she will just forget about what she did and go on with her life?"

"I doubt very much she will just go on with her life as if this never happencd. But yes, once she is treated for mental illness and her doctor says she is recovered, she will not be prosecuted."

"Well, *that* is crazy. You mean a person who put a baby at risk of death, a person who takes from a mother her child, her *child*, just goes free?"

"If it makes you feel any better, Mrs. Lamarato, once Mrs. Kerber is well again, it is very unlikely she will just 'forget about it,' as you say, forget about what she did. But she will not be prosecuted."

"Bullshit! Bullshit! There's no way I am just going to lie down and take this. There's no way I'm going to let my child, my family, get attacked and no one pays."

And with that, she marches out of his office.

LATER THAT DAY, RENEE LAMARATO CALLED REQUESTING another appointment, and the chief prosecutor, with a prolonged sigh, signaled his assistant to set one for the following week. Now, she is back in his office, with her husband in tow. She sets her large black tote bag, over-flowing with typed papers and writings on yellow legal pad paper, right on his desk, disregarding propriety or respect.

"So, Mister Prosecutor, what do we do now, since you refuse to prosecute?"

Charles Annison studiously avoids looking at the bag. "You may file a civil suit for damages. I don't recommend it, though, since it is highly likely you will not prevail."

Renee thrusts herself from her chair and motions her husband to rise as well. She plants her palms on the table and pushes her face closer to his. "Thanks so much for your wonderful advice," she says witheringly, "but we've already learned your recommendations are full of shit."

She yanks her bag off the desk and walks out.

SEVERAL WEEKS LATER, RENEE MEETS FOR A SECOND time with Stewart Larkin, the lawyer who has been recommended to her by a friend of a friend. He's a small man, but his voice is deep and resonant and he carries himself in a way that inspires confidence. Renee also approves of the look of his office, with traditional furniture in traditional colors—a lawyerly look, not like the metal and the cheap orange upholstery in the chief prosecutor's office.

"Let's consider where we're at," Mr. Larkin says. "Last week you came to me requesting I assist you in filing a civil suit for damages. Clearly, you are bitter, and it is completely understandable that you are. Your baby was wrenched away from you. He was put in mortal danger. Your agony was surely immeasurable."

"Yes! And nothing has been done about it, nothing at

all. And nothing is *going* to be done about it—not unless I do it myself. The legal system stinks. It did absolutely nothing, like this never happened. So where's the justice in that? And it's not for the money—how could money make up for what happened to us? It's for my child. He's just a baby, but he deserves respect. He didn't deserve to be treated like that woman's toy!"

"Mrs. Lamarato, I understand both your feelings and your reasoning. Now let me give you my best advice, based on years of experience with civil suits, many involving minors, and very young ones at that. Your baby will not re-member the hours he was away from you, or the hours of hunger he felt. Those experiences will not substantially affect him in the future. Furthermore, there is no evidence they have substantially affected him even now, this close to the events. Fortunately, neither of you has been seriously or permanently harmed. The baby is safe and healthy, accor-ding to the pediatrician's reports, and you've resumed your mothering. And that is the crux of the law. Whether one likes it or not, harm is the issue here. Without it, pain and suffering is just not sufficient."

Renee's eyes grow big, her lips part, and she seems about to speak. "I see you disagree," the lawyer quickly interjects, "and that's understandable. But that is the legal position in these matters."

"Pain and suffering is not enough? I don't buy that. I don't accept that. What kind of laws do we have in this country? I will keep on fighting for my child's rights. It's my duty, as his mother."

"Mrs. Lamarato, I've given advice to parents in similar —not the same, but similar—situations. So let me give you the benefit of my experience. The main thing is for families to get back to normal life as quickly as possible. If you can put aside the desire for retribution and instead try to move forward, that's the best thing you can do for your child and your family. You could go on trying to file a suit, but it will be an exercise in frustration for you. And it will delay your ability to put this behind you, which will have deleterious effects on you, and thus on your child." He nods a few times, as if by nodding he can add more weight and impact to his words.

"But how am I supposed to put this behind me if nothing gets done to make this right? If she just walks away from this as if she's done nothing wrong? That woman almost destroyed our lives."

"That's my point, Mrs. Lamarato. The operative word is 'almost.' You also said that no amount of money could wipe out the pain. That's true. And what's more, a few years from now, realizing that you sued a woman who is mentally ill won't necessarily make you feel wonderful about yourself. Instead, try to think about your son. Your job as his parent is to ensure he has a mother who lives fully in the present and is not chained to the past. You can best make that happen for him by letting go of that past."

Renee's mouth pinches itself so tightly that white edges appear around her lips.

Accustomed to scanning jurors' faces for signs of the effects of his arguments, the lawyer notices this and concludes he has not yet sufficiently persuaded her. "You came to see me because of my reputation and my experience, correct? So let me tell you I've seen many people in situations similar to yours, where the chief prosecutor has decided not to prosecute. They are often extremely angry, with the same wish that you have to retaliate in a substantial way. This time, they want to be the ones taking the offensive. This time, they don't want to be the victim. But what is more important, Mrs. Lamarato? Revenging yourself on this ill woman by exposing her to a drawn-out, painful civil suit? Or letting go now and healing yourself for the sake of your son?"

"You're asking me to be a saint, Mr. Larkin."

"No, I'm not. I'm asking you to be a mother."

70

————

*M*any months and many sessions with Dr. Taynor have passed. Margo is feeling a great deal better. She sleeps deeply now, has regained most of the weight she lost, and her concentration is good. Her mood is only intermittently sad. She has much more energy, and she's better able to use it productively.

Margo is feeling more like herself again. Her mind is filled with thoughts that make her feel grounded rather than adrift. Sometimes, though, the awareness that she stole a baby jams into her mind and guilt grips her hard. I just can't believe I did that, she thinks. Then, part of her longs to believe it was half-nightmare; part of her longs to stuff the tormenting knowledge into a box and bury it in some inaccessible place in her mind. But then she thinks: I can't hide uncomfortable things from myself anymore. I don't really *want* to do that anymore.

From the beginning, Dr. Taynor urged her to exercise. "Try and do a little every day," she'd said. "Whatever you can do, just walk ten steps in place if that's all you have the energy for. Exercise is like fertilizer for the brain and improves its biology. It has a strong antidepressant effect, so take it like a medicine." By now, Margo is walking for half an hour a day around her neighborhood, and enjoying both the fresh smell of the outdoors and the fluid movements of her body. On the weekends Kate comes to join her, and their easy camaraderie and lively talk of hospital goings-on, gossip, new books to read and movies to see immeasurably enhance the pleasure of the walk.

Margo looks forward to her sessions with Dr. Taynor, and awaits them so eagerly that on each appointment day she checks her watch frequently to be sure she won't be late and miss even a second of the forty-five minutes allotted to her. Not that Dr. Taynor makes the work easy; while she never presses Margo to stay with emerging unpleasant feelings or thoughts longer than she can bear, she also encourages Margo not to dodge them either.

Today, Margo is midway through her session, although she has no sense—at least, no conscious sense—of how much time has elapsed and how much remains. The room is quiet, because the next thought has not yet formed in her mind, much less been expressed. The silence doesn't feel uncomfortable to her because, as always, Dr. Taynor respects it and doesn't intrude or pressure her to speak.

Margo gazes at Dr. Taynor. She looks so serene and so attentive at the same time, Margo thinks. One thing she knows for certain: Dr. Taynor understands her, truly and deeply. She feels reassured to have a reliable, wise, and compassionate companion on this difficult journey deep into herself.

Margo returns again to the issue she has been struggling with during the last few weeks, returning to it and each time digging ever deeper. She took the baby. No, not took—stole. She will not use that self-protective euphemism anymore.

"How could I do that to another woman? I wanted a baby so much, but to steal her child? Is there anything worse?"

"It's not just that you wanted a baby. You *needed* a baby."

"I *needed* a baby?"

There is silence in the room again as Margo grapples with this idea.

"To show the world that I, too, was a real woman with her own baby," Margo muses, half to herself.

"To show the world, and prove it to yourself," says Dr. Taynor.

"Even though it meant ignoring how I got it," Margo says quietly. "Maybe even pretending my body made it, like my mom and other women's bodies made theirs," she whispers.

"You also needed to nurse the baby," continues Dr. Taynor. "You could have done the far easier thing, which was to buy bottles and formula. But you didn't."

"Well, don't the experts say that's the best thing for babies?" Margo says, defensively. "And isn't that what breasts are for?" Mine started out smaller than Lucille's but they are big enough now, she thinks.

"Nursing would prove to you that you were a real

woman after all, with womanly parts like breasts that work," Dr. Taynor says.

Vivid and electrifying memories flash through Margo's mind. Mama's swollen belly, and then the baby sucking on her chest. Daddy looking on, his face happy and proud. Sitting on the porch plucking her own tiny nipples to make them pointy. Arthur Meese from the supermarket walking alongside his new baby in its big, shiny carriage.

A long silence, as Margo turns the new ideas Dr. Taynor just presented to her around and around in her mind.

"Okay."

A sigh. "Okay."

Another long silence, and then Margo addresses the next thought that comes into her mind, as if she has gone as far as she can tolerate with these ideas right now.

"There's another thing I feel really bad about. Steven, because of what I put him through. Especially that I ran away when he was responsible for me. And because of that, now he needs to see a therapist."

"How can you be so sure his need for therapy is because of that?"

"I guess I can't."

Dr. Taynor says nothing more, letting Margo draw her own inferences from that observation.

"Well, maybe his therapy *is* a good thing. He must think it's helping him, because he keeps on going. And I think it's getting easier now for him to show his feelings to me. The other night when he came home from work, he came right over and gave me a big hug, a hard hug. And the thing about it was, it was different than usual because it wasn't just him giving something to me. He was actually clinging to me, kind of in a needy way.

"So I hugged him back. I kissed him and smoothed his hair. And I think he realized I understood and accepted that, because I felt his body relax."

Dr. Taynor steps in here to highlight something important. "At that moment, you not only understood him but you were able to help by accepting his need. You helped him by signaling your acceptance, and that was a support he felt physically and was soothed by."

And Margo realizes that yes, she had done that. What Dr. Taynor was saying was true.

---

71

*T*ime has passed—but it has not healed all wounds. Margo has come to understand that therapy is a slow, steady process with few sudden breakthroughs, and so continues working with Dr. Taynor with serious dedication and effort. Time has passed too rapidly for the chief prosecutor, who continues to not have enough of it to deal with the overload in his office. Time has passed too slowly for Renee Lamarato, who is still waiting for some action, almost any action, to redress what had happened to her.

Mrs. Lamarato keeps pressing for a meeting together with Mrs. Kerber under the auspices of the chief prosecutor's office. The chief prosecutor repeatedly tells her that while he supports having such a meeting, he will not be pressured into setting a date, citing Dr. Taynor's continuing opinion that Margo is still not ready for such a meeting and it isn't yet clear whether or not a meeting would have therapeutic benefits for her.

Charles Annison, in fact, hopes to arrange such a

meeting. He takes pride in his division's concern for the needs of the victim, and free counseling from a social worker on call to his office is available for just that. Not that Mrs. Lamarato would accept anything that smacked of counseling; he has never suggested she could avail herself of it through his office, knowing she would see it as just another example of his disrespect. But he sees a possibility, however slight, that a meeting between the two women might help them both, and he meant it when he told Renee Lamarato he would try to arrange it.

Charles Annison waited out the weeks until Margo Kerber came home from the hospital. He also waited through the months of outpatient therapy that followed, until Dr. Taynor informed him that a meeting held under the supervision of a social worker would be all right. A few weeks prior, Dr. Taynor had written that Margo was sufficiently strengthened by the ongoing therapy to withstand a difficult confrontation, and that with proper preparation beforehand and more therapeutic work afterward, she might, in fact, benefit from it. And Dr. Taynor thought it was worth the risk.

Margo is not so certain.

Dr. Taynor has explained to her that she's been quite ill with a depression that has responded very well to medication, and through her own hard work in therapy has developed new insights and new strengths. Okay, Margo thinks, I *do* feel better and mentally stronger. I've been able to go back to work and I'm doing the job well. I can cope with knowing everyone there knows absolutely everything that happened. I'm almost not even thinking about that anymore when I'm talking to them.

I know I'm more flexible. When I talk with Steven about our options for becoming parents, I'm willing to consider a surrogate mother, just like he's getting okay with possibly adopting. I know we'll be able to figure out the best path for us.

And I accept that human life is filled with disappointments and sorrows, and that does not exclude me. It's not fate, or punishment, or the Evil Eye—it's just life.

But Margo is also beset by doubts.

Maybe Doctor Taynor is being overly optimistic, she worries. Suppose she's missed something important I still need to work on to be ready? I know I need to do this, but when Renee Lamarato hits me with her accusations and her anger, will I just crumble?

Really, she thinks, I'm scared to death.

EDNA SULLIVAN, THE SOCIAL WORKER, IS ARRANGING the chairs in the conference room with great care. She plans for each of the women to be seated at one or another end of the rectangular table, with Renee's husband seated to her left, and Margo's husband seated close by her side to provide the support of physical proximity.

She scheduled the couples to come in fifteen minutes apart, with the Kerbers coming first to give Margo the opportunity to become familiar with the surroundings and compose herself. As they walk in, Edna Sullivan notices how Mr. Kerber has his arm linked through his wife's and how his hand touches her forearm.

The Lamaratos arrive too soon, however, twelve minutes earlier than their assigned time, while Edna is still greeting Margo and her husband. So she simply ushers all four of them into the conference room before anything untoward or uncomfortable can unfold in the small room where they're assembling.

After the initial introductions, Edna offers a few remarks designed to create a safe and accepting environment. Then she leads them to the heart of the matter.

"Mrs. Kerber," Edna says from her seat midway along the table's length, turning to face Margo. "I know you are continuing with your outpatient psychotherapy—and making good progress, according to Dr. Taynor's report."

Margo hears Steven's chair scrape the floor as he moves closer to her. "I think so," Margo says. And then, "Yes. I am."

"Mr. and Mrs. Lamarato, I know you considered filing a civil suit on grounds of your son's physical suffering and your emotional distress. Where are you with that?"

"We did consider it, Ms. Sullivan," Mr. Lamarato replies. "We consulted a lawyer about it, and our friends, and our priest. And we decided not to."

"Though maybe we should have," Renee interjects. Her lips are so tightly pursed together it's a mystery how any sounds emerge. "Maybe we should have, because we owe ourselves at least that. But we decided not to. And we won't.

"But how is this meeting supposed to help?" she presses Edna, bitterness in her face. "This woman should be prosecuted in court, and she won't be. My family deserves some justice for what was done to us, and we won't be getting it."

"The legal system made what it considered the most just decision, Mrs. Lamarato. You don't agree, and you feel that now you have even more to be angry about."

"You bet I do."

"That decision won't be changed. But what the chief prosecutor hopes is that you will understand this meeting is in recognition of your need for something that will be of help to you, and will hopefully provide you with some closure."

"And what about *her*?" she says, glaring at Margo. "This meeting is supposed to be of help to her, too, right? Does she deserve to have some 'closure'? No. Being let off the hook is what I call it."

Steven squeezes Margo's arm and whispers in her ear. She looks at him, and he nods encouragingly. There is silence for a moment, and then Margo sits upright in her chair and looks directly at Renee Lamarato, even as the blood pounds in her ears.

"Mrs. Lamarato, I hope you'll listen to me. I know what I did hurt you terribly. There's probably not much worse than having your baby taken. I know that."

Renee stares stonily down at the table, as if nothing has been said—or, if it had, as if a person who deserved no reply had said it.

Margo doesn't waver, continuing on nevertheless. "I'm very, very sorry," she says softly. "Truly, I am."

"You're sorry?" Now Renee is looking Margo in the face. "That's it? You just have to say you're sorry, and justice is done? And you get off the hook, just like that? And never have to think about it anymore?"

"I'll always think about it. I'm the one who took your baby from you. I can never forget that."

"And how about our agony, our worrying about his health? And the threat to his life?"

"I want you to know that I took care of him the very best I could," Margo continues, her voice increasingly stronger. "That's not an excuse, and I don't mean it to be. But please know that I cared about your son and protected him the best I could. I can't imagine the pain I caused you. When I did what I did, my mind just didn't think about you or your feelings. I should have, but I didn't. It was just the baby and me. I wish I could change what happened, but I can't."

"Well, that's one thing we agree on," says Renee. "That it never should have happened."

"Please. Your baby, he's okay? He's doing fine?"

For a moment Renee hesitates, and then answers sharply, "Yes," almost spitting out the word.

Margo senses the rebuff, the rebuke. Still, though, she doesn't flinch, doesn't avert her gaze from Renee's pinched face.

A long moment passes.

"He's all right," Renee says. "All right," she repeats, less stridently now, seemingly moved, in spite of herself, by Margo's earnestness and concern. "Plump and round, and he gets into everything. He crawls fast as lightning."

"He does?" Margo responds eagerly, as invisible bands of guilt begin to fall away. "Really? Fast as lightning?"

72

After the meeting ends, Margo and Steven walk hand in hand through the lobby and out into the street. The air carries the scent of late autumn and richly colored leaves crackle underfoot. They walk through them together, in comfortable silence.

As she walks, Margo is experiencing herself in a new way. She feels buoyant, yet at the same time more solid, more grounded. Her breathing has an easier, fluid rhythm to it, beginning deep in her belly and expanding her lungs fully to receive the energy-giving air. She feels Steven's hand clasping hers, and she squeezes it back with a firm, responsive grip.

As Margo walks, she marvels at what has just taken place. She rolls the memory around and around in her mind, reviewing and reexamining its every facet.

The essence of it is that she tapped into an inner core of strength and effectiveness that is new—or, at least, newly accessible to her. She had pressed Renee Lamarato for a measure of forgiveness and had received it. And, even more —she had allowed herself to accept and be comforted by it.

Margo can scarcely wait to meet with Dr. Taynor the following afternoon. She visualizes herself in the office, sitting in the chair across from the bromeliad and the ivy and philodendron plants that flow down their stands like rivers of green, and telling Dr. Taynor all the good news.

"The baby is fine. Mrs. Lamarato is fine. And I, Margo Kerber, am well on my way to being fine."

acknowledgments

It takes a village to raise a child—and to write and publish a novel.

Many thanks to the writers who graciously gave invaluable editorial suggestions at various points during the long writing process. These talented and generous people include Harriette Simpson Arnow (sadly, posthumously), Elizabeth Kostova, and Rochel Urist.

I am also grateful to the professionals in the world of books and publishing who provided me with important comments and editorial recommendations: Susan Golomb, Stephanie Cabot, and Polly Rosenwaike.

I am greatly indebted to the indomitable publisher of She Writes Press, Brooke Warner, who offered expert and unflagging guidance during the steps to publication and distribution, and to her excellent editorial, design, and production staff.

A special thanks to those who read the manuscript with professional attention to psychiatric, obstetric, and legal issues: Drs. Cassandra Klyman, Michelle Riba, Timothy Johnson, and Lynn Blunt. The expertise is theirs, while any mistakes are mine.

An enormous thank you to the talented people not in the writing professions who read manuscript drafts, gave excellent suggestions—often of professional quality—that led to marked improvements in the manuscript, and slogged through proofreading. These people include my three children, Daniel, Judith, and Miriam; my sister Reeva Starkman Mager; and my very good friend Mickey Katz-Pek.

And most of all, my deepest gratitude goes to my beloved husband, Eduardo, who walked together with me through life and the birth and development of *The End of Miracles*, until he went ahead of me on the path that awaits us all.

about the author

DR. MONICA STARKMAN is a psychiatrist who is a faculty member of the University of Michigan Medical School Department of Psychiatry in Ann Arbor, Michigan. She is a clinician and a scientific researcher. Many of her publications in the scientific literature highlight concerns and conditions of women. She has served on the editorial board of the Journal of Psychosomatic Obstetrics and Gynecology. She is a recognized expert on mind-body interactions and the effects of stress hormones on mood and on brain structure. Dr. Starkman has also published in *The New Republic* and *Vogue* magazine.

SELECTED TITLES FROM SHE WRITES PRESS

She Writes Press is an independent publishing company
founded to serve women writers everywhere.
Visit us at www.shewritespress.com.

Shelter Us by Laura Diamond. $16.95, 978-1-63152-970-2.
Lawyer-turned-stay-at-home-mom Sarah Shaw is still struggling
to find a steady happiness after the death of her infant daughter
when she meets a young homeless mother and toddler she can't
get out of her mind—and becomes determined to rescue them.

How to Grow an Addict by J.A. Wright. $16.95,
978-1-63152-991-7. Raised by an abusive father, a detached
mother, and a loving aunt and uncle, Randall Grange is built
for addiction. By twenty-three, she knows that together, pills
and booze have the power to cure just about any problem she
could possibly have . . . right?

Play for Me by Céline Keating. $16.95, 978-1-63152-972-6.
Middle-aged Lily impulsively joins a touring folk-rock band,
leaving her job and marriage behind in an attempt to find a
second chance at life, passion, and art.

Stella Rose by Tammy Flanders Hetrick. $16.95,
978-1-63152-921-4. When her dying best friend asks her to
take care of her sixteen-year-old daughter, Abby says yes—but
as she grapples with raising a grieving teenager, she realizes
she didn't know her best friend as well as she thought she did.

Again and Again by Ellen Bravo. $16.95, 978-1-63152-939-9.
When the man who raped her roommate in college becomes a
Senate candidate, women's rights leader Deborah Borenstein
must make a choice—one that could determine control of the
Senate, the course of a friendship, and the fate of a marriage.

The Geometry of Love by Jessica Levine. $16.95,
978-1-938314-62-9. Torn between her need for stability and
her desire for independence, an aspiring poets grapples with
questions of artistic inspiration, erotic love, and infidelity.